Dave

2d6

by

ROBERT BEVAN

CONGRATULATIONS!

YOU JUST GOT CORNHOLED BY ROBERT BEVAN.

Caverns & Creatures logo by EM Kaplan.
Used with permission by the creator.

C & C Gang Illustration courtesy of evilgiggles.com.
Used with permission by the creator.

20-Sided Die icon provided by Shutterstock.com and used and adapted in conjuction with its licensing agreement. For more information regarding Shutterstock licensing, visit www.shutterstock.com/license

All content edited by Joan Reginaldo.
Layout design by Christopher Dowell.

ISBN: 1499238460
ISBN-13: 978-1499238464

SPECIAL THANKS TO:

Joan Reginaldo for her invaluable criticism. It's tough to find a good beta-reader. I went through a few before I met Joan. I can't stress enough how important it is to find someone who understands your vision and is able to help you achieve it. There's so much more involved than pointing out misplaced commas (though she did a lot of that, too).

No Young Sook, for her constant support, and for getting up to get the kids ready for school every morning because I left early to go to the office to write some books.

No Hyun Jun. Every cover of mine you see is the end product of a communication struggle, his English being about on par with my Korean. But the guy can work some Photoshop magic. And he also helps out with the kids quite a bit. Thanks, Hyun Jun.

Finally, I'd like to thank all of you wonderful people who like my Facebook page (www.facebook.com/robertbevanbooks).

TABLE OF CONTENTS

Nymph-O-Maniacs
ROBERT BEVAN

NYMPH-O-MANIACS

(Original Publication Date: February 24, 2014)

"I was thinking," said Julian.

"Well maybe you should stop," said Tim, stomping through the woods ahead of the group. Whatever was on Julian's mind, he was sure he didn't want to hear about it.

"Maybe we could take up trades," said Julian. "You could be a tailor's apprentice or something. You've got nimble fingers. With Cooper's strength, he could train to be a blacksmith. Dave could probably find something to do in the clergy. And with my high Charisma score, I could... I don't know... tend bar or something."

Tim slashed through the underbrush with his shortsword as he marched forward. "I've had it with honest work. Back in the real world, all it ever did was slow my descent into debt. Here in this stupid game, it only ever gets me into trouble."

"How much trouble could you get into being a tailor's apprentice?"

That was it. Tim stopped and turned around. "I—" He got a faceful of filthy half-orc loincloth and fell on his ass.

"Oh shit," said Cooper. "Sorry. You shouldn't have stopped so suddenly."

Tim sat on the ground and spat repeatedly, trying to get the taste of sweat, shit, and HOBO (half-orc body odor) out of his mouth. He scrambled through his backpack until he found his emergency hip flask full of stonepiss. The emergency it was normally reserved for was the necessity to get extremely fucked up in an extremely short amount of time. This emergency, however, had less to do with getting fucked up, and more to do with getting the taste of Cooper out of his mouth. He gargled the stonepiss and spat it out. It worked insofar as his tongue was now completely numb to taste.

"Are you okay?" asked Julian.

"I didn't start playing Caverns and Creatures to be a tailor's apprentice," said Tim. "And we'll never get back home if we don't start making some real money."

"What if going back home isn't an option?"

"So what if it isn't?" said Tim. "Do you think I want to spend the rest of my fake life sewing fucking pantaloons for rich assholes?"

"I don't —"

"And Cooper," Tim continued. "Do you want to be a blacksmith's apprentice, pounding the shit out of metal with a hammer in the blazing heat of a forge?"

"I dunno," said Cooper. "It sounds kind of cool."

"Dave," said Tim. "You're an atheist. How do you feel about getting a job in the clergy?"

"If I can learn more powerful spells, it actually sounds kinda neat."

Tim closed his eyes, trying to shake off the small buzz the stonepiss had given him. He looked up at Julian. "And I suppose you think tending bar is a nonstop party, right? What are you, seventeen?"

"I'm twenty-two," said Julian.

Tim got to his feet. "Well let me tell you something. I've tended bar. It's no party. Back home, what's the worst that could happen? You say 'I'm sorry, Mr. Ratcliffe. Some of the other customers are complaining. Please keep your voice down, or I'm going to have to cut you off.' Maybe you'll get a little attitude. If the shit gets too thick, you call the police in. What do you think will happen here when you say 'I'm sorry, Mr. Scarfang. Would you please stop raping the barmaid. She has a full shift ahead of her.' I'll tell you what will happen. You'll get a fucking axe to the face,

that's what."

"It's still less dangerous than this," said Dave. "I mean, what are we doing out here? We're just wandering through the woods looking for a fight."

"That's right," said Tim. "If we're ever going to get home, we're either going to need a shitload of money to pay some wizard to teleport us back there, or we're going to need Julian to level up enough to do the job himself."

Julian looked at Tim with sad eyes. "But—"

"I know," said Tim. "But what if none of that works? Well fuck it. If I'm going to spend the rest of my life in a fantasy world, then I'm going to live a fantasy fucking life. I want levels, gold, whores, whatever passes for the good life here. And we all know the best way to get it."

"Killing monsters," said Dave.

"That's right," said Tim. "Julian. Call your bird and see if he's spotted anything."

Julian inserted two fingers into his mouth and let out a long, loud whistle. "Ravenus!"

"Here I am, sir," said Ravenus, flapping down from behind them. He landed on a low-hanging branch of a nearby oak tree.

"Ask him if he's seen anything," said Tim.

"Why don't you ask him yourself?" said Julian. "You speak Elven."

"Because I'm in a lousy fucking mood. Forcing myself to speak in a British accent is only going to make it worse."

Julian sighed and looked up at Ravenus. "Did you see anything?"

"There's a lovely oak grove about half a mile northeast of here."

"Monsters, you stupid bird!" said Tim. "Did you see any monsters?"

Ravenus cocked his head sideways, looking at Tim. "I beg your pardon?"

"Jesus Christ," said Tim. He repeated the question in Dick Van

Dyke Cockney.

"Oh, no. No monsters at all. The forest is calm and quiet."

"The oak grove sounds nice," said Dave. "Maybe we could break for lunch."

"I am getting hungry," agreed Julian.

"I just shat out a log as big as Tim," said Cooper. "I could eat."

"Fine," said Tim. He looked up at Ravenus. "Lead the way."

"Come again?" said Ravenus.

Tim gave him the finger.

"Well that was uncalled for."

"Could you lead us to the oak grove?" asked Julian.

"Very good, sir! Follow me!" Ravenus flew from tree to tree, waiting for the others to catch up.

Tim knew where they were headed from a hundred feet away. He spotted a clearing through the trees, bathed in golden sunlight, as if the sun itself favored this particular patch of land above all others.

As they walked closer, Tim heard the playful twitter of birds. He'd been quite content to remain bitter and sullen all day, but the closer he got to the grove, the more his spirits lifted, even against his will.

"This place is beautiful," said Julian, stepping onto the fluffy carpet of grass which separated the grove from the rest of the forest.

When Tim stepped onto the grass, it was as if all of his worry, stress, and frustration were absorbed into the earth through his bare feet. The void left in their place was filled with the warmth of the sun and the freshness of the air. "I never want to leave."

The air was alive with butterflies and dandelion tufts. Eight oak trees provided a roughly octagonal border around the grove, but the tree at the center was a truly impressive specimen. It was wide enough at the base that, if all four of them surrounded it, they might be able to join hands, but only just. Its huge bottom branches drooped gently down to the ground before curving back up again. Tim reckoned he could be twenty feet high in the

tree without even using his hands.

A dozen or more species of bird fluttered among the higher branches, each singing a distinct song, but all contributing to a greater chorus of good cheer. Ravenus disappeared into the treetop to join them. Squirrels chased one another up and down the mighty trunk without a care in the world.

Julian spread a blanket on the ground, and began setting out the lunch boxes he had prepared. Dave unbuckled his breastplate and backpiece, and lay on his bare back in the soft grass.

Cooper lifted the front of his loincloth to have a piss on the great oak. After he finished watering the tree, he pulled a dagger out from the sheath he had strapped to his leg and began scraping it against the trunk.

"What are you doing?" Julian asked Cooer.

Cooper giggled like an idiot as he carved into the tree trunk. "I'm drawing a picture. Hey, how do you spell Dave?"

"What difference does it make?" asked Julian. "You don't know how to write."

"You make a fair point."

"How's that supposed to be Dave? It looks like a giant flaccid penis with a beard to me."

"Who are you to question my art?" asked Cooper. "This is my interpretation of Dave."

A chill breeze blew through the air, and the sunlight was temporarily obscured by shadow. Cooper's carving began to bleed dark orange sap.

"Awesome," said Cooper. "It looks like he's puking up infected jizz."

"Not awesome," said Julian. "Something's wrong."

"Who are you?" said a female voice.

Tim turned toward the voice. A woman sat in one of the lower branches of the great oak. She was tall and slender, with long, pointed ears, like Julian. Unlike Julian, however, she was stark raving naked. She had dark skin, somewhere between tanned white woman and Halle Berry. Her hair was green like the underside of a leaf. Tim assumed that was its natural color, as the carpet matched the drapes. Her breasts were like songs sung by angels. They defied gravity. They were like the effect of a Wonderbra without all the pesky fabric. So mesmerized was he that he could scarcely follow the rest of the conversation.

Dave and Cooper stared unblinkingly at the woman, mouths hanging open. They were obviously under the same trance that Tim was caught in. The only one who seemed to be functioning normally was Julian.

"I'm Julian," said Julian.

"What business do you have in my grove?" said the naked green-haired woman in the tree. "What is it you want?"

A long, thick line of drool spilled out of Cooper's open mouth. "I want to put my ding-dong in your hoo-ha."

Julian looked up at Cooper's face. "What the fuck does that even—"

Without taking his eyes off the woman, Cooper punched Julian lightly on the head. "Dude, mind your language. There's a lady present. Try to show a little class, huh?" His hand, as if acting on its own will, began to creep under his loincloth.

"Enough!" said the woman. She smiled and batted her long, green eyelashes.

Tim was suddenly out of his trance, but engulfed in darkness. "What's going on?"

"I can't see anything!" Dave called out.

"Oh my god!" cried Cooper. "Sister Mary Francis was right!"

"What have you done to my friends?" asked Julian.

"They were blinded by my beauty," said the woman. "And yet you were not. How interesting."

"I have a bonus against enchantment spells and effects," said Julian. "It's because I'm an elf."

"It's because you're a fag," said Cooper. "Ow! Hey man, it's not cool to hit a blind man."

"Which one of you defiled my tree?" asked the woman.

"Cooper," said Tim, Julian, and Dave simultaneously.

"You guys are dicks," said Cooper. "We don't even know what she means by defiled. She might be referring to pissing on the tree or she might be referring to carving a picture of a dick onto the trunk."

"You did both of those things," said Julian.

"Fuck."

Suddenly, Tim could see again. Light flowed into his eyes, warm and gentle. He looked around.

Dave rubbed his own eyes, and then opened them wide. His smile shone through his bushy auburn beard. "Ha ha!" he cried. "I can see again!"

"Me too!" said Tim.

"Thank you ma'am," said Dave to the tree woman. "I'm really sorry we've offended you. It won't—"

"I still can't see shit," said Cooper.

Tim turned from Cooper to the... "I'm sorry, miss. What are you exactly? A dryad?"

The woman let out a chirpy laugh, like the twitter of birds. "Heavens no, child. I'm a nymph."

"Why is it that my friend still can't see?"

"He must be punished, for he has shed the blood of the Life Tree."

"Will I be like this forever?" asked Cooper.

The nymph laughed her chipper laugh again. "Of course not, my child."

"Thank fuck."

"I expect that you will eventually grow old and die." Again with the laugh.

"You think that's funny, you skanky tree bitch?" Cooper walked unsteadily toward the sound of her voice. "You just keep right on laughing." He reached for the greataxe strapped to his back.

"Sorry, Coop," said Julian. He whacked him in the shins with his quarterstaff.

"Son of a mother fucker!" cried Cooper, collapsing on the soft grass.

"Miss Nymph," said Julian. "Surely there can be something we can do to make amends for our friend's transgressions."

"Amends," said the nymph thoughtfully, nibbling on her lower lip. "Let me think... hmmm...." Her eyes flashed wide. "I've got just the thing."

"Before you go on," said Dave, "I feel it's fair to warn you that there is a limit on how much we value Cooper's eyesight."

"Fuck you, Dave."

"Shut up, guys," said Julian. "Let her talk. Please, ma'am. State what you'd have us do."

"Not far from here is a stream running north to south," said the nymph. "If you listen, you can hear it from here."

"I can hear it," said Julian. "Would you like us to fetch water for your grove?"

The nymph laughed. "No, child. The Life Tree's roots spread far and wide. We have all the water we need. The stream flows north and slightly to the east. About a mile upstream, there is a small cave. My little birdies tell me a group of seven hobgoblins have recently taken an interest in the cave."

"What's a hobgoblin?" asked Julian.

"They're related to goblins," said Tim. "Only they're bigger, stronger, and hairier."

"They are an evil race," said the nymph. "They have no respect for the forest. I cannot risk them discovering this grove. I need you to destroy them."

Julian frowned. "That seems like kind of a severe solution to your problem."

"And if they're such a threat," said Tim, "why haven't you gone and taken care of them yourself? You're what? Like a Challenge Rating 7 Monster, aren't you?"

"I beg your pardon?" said the nymph, her tone a mix of confusion and contempt.

"Sorry," said Tim. "That came out wrong. What I meant to say is that you're very powerful. A few hobgoblins are nothing to you. You could deal with them as easily as if you were swatting flies."

"Your words are true, little halfling," said the nymph. "They are no real threat to me. Not in such small numbers anyway. But you require a quest to make amends, do you not?"

"I don't suppose we could get by with a sincere apology?" offered Julian.

The nymph laughed her chirpy, high-pitched laugh. "You are a cute one, young elf. I'm afraid I will require something more amusing. As beautiful as this grove is, there is precious little in the way of entertainment."

"You want us to commit murder for your amusement?" said Julian. "I won't do it. There has to be a line somewhere. If you have a problem with hobgoblins in the vicinity, there are other ways to handle it. Diplomatic ways."

"Do you think you can talk them into leaving?" asked the nymph. She smiled slowly. Tim thought he could almost see the wheels turning behind those bright green eyes. "I'll tell you what. You may try it your way first. But you alone, young elf, must do the talking."

"That's not a problem," said Julian. "I am accustomed to acting as the face of the party."

"And an adorable face it is," said the nymph. "If, for whatever reason, you fail to persuade them to leave, I require you to return here with their heads."

"Their heads?" said Dave.

"If you return with seven hobgoblin heads, I shall restore your friend's sight."

"Wait, what?" said Cooper. "You're sending me out there blind? How the fuck am I supposed to fight hobgoblins without my eyes?"

"I recommend you use your axe," said the nymph. "Return with less than seven heads, and I'll blind the rest of you as well. Now be gone!" There was no mirthful laugh this time. Even the birds in the Life Tree fell silent as she raised her hands to the sky.

The temperature dropped as a black cloud swirled into existence above the grove. It crackled with electricity.

"What's going on?" asked Ravenus, flying down from the Life Tree. "What happened?" He let out a loud caw when a small bolt of lightning struck the ground next to him and Julian.

"Okay," said Tim. "We're going!" He ran as fast as he could out of the grove. Julian, with his longer, more slender legs, beat him to the edge.

From the relative safety of the forest outside the nymph's grove, Tim watched Dave waddle toward him.

Cooper ran in an entirely different direction as the nymph called small bolts of lightning down, not quite on him, but near enough so that he could feel they were there. Every time he was nearly struck, he changed direction, zig-zagging his way out of the grove. He ran face-first into one of the smaller oaks marking the border and fell on his ass.

The nymph laughed and the birds resumed their treetop chatter as Cooper crawled past the grassy border.

"She really cranked up the bitch knob toward the end there," said Tim as he, Julian and Dave circled the perimeter of the grove to find Cooper.

"She was getting bored with us," said Dave.

"How do you know?" asked Julian.

"My high Wisdom score sometimes allows me certain insights into people's behavior. Maybe it's an untrained Sense Motive check. I don't know. Anyway, you heard her yourself. She seeks to be entertained. She toyed with us, like a cat plays with a mouse, until it just wasn't fun for her anymore. Then, instead of eating us, or whatever—"

"I think this is where your cat analogy breaks down," said Tim. "We get it."

"Right," said Dave. "She sent us to go find new toys for her to play with."

"Gobstopper heads?" said Julian.

"Hobgoblin," said Tim.

"Tim?" Cooper called out. He was sitting against a tree, his head facing in their general direction.

"We're coming," said Tim. "Stay there."

"Are you okay?" asked Julian as they got closer.

"My head hurts," said Cooper. His right eyebrow was bleeding and dirty with tree bark.

"You hit that tree pretty hard," said Tim. "Dave, patch him up, will you?"

"We may have a fight coming up," said Dave. "Are you sure we should be using up my Heal spells already?"

"Jesus, Dave," said Tim. "Just give him a Level Zero heal, huh? Something to take the edge off. He just slammed his face into a fucking tree."

"Sorry," said Dave. "I'm just trying to think ahead." He touched Cooper's forehead. "I heal thee."

The cut sealed itself up, and Julian wiped the spilled blood out of Cooper's useless eye.

"What's the plan?" said Cooper.

"It would make the most sense to have Ravenus scout the area first," said Tim. "If we can catch one or two of them alone, then we stand a better chance of taking them down at minimal risk to ourselves."

"What happened to Diplomacy?" said Julian.

Tim and Dave exchanged a quick glance.

"Listen," said Dave. "I know you're new to all this, but we've been playing this game for a long time. You can't settle every problem that comes your way by talking. Most of the time, violence is the best answer. No loose ends. No future betrayals. Just nice and simple."

"What loose ends or future betrayals?" asked Julian. "These Hip-hoppins—"

"Hobgoblins," said Tim.

"Whatever. They haven't done anything to us. We're going out to murder them for the amusement of some sadistic magical hippie. What harm could it do to talk to them first?"

Dave scratched under his beard. "What if they only say they're going away, but then they come back with a bunch of reinforcements?"

"What if they do?" said Julian. "We'll have returned successfully to the grove, gotten Cooper's vision sorted out, and be well on our way to getting shitfaced at the Whore's Head long before they come back."

"He makes a good point," said Cooper.

"You're using it right now, aren't you?" said Dave.

Julian looked at him innocently. "What?"

"Diplomacy."

Julian looked at the ground. "Yes."

"Fine," said Tim. "We'll try it your way. But I still want to try and find one or two of them alone. If Diplomacy doesn't work, then we don't need all of them alerted to our presence at once."

"I'll agree to that," said Julian. "Let's go find the stream, and I'll have Ravenus scout north from there."

Finding the stream was no big challenge. Julian followed his long ears, leading Cooper by the hand as he stumbled through the undergrowth.

After about ten minutes of walking, Tim could hear the babble of the water. Twenty minutes after that, they arrived. If the stream flowed north and slightly to the east, as the nymph had told them, it didn't do so in a straight line. It was full of twists and bends, some of the larger trees in the forest diverting its route. It was impossible to guess an average width or depth. At some points, Tim guessed he could jump clear across it with a running start. At other points, it formed pools twenty feet wide.

"Ravenus," said Julian. "Fly downriver until you spot the cave or the hoprobbins."

"Hobgoblins," said Tim.

"Right away, sir," said Ravenus. He flapped off down the river and disappeared above the treetops.

"Cooper should walk in the stream," said Tim.

"Why?" asked Cooper.

"Because you're blind."

"Of course," said Julian. "Everyone knows that blind people travel best in running water."

"Seriously?" said Cooper.

"No," said Julian.

Tim threw an acorn at Julian's head. "It's for your safety," he said to Cooper. "You'll be quieter in the water than you would be crashing into every low-hanging branch you pass. And you won't need anyone to guide you. Just follow the direction of the current. And if it does come to a fight, well... maybe you can stay hidden."

"Fuck that," said Cooper. "I'm not going to hide from a fight. Fighting is the only thing I'm any good at."

Tim was getting ready to argue again when Ravenus flew down from the trees.

"That was fast," said Julian. "Did you find the cave already?"

"No, sir," said the bird. "But I spotted two hobgoblins just downstream from here. Looks like a patrol."

"Perfect," said Tim. "That's just what we were looking for. Cooper, no arguments from you. Get in the river and keep your big head down. If you hear any fighting, you can come join in, but don't use your axe. You'd be just as likely to chop one of us in half."

"Fine," grumbled Cooper. He trudged toward the stream, waving his hands out in front of him. It was his foot, however, that found an obstacle. He tripped over a log and belly-flopped into the water.

"Dude," said Dave. "Keep it down!"

"Fuck you," said Cooper, wiping water off his face. It came off slimy and sticky, stringing from his face to his hands.

"Ew," said Julian. "What kind of water is that?"

"It's not the water," said Tim. "That's just Cooper's filth getting wet."

Tim, Julian, and Dave crept forward, moving from tree to tree as quietly as Dave's armor would allow.

Before long, Tim spotted the two hobgoblins about sixty feet away, sitting on a freshly chopped tree trunk, facing away from him. Thick, reddish-brown fur poked through the joints of their plate armor. Their boots sat unattended next to them as they dangled their feet in the water. Battleaxes and longbows also lay on the ground nearby.

"We should get moving," said the hobgoblin on the left. "If Snarlgore catches us sitting on our asses, he'll thrash us for sure."

"How's he going to find out?" asked the hobgoblin on the right, the slightly larger of the two. "We're the only ones on patrol. You worry too much, Grimblart. It's important to clear your mind every once in a while. Just take in the world around you." He took a long, deep breath. "Smell the fresh air. Feel the cool water as it runs between your toes."

"These guys seem perfectly reasonable," Julian whispered.

The hobgoblin called Grimblart removed his skullcap and dipped it into the stream. He brought it to his mouth and drank. Then he spat out the water and started to choke violently.

The other hobgoblin laughed at him. "You fool! You're supposed to drink the water, not breathe it."

Grimblart's choking eventually subsided. "This water tastes like elf shit!"

Tim face-palmed himself. "Fucking Cooper."

"Why elf shit?" asked Julian. With such a wide diversity of life in this world, it was a fair question.

Dave shrugged. "Just a figure of speech?"

The other hobgoblin sniffed Grimblart's head. "Well no wonder. You've been wearing that helmet on your sweaty, flea-ridden head all day. You need to rinse it out first." He removed his own helmet and demonstrated, rinsing it in the stream a few times before taking a cautious sip. He immediately spat it out. "By the scars my father left me, you're right. This is bad water indeed. Perhaps a bear died upstream. Let's have a look."

The two hobgoblins pulled their feet out of the water and re-donned their helmets.

"It's now or never," said Tim. "If they spot Cooper, your Diplomacy isn't going to do shit."

"Okay," said Julian. "Wait here."

Julian stepped out from behind the cover of the oak as the two hobgoblins were fastening their bootstraps. "Excuse me, gentlemen."

The hobgoblins instinctively reached for their bows. When they looked up and saw Julian, they threw the bows down and picked up their axes. "BRRAAAWWWWRRRRGGGHHHH!" they roared as they charged at him, axes held high in the air.

"The fuck?" said Julian. He stumbled backward. "M-m-magic Missile!"

A glowing bolt of magical energy burst out of Julian's outstretched palm, flew through the air, swerved around a tree, and struck the larger hobgoblin in the thigh, through a gap in his armor. Burnt bits of flesh exploded from his leg, but he didn't even slow down.

Tim readied his crossbow and aimed it at the injured hobgoblin. He took care to remain concealed as best he could, but the precaution was probably unnecessary. The hobgoblin was rabidly focused on Julian. He waited for it to close in to within thirty feet of his position, so that he would get his Sneak Attack Bonus.

THWACK!

The bolt caught the hobgoblin in the throat. He dropped his battleaxe and clutched at the bolt, gurgling up blood from his mouth. He managed to pull the bolt out, and a fine, pink mist escaped from his neck. He collapsed on the ground and was no longer a problem.

His friend, Grimblart, didn't even seem to notice his fallen comrade. He kept running after Julian, who was now running as fast as he could in the other direction.

Dave jumped out from behind the tree to intercept Grimblart. "Yah!" he cried, swinging his heavy mace. He swung a little too high, allowing the hobgoblin to easily duck under the blow, punch him in the face, and continue stalking Julian.

"Surprise, motherfuckers!" shouted Cooper as he jumped out of the stream. It was unclear as to what he thought he was running toward, but he didn't get more than two strides in before running straight into Dave. They both fell to the ground, and Cooper grabbed a handful of Dave's beard.

"Wraaa!" cried Dave. His right arm was pinned down by Cooper's knee, so he gave a weak swing at Cooper's face with his left hand. Cooper caught him by his leopard-furred forearm.

"You hairy son of a bitch!" said Cooper. He lifted Dave off the ground. "This is what happens when you fuck with one of my friends!" He threw Dave into the stream and jumped onto his back.

Tim's eyes darted back and forth as he tried to determine who needed his help the most. He'd never be able to catch Julian and the hobgoblin, not with his tiny legs. And Ravenus had already flown off that way, for whatever help he could provide. He ran toward the stream.

When he arrived at the bank, Dave was face-down in the water, and Cooper was sitting on his back, punching the shit out of him.

"Cooper!" cried Tim. "Knock it off! That's Dave!"

Cooper raised his head, looking around blindly. "Huh? Where?"

"You're sitting on him, you stupid asshole!"

"Oh shit," said Cooper. He stood up, grabbed Dave by his normal, non-furry arm, and pulled him up. "My bad, dude."

Dave coughed up what looked like four gallons of mud and sand, and then sucked in about ten times that volume of air. He raised a shaky index finger to his bleeding temple. "I heal—" The rest of his incantation came out as another gush of mud-vomit, but it must have been good enough. The bleeding stopped, and the back of his skull cracked back into its proper form.

Cooper reached out to feel Dave's face. "Are you okay?"

Dave jerked away. "Don't touch me."

"Hey man," said Cooper. "I said I was sorry."

"No you fucking didn't, shithead." He kicked Cooper in the shin, right in the lump where Julian had hit him with his quarterstaff.

"Ow!" cried Cooper, bending down to grab his shin. "Not cool, man! I'm fucking disabled!"

"Wait," said Dave. "Where's Julian?"

"How the fuck should I know?" said Cooper. "I'm fucking blind."

"Shut up. I wasn't talking to you."

"I don't know," said Tim. "I guess he's still running from the hobgoblin."

"Well what are we waiting for?" said Dave. "Let's go help him!"

"We'll never find them," said Tim. "We're too short and slow, and Cooper's blind. Julian's just going to have to fend for himself this time."

"So we just sit here and do nothing?"

"If we wander off, and he comes back, then we'll all be screwed," said Tim. "We need to stay put and wait for him. It's just one hobgoblin. He'll be fine."

"You don't know that," said Dave. "That thing was three times the size of Julian, and it was pissed the fuck off. You stay here if you want to. I'm going to go find him."

"Didn't you ever see any PSA's as a kid? What were you supposed to do when you get lost in the mall?"

"Stay where you are and wait for your parents to find you."

"That's right," said Tim.

"But who's to say who the parents are in this analogy?"

"Look," said Tim. "Julian knows where we are. We have no idea where he is. It makes more sense to let him come to us." He rummaged through his bag until he found his small leather tobacco pouch. It wasn't really tobacco. It was some kind of plant the locals smoked. They called it snotgrass, or something to that effect. That would probably change once large corporations became a thing in this world. Tim rolled up three fat cigarettes. "Julian will be back before these are finished."

They smoked in silence. Tim hoped that his prediction would be accurate.

They didn't have to wait long. Before their cigarettes had burned down halfway, Julian came trudging through the underbrush. Blood was smeared across his face, splattered all over his serape, and dripping from his limp left arm. In his right hand he carried his quarterstaff, the head of which was also coated in a thick layer of red. It ran down the shaft and pooled on his hand. Ravenus perched on his shoulder, his beak and neck sticky with some clear liquid. Somewhere, out in the woods, was a dead hobgoblin with no eyes.

"Julian!" said Tim. "You're all right!"

"No thanks to you dickholes," said Julian. "Have you guys seriously been sitting around getting stoned while I was out fighting for my life?"

"I wanted to go out and look for you," said Dave. "But Tim said... Um, that is, we thought it would be best to let you come back to us. So we wouldn't get lost. You know?" He held out his half-smoked cigarette. "Want some?"

"Just shut up and heal me."

"Is that your blood?" asked Tim.

Julian shook his quarterstaff. "This isn't." He waved it in front of his face and serape. "This isn't." He pointed at his left arm. "This is. He got me pretty good with his axe. I'm lucky I still have an arm at all."

Dave touched Julian's limp arm. "I heal thee."

Julian's eyes rolled up, and he sighed ecstatically. The fingers on his left hand started to wiggle. "Oh my god that feels good." When he was finally able to make a fist and move his arm properly, he reached out to Dave. "Okay, you're forgiven. Hand it over."

Dave handed him what was left of his cigarette. "What happened to your quarterstaff?"

Julian took a few puffs on the cigarette to keep it burning. "I wanted to make sure he was really dead. You know, below-negative-ten-Hit-Points dead. I didn't want him getting back up and

chasing me again. So I beat his skull in until it was a pulpy mess."

"That's kind of fucked up," said Cooper.

"I'll admit, it was probably overkill, especially considering that Ravenus had already eaten his eyes by that point. But I was angry."

"We've got to bring those heads back with us, you know," said Dave.

"Oh shit," said Julian. "I forgot about that."

"Is it still recognizable as a hobgoblin head?" asked Tim.

Julian shrugged. "I guess."

Tim started rolling another cigarette.

"Dude, take it easy," said Dave. "You're not even finished with the one you're smoking."

"I've got an idea," said Tim. "Remember that campaign we played last year when we stormed the bandit camp? I think Cooper was the Cavern Master."

"Vaguely," said Dave. "Was that the game where we were supposed to rescue the gnome princess from the high tower?"

"I remember," said Cooper. "I spent like four hours mapping out that goddamn tower, and you dickheads never went in there. You just took the prince's giant cigars and fucked off into the forest."

"That's right," said Tim. "And you were so butt-hurt about it that you had some bandits show up and steal all our money and our giant cigars. Do you remember how we defeated the bandits?"

"Not really," said Cooper. "I was pretty wasted at that point."

"I remember," said Dave. "I think I like where you're going with this."

"What did you do?" asked Julian.

"We found their campsite," said Tim. "And we stayed hidden until nightfall. We waited for all the bandits to go to sleep, except for the two on watch duty."

"Okay," said Julian. "What then?"

"It was dark. Nobody could see shit. But then Cooper did exactly what I was counting on. He had the two poor fuckers light up the cigars they stole from us, just to rub it in our faces."

"So what?" said Julian.

"So we didn't need to see them in order to shoot them. We just aimed at the cigar embers. We took out the two guards on watch duty, and then went and slit everyone else's throats while they slept."

"I may have been a bit generous with what I let you get away with," said Cooper. "I was probably just drunk and tired, and wanted to go home and go to bed."

"So what about the princess?" asked Julian.

"What princess?" said Tim.

"The gnome princess you were supposed to rescue from the tower," said Julian. "Did you go back for her?"

"No," said Dave. "The week after that Cooper got tired of running the game and had a dragon fly down and eat our characters."

Tim finished rolling a particularly fat cigarette— closer to a cigar really— and set to work on another one.

"It was a good plan then," said Dave. "But here and now it hinges on the contingency that any hobgoblins we run into are just going to steal our shit rather than flat-out try to murder us, which didn't work out so well for Julian."

"Yeah," said Julian. "What was up with that? Those guys were perfectly chill, and then they went all apeshit as soon as I opened my mouth. Did I fail a Diplomacy Check?"

"No," said Tim. "Even if you rolled a 1, you would have inadvertently said something offensive, or farted or something."

"Maybe the words 'Excuse me, gentlemen' sound like 'Your mother's a whore' in the hob-knobbin' language."

"It's hobgoblin, and no. I don't think so. That's not how language works here. It must have been something else."

"I think it was your race," said Cooper.

"They hate Jews?"

"No, fucktard. They hate elves."

"Why didn't you tell me this before you sent me out to talk to them?"

"I thought it was bugbears who hated elves," said Cooper. "I always get the two confused."

"What the fuck is a bugbear?"

"Would you guys shut up?" said Dave. "I'd still like to know who's planning to walk around flaunting a couple of fat doobies in the hopes that a group of hobgoblins is just going to confiscate them and send us on our way."

"Nobody's going to flaunt anything," said Tim, finishing up the second cigarette. "We're going to make it look like the hobgoblins caught us by surprise while we were camping, and we were forced to flee in a hurry, leaving some of our shit behind."

Dave gathered some sticks, built a small campfire, and doused it with water once the wood was sufficiently blackened.

Cooper chopped off one of the hobgoblin's arms. It took a few tries because he couldn't see what he was doing, but he managed to get in a good enough chop above the elbow so that he could just rip it the rest of the way off. He held it by the hand and swung it around over his head, spraying the whole area in blood.

Julian spread a few non-essential items around the site. A spare dagger here. A tinderbox there. An empty waterskin. Whatever they would be able to do without for the upcoming battle. He even talked Tim into leaving his flask of stonepiss.

"If they're wasted," he argued, "they'll be even easier to kill."

"Fine," Tim said, handing over the flask.

For Tim's part, he took off his clothes, soaked them in the stream, and laid them out to dry on the fallen tree trunk.

"You're getting pretty comfortable with being naked around us these days," said Julian, looking slightly to the left of Tim.

"I'm trying to make it look like we were caught off guard," said Tim. "I can't afford the luxuries of dignity and shame."

"Oh, I wasn't suggesting you should be ashamed of your body. I just—"

"This isn't my body," snapped Tim. "My body is more than three feet tall, and my dick is more than an inch long. Take off your serape."

"What?" said Julian. "I've got to strip down too?"

"You can keep your shirt and pants on, Mr. Modest. "But at least take off the serape. Details sell the story."

Julian pulled his serape over his head. "What's the genre? Gay erotica?"

Tim snatched the garment out of Julian's hand and turned toward the river. He was barely able to stop himself from running straight into Cooper's disgusting half-orc dick. "Jesus, Cooper! What the fuck?"

Cooper held up his loincloth. "I was just trying to help."

"Sorry," said Tim. "Would you please put that back on."

"My clothes aren't good enough for your story?"

"No," said Tim. "That doesn't even look like clothes. It looks like a giant sewer rat died of AIDS. Now put it back on." He dunked Julian's blood-spattered serape into the stream and then spread it out on the fallen tree. He surveyed the fake campsite. A CSI team might spend a day wondering what the fuck had happened here, but it looked good enough to fool a couple of hobgoblins. "That should just about do it. Cooper, toss that arm in the stream."

"What for?"

"With any luck, the other hobgoblins will spot it and come to investigate."

"Good thinking," said Cooper. He tossed the arm. It hit Dave in the face.

"Dammit, Cooper!" said Dave. He kicked the arm into the stream.

"Sorry, dude. I can't see."

Tim placed his two giant snotgrass cigars on his empty tobacco pouch and set it gently on the ground next to the dead hobgoblin, where it stood a better chance of being noticed. "Let's go get that other hobgoblin head."

They followed Julian, who zigged and zagged through the forest, trying to remember where the fight had taken place, until he finally conceded that he had no idea where he was going. In flight, Ravenus was able to find the spot almost right away.

It was a grizzly sight indeed. Julian had been nothing if not thorough. The hobgoblin lay dead in a pool of its own congealing blood. Of course, its eyes were missing. The top of its head was completely caved in, as was the left side of its face. Its bearded jaw was still intact, pointy lower-canines jutting up from its underbite. The poor bastard might not be recognizable as Grimblart, but he should at least be identifiable as a hobgoblin.

"You really went to town on this guy," Tim said to Julian. He pointed to a scorched hole in the leather covering the dead hobgoblin's groin area. "Did you Magic Missile him in the nuts?"

"Yeah."

"How do you even do that?"

"It was close combat at that point. He'd already broken my arm, so I grabbed his crotch while I said the incantation."

Dave winced. "Lucky for us the nymph didn't ask us to bring back seven hobgoblin dicks."

"This is disgusting," said Tim. "Cooper, chop its head off. And for fuck's sake be careful. We don't need it anymore damaged than it already is."

Cooper knelt next to the body, feeling it with his hands. "Okay. I think I've got it." He stood up, raised his axe in the air, and brought it down hard on the hobgoblin's chest. "How close was I?"

"Not very," said Dave.

After seven more tries, Cooper had chopped the torso of the creature into hamburger, severed an arm at the shoulder, and finished off the work Julian had started on its dick.

"Stand back," said Dave. "Let me try." He picked up the dead hobgoblin's battleaxe, and removed the creature's head with one blow.

"We really need to start remembering to utilize all of the resources available to us," said Tim. "Julian, ask Ravenus to go find the cave, would you? If this cigar thing works, I'd like to scout out the terrain while there's still some daylight left."

Julian sent Ravenus on his way, and Cooper stuffed the battered hobgoblin head into his bag.

Ravenus returned a few minutes later.

"Bury this body," said Tim. He let Ravenous lead him toward the hobgoblin cave. As an extra precaution, he used his Move Silently rogue ability, making him even slower than usual. But there were still a few hours of daylight left, and being alone in a forest with a bunch of angry hobgoblins with only a crossbow and a bird for protection was not a time for impatience.

He snuck silently from tree to tree until, about thirty minutes later, he ran out of trees. Peeking out from behind the last one, he saw the cave. The site looked to be the result of a fault shift or something. One chunk of the ground jutted up sharply against the ground next to it, leaving a fifteen foot wall of sedimentary rock exposed. It was in the face of this rock that the entrance of the cave had been carved. Just a rough hole in the rock about eight feet tall at its highest point, just slightly above the head of the lone hobgoblin standing guard outside it. A grey and white wolf sat beside him, tethered to an iron stake in the ground. Shit. The wolf would be a problem.

The purpose of the cave was not readily apparent. Maybe someone had been mining for gold or gems. Maybe it was a tunnel leading somewhere else. Maybe it had served a military purpose some time ago, or been a temporary home to a group of bandits on the run from the law. It was as defensible a location as one was likely to find in this forest. The rock wall would prevent any attacks from directly behind, and the stream cut sharply to the left, ballooning out in front of the cave, before turning northward again, like a giant Omega symbol. Anyone attempting a direct assault on the cave would have, at best, wet feet and twenty yards of open ground to cross.

Tim would have to cross the stream in order to get close enough to use his Sneak Attack bonus, but that shouldn't be a problem. The water ran slowly, and it probably wasn't deep enough for him to drown in anyway. The Difficulty Class for an Untrained Swim Check should be pretty low.

The wolf barked sharply and stood up. Another hobgoblin was approaching quickly from the right..

"Elfgina," said the hobgoblin on duty. "What's that in your hand?"

"It's an arm," said the other hobgoblin. "And I wish you'd stop calling me that. My family name is Bloodfang."

"You will earn your name once you've proved yourself in battle. Until then, you'll be known as Elfgina. Now give that here."

Elfgina handed over the severed arm.

"Hell's fury!" said the hobgoblin standing guard. "Where did you find this?"

"I was having a piss in the stream, and it just floated by."

"This belongs to Rothgar. It still bears his father's ring."

Fuck. It was wearing a ring? Tim made a mental note to check the other body more thoroughly when he returned to the others.

"What's going on out here?" said one of two hobgoblins emerging from the cave. That accounted for six of the total seven.

"Bonecrusher," said the hobgoblin who had been standing guard. "You and Elfgina go upstream and see if you can find out what happened. Take Pepper with you."

The hobgoblin called Bonecrusher untied the wolf from the stake. He crouched down, whispered something in its ear as he stroked its fur, and held the severed arm out for it to sniff. The wolf sprang forward toward the stream, dragging Bonecrusher behind with its leash. Elfgina followed after them.

That left two hobgoblins alone in front of the cave. If he'd brought just one more person, it might have been worth risking a direct assault. Tim briefly toyed with trying to pick them off one by one from where he was, but quickly dismissed it.

He wasn't sure how good a nose a wolf had, but if it had any sense of smell at all, it would be able to pick up Cooper's stench, not to mention the trail of destruction he left while stumbling blindly through the forest.

"Ravenus," Tim whispered in a British accent. "We've got to get back to the others. Let's go."

Tim Moved Silently for about the first fifty yards, and then broke into a run. They made it back to the group in what seemed like no time at all.

Cooper's entire body was covered in sweat and freshly turned earth. He stood over what Tim assumed to be the grave of a headless hobgoblin. "Hey guys," he said. "Look. I soiled myself. Get it? 'Cause I'm covered in soil."

"Fucking hilarious," said Dave.

Cooper let out a fart that sounded too wet to just be a fart.

"Jesus, Cooper!" said Julian.

"Shit," said Cooper. "I soiled myself for real this time." He stumbled around, waving his arms until he found a tree.

"You're so disgusting," said Dave.

Cooper lifted the back of his loincloth and rubbed his ass against the tree trunk. "Screw you, man! It's not me. It's my Charisma score. You know I can't help it."

"Ahem," said Tim.

Julian and Dave quickly turned their heads toward him. Cooper raised his head toward somewhere to the left of him.

"Did you find the cave?" asked Julian.

"Yeah," said Tim. "And they found the arm."

"That's great," said Dave. "Everything's going according to plan then."

"Not quite," said Tim. "They've got a wolf with them, and it looks like one of them has at least a few ranks in the Tracking skill. They'll probably hunt us down."

"Shit," said Julian. He thought for a moment. "Couldn't we just move?"

"We're too slow as a party," said Dave. "We'd just put off the inevitable by a few minutes."

"So what do we do?"

"We get ready for a fight," said Tim. He'd been looking forward to seeing how his cigar trick would play out, but they'd just have to adapt. "We'll be up against two hobgoblins and a wolf, so we still outnumber them. Since they're coming toward us, we can

have the home field advantage as well."

"Is there really such a thing?" asked Julian.

"As what?" asked Tim..

"A home field advantage. I mean, is it a game term? Do we get bonuses to our Attack Rolls or something?"

"No," said Tim. "It's not a game term. It is what it is. We can prepare for them. Set a trap. That sort of thing."

"Awesome!" said Julian. "We could dig a big pit, and put spikes on the bottom, and then cover it with branches. Then when they come, I'll stand on one side of it and say 'Hey fellas! Were you looking for some hot elf love?'"

Tim shook his head. "That's—"

"Hold on!" said Julian. "I've got a better one. I'll hold my hands up and say 'I'm unarmed... and so is your friend!'".

"Yes," said Tim. "That's very funny, but—"

"Ooh! Or how about this one. I'll point at my balls and say—"

"Would you shut the fuck up?" said Cooper, returning from defiling yet another tree. "Do you know how long it would take to make a trap like that?"

"A couple of hours?"

"More like a week," said Tim. "And I reckon we've only got maybe thirty minutes to come up with something that's not incredibly stupid."

"Ambush," said Dave.

"Keep talking," said Tim.

"They don't know how many we are, or in what condition we're in. You and Julian take positions up in the trees." He pointed up at two trees he thought would make good candidates. "I'll hide behind one of the trees, and Cooper will stand out in the open as bait."

Cooper raised his head. "Wait, what?"

"I like it," said Tim. "We should be able to take down at least one of them before they even know they've been ambushed."

"You like it because you get to be up in a tree," said Cooper. "Let's use the blind guy as bait."

"You've got a ton of Hit Points," said Tim. "You'll be all right. And let's face it. This is really the only opportunity you have to be useful in your present condition."

"Thanks."

Julian sent Ravenus to keep an eye on the hobgoblins. Then he took Grimblart's bow and quiver which, thankfully, they'd had the presence of mind not to bury him with, and climbed up one of the trees that Dave had pointed out. He nestled himself into the fork of a large branch and tested his line of sight. Tim did likewise in the tree Cooper was standing next to. With Dave's help on the ground, they mapped out an ideal area for Cooper to lure the hobgoblins into which both Julian and Tim could see from their positions.

Dave hid behind the thick trunk of Tim's tree, and Cooper stood out in the open like a vulnerable jackass who was waiting to get murdered.

"That's perfect," said Tim. "Just act natural and... I don't know. Try not to let on that you're blind."

"How the fuck am I supposed to do that? You want me to juggle?"

"Here," said Julian, tossing down a scroll tube. It hit Cooper in the head.

"Ow."

"Pretend you're reading."

"But I'm illiterate."

"You're blind, too, dumbass," said Julian. "That's why I said 'pretend'."

"Oh, right." Cooper crouched down, feeling the ground until he found the tube. He opened it and pulled out a sheet of parchment. Standing back up, he unrolled the parchment and cleared his throat. He spat a fist-sized gob of rusty-brown phlegm on the ground.

"Ew," said Dave. "Watch where you spit. I've got to hide over here."

Cooper held the blank parchment out in front of him. "We the people, of the United States of America..."

Ravenus flew in like a rocket, stumbling as he landed. "They're coming!" he said to Cooper.

Unable to understand the bird's Elven language, Cooper ignored him and continued reading. "...and to the republic for which it stands, one nation..."

"Hey!" said Ravenus. "Hang on. Where is everybody?"

"...our four fathers hold these truths to be self elephants..."

"Ravenus," whispered Julian. "Up here!"

"...will not be judged by the color of their skin, but by the contents of their character sheets..."

Ravenus flew into Julian's tree. "One of those bastards fired an arrow at me!"

"...anything you say can and will be used against you in a court of law..."

"Cooper," Tim whispered. "Get ready. Here they come!"

"...One small step for man. One giant leap for—"

Snarls and barks announced the wolf's arrival. "You there!" shouted the hobgoblin called Bonecrusher, barely able to hold his wolf's leash. "Who are you?"

Cooper threw down the parchment and roared, "ICH BIN EIN BERLINER!"

Bonecrusher and Elfgina looked at one another uncertainly. Even Pepper stopped barking.

"Sorry," said Cooper. "I got a little carried away."

Julian looked at Tim. Tim shook his head. The hobgoblins were still about forty feet away. He wouldn't get his Sneak Attack bonus at this range. While he was guaging their position, Tim noticed his tobacco pouch slung around Elfgina's neck. The ends of two fat cigars poked out of the top of it.

"I'll ask you one more time, half-orc," said Bonecrusher. "Who are you?"

"My name is Cooper."

Bonecrusher held up the severed hobgoblin arm. "Are you responsible for this?"

"For what?"

"Have the gods removed your eyes as well as your wits?"

"My vision isn't what it used to be."

That's it, Cooper. Draw him in a little closer.

Bonecrusher lobbed the severed arm at Cooper. It bounced off his chest and fell to the ground.

Shit.

"Neither are my reflexes." Cooper bent over and felt for the arm.

"I think he's blind," said Elfgina.

Cooper found the arm and stood up. "Oh, this," he said. "Yes. I'm totally responsible for this." He tossed the arm back toward the hobgoblins. They watched as it arced high over their heads.

Bonecrusher unstrapped his battleaxe. "That arm belonged to my cousin."

Cooper took a step backward, and another. "Sorry about that," he said. "I used it to whack off." He performed the universally recognized 'whacking off' gesture in case the hobgoblins were not familiar with the term. "Pro tip: If you use someone else's hand, it feels less lonely."

"Why you vile piece of..." Bonecrusher let go of the leash. "Pepper, get him!" Bonecrusher followed, holding his axe with both hands, as Pepper launched into Cooper.

It all happened so suddenly that by the time Tim shouted "Now!", the hobgoblin was practically right under his tree.

Tim's bolt caught Bonecrusher right where his neck met his chest. Julian's arrow pierced the hobgoblin's leg. Dave stepped out from behind the tree and smashed his mace into the creature's gut with a mighty, all-or-nothing two-handed swing. It was impossible to say which was the killing blow, but Bonecrusher didn't even have time to grunt before collapsing dead to the ground.

Cooper continued stumbling backwards until Pepper leapt up and tackled him.

"Dave? Is that you?" said Cooper, grasping at the animal on

top of him. The wolf bit his hand and clawed his face.

"Ow!" said Cooper. "Fuck you, Dave!" He grabbed the animal by the throat and punched it in the face.

"Shit!" said Elfgina, who hadn't even readied a weapon. He bolted off in the other direction.

Tim climbed down from his branch, and Julian hopped down from his. Julian had an arrow nocked and aimed by the time Tim got down.

"Wait!" said Tim. "Let him go."

"What? Why?" Julian lowered his bow.

"He's got my tobacco pouch."

"Fuck your tobacco pouch!" Julian raised his bow again, but Elfgina was gone. "Dammit!"

"Come on," said Tim, running toward Cooper.

Dave stood over Cooper and Pepper as they wrestled on the ground, looking for an opportunity to strike. Tim saved him the trouble. A single bolt to the chest was all it took. The wolf gave a last, whiny bark and fell to Cooper's side.

Cooper stood up on his massive, but trembling, legs. His face and chest were scratched up pretty bad, and his hand was dripping with blood.

"You okay, Coop?" said Tim.

"I'll live."

"I've got one more Heal spell," said Dave.

"Save it," said Cooper. "Just give me a zero-level Heal to stop the bleeding."

Dave touched Cooper's arm. "I heal thee."

"Thanks." Cooper opened and closed his hand a couple of times. It still looked pretty bad, but no more blood was dripping out of it. "So, that's four down?"

"Three," said Julian with more than a trace of annoyance in his voice. "Tim let the other one get away."

"What the fuck for?" said Cooper.

"He had my tobacco pouch," Tim explained. "There's still a chance for my cigar plan to work."

"Fucking hell," said Cooper.

"Tim," said Dave. "That plan was clever in a what-harm-could-it-do sort of way, but it's not something you'd want to count on. Not when we could have just tipped the odds in our favor. We could have probably taken out three hobgoblins in a straight-up fight. Having a fourth one there, who can give the others a full report on us, well... you may have just fucked us."

"You make a fair point," said Tim. "But if my plan works, there won't even be a fight."

"Okay," said Julian. "I'm going to jump in and be totally honest for a second. I think your plan is stupid. In fact, I think it's the stupidest fucking plan I've ever heard. What if none of those guys smoke? What if they like to smoke in the morning? What if they've got a big campfire going and we can't even get close enough without them spotting us? There's so much about this plan that has to go precisely the way you want it to for it to have any prayer of working. If your plan was a person, it would be riding the short bus to school."

An awkward moment of silence followed while Tim waited for someone to speak up in his defense. Cooper farted.

"I appreciate your honesty," said Tim. "I made a split-second decision. Had I had more time to think about it, I might have chosen differently. But that's neither here nor there. What's done is done, and my plan, stupid or not, is the only one we've got."

As the sun set, the oak tree shadows grew larger and darker. Ravenus led the group to a safe distance from the hobgoblin cave. Just before evening turned completely into night, Tim led Julian to a not-quite-as-safe distance from the cave.

"Do you really think it's wise to have me be your backup?" asked Julian. "Those guys really hate elves."

"I think it's a safe bet that they hate all of us right about now," said Tim. "And if this works, they won't see you at all. I need you because you're the only one who can at least try to walk quietly, and you're decent with a bow."

When they reached the last tree before the stream, Tim

crouched down and gestured for Julian to do the same. Two hobgoblins stood outside the entrance of the cave.

Tim spoke just above a whisper. "We'll cross the stream here. Do your best not to splash, but the babble of the water should cover us pretty well. Then we'll make straight for the cave entrance. If there's only one hobgoblin standing guard, we'll both fire at the same time. If there are two, we're going to have to split our attacks and hope we kill both of them on the first try."

Julian shrugged and nodded.

"Take one more look," said Tim. "Try to remember the layout of the land as best you can."

Julian stared for a little while. "Okay. I've got it."

Tim stood up. "Good. Now let's go back and—"

"They came out of nowhere!" said Elfgina, running toward the two hobgoblins standing outside the cave.

"What are you talking about?" asked the larger of the two. "Where is Bonecrusher? Where is Pepper?"

"They're gone, Snarlgore," said Elfgina. "I'm sorry, but there was nothing that could be done. They jumped out of the trees, half a dozen or more."

"You are lower than a dog," said Snarlgore. "Elfgina is too good a name for you. We'll have to think of something better."

"Please, sir," pleaded Elfgina. "You don't understand."

"I understand perfectly," said Snarlgore. "The dog stayed to fight. You did not. Therefore, you are lower than a dog. Hammerfist," he said to the hobgoblin standing next to him. "Is there some flaw in my reasoning?"

"Your logic is sound, sir," said Hammerfist.

"You must listen to me!" said Elfgina. "They may be coming this—"

"Have I completely lost my senses," said Snarlgore, "or did the dog just presume to give its owner a command? Have you ever heard of something so preposterous?"

"Never in my whole life, sir," said Hammerfist.

"See if perhaps you can demonstrate to him his proper place, would you?"

Hammerfist stepped up to Elfgina.

"Come on, Hammer," said Elfgina. "Those guys are coming for us. We need to—"

His words were interrupted by a gauntleted backhand slap to the face.

Elfgina dropped to his hands and knees, out of breath and drooling blood.

"That's better," said Snarlgore. "Now, what does a good doggie say?"

"P-p-please."

"If I have to unsheathe my short sword, I shall sheathe it through that soggy noodle you call a spine. Now what does the good doggie say?"

"Woof?"

"Very good."

"I don't think I can watch anymore of this," said Julian.

"Okay," said Tim. "I can barely see anything anyway. I was hoping we'd catch a glimpse of the seventh hobgoblin." He put a hand on Julian's elbow for guidance.

"He may be inside the cave," said Julian. "Like maybe he's the big boss or something."

"I hope not."

About thirty yards further away, they met the rest of the group and explained the current situation.

"So now what?" asked Dave.

"Now we wait," said Tim. Give them an hour or two, hope that at least one of them goes to sleep. And then we make our move. Julian and I will go in alone. You and Cooper will stay on this side of the stream unless shit really goes south." He put his hand on Cooper's. "If that happens, I'll need you to go into your barbarian rage."

"You want me to fight?"

"No," said Tim. "I want you to look big and scary so that they'll all shoot at you while we pick them off."

"Being blind sucks."

About twenty minutes passed before Tim finally said, "Fuck it. I'm tired of waiting. Ready?"

Julian shrugged. "As ready as I'll ever be."

The whole group crept back up toward the stream so slowly that even Cooper was quiet. When they finally made it to the stream, Tim scanned the darkness beyond until he saw what he was looking for. A beautiful solitary glow, like the Star of Bethlehem. Someone was smoking one of his cigars.

"Way to go!" whispered Dave, giving Tim a friendly punch on the arm.

"I'll admit when I'm wrong," said Julian. "I honestly didn't think this plan had a chance of working, but it looks like it might actually work out pretty well."

Tim took a moment to bask in some well-deserved I-told-you-so satisfaction, before calibrating some of the finer details of his plan.

The glow of the cigar was red and irregular. It wobbled around, and didn't appear to be likely to guarantee a hit as well as he'd imagined it would. As he stared at the light, contemplating on how best to shoot at it, it suddenly grew brighter, and quickly dimmed again.

That was it. The light would grow brighter when air was being sucked through it... when the hobgoblin was inhaling. That's when it was guaranteed to be right in their face. "Keep your aim on the light," he said to Julian. "Fire when it glows brightest."

"Okay," said Julian.

"We'll be back in a few," said Tim.

"Good luck!" said Dave.

"You don't need luck if you've got a solid plan," said Tim. "Come on, Julian. Let's go."

Tim and Julian waded silently through the water, carefully holding their weapons over their heads. When they made it to the other side, they lowered their arms and relaxed.

"Okay, perfect," whispered Tim. "Now let's just keep going

like that for another ten yards. We've got to get within thirty feet of him for me to get my Sneak Attack bonus." Julian nodded and took a step forward.

"Elf!" Cried a hobgoblin voice from the direction of the cigar.

Thunk. The back end of an arrow suddenly appeared poking out of Julian's chest.

"Yow!" said Julian.

"The fuck?" said Tim.

"I'm really angry!" Cooper's voice bellowed out from behind them.

"Hang on, guys!" said Dave. "We're coming!"

Tim shot at the cigar light. The light neither flickered nor flinched. Whoever had been smoking the cigar had obviously put it down. Shit.

"How did they see us?" said Tim.

Julian nocked an arrow. "They must have Darkvision. You know, like Dave and Cooper have."

There was a giant splash behind them, followed by a "Fuck!"

"Well," said Julian. "Like Dave has anyway."

"Am I the only goddamn creature in this world who can't see in the dark?" asked Tim, his crossbow loaded but nothing to aim at.

"I'm about to help you out with that," said Julian. He whispered at the fletching of his arrow, "Light." The feathers grew as bright as lamplight, revealing an approaching hobgoblin, battle-axe raised, charging silently toward Julian. Julian shot it in the throat.

Tim, who had been looking and listening for something to shoot, wasted no time pulling the trigger. He caught the hobgoblin in the leg.

Julian stepped nimbly out of the way when the axe came down. Tim dropped his crossbow, jumped on the shaft of the axe, and grabbed for the small dagger he kept hidden in his boot. Before he could get a stab in, however, the hobgoblin pulled him off and cocked his arm back to throw him.

"Magic Missile," said Julian. Tim was not in an ideal position to see the magical glowing arrow, but he had a pretty good idea of what happened when his captor's arm went limp.

Tim managed to land in a crouching position right beside his crossbow. He had it loaded just in time to fire at one of the two hobgoblins entering the sphere of light radiating from their fallen comrade's throat. The bolt glanced off the gauntlet of the hobgoblin Tim now recognized as Hammerfist, and bounced away into the darkness. The other hobgoblin was Elfgina, which meant that the one they'd already killed was Snarlgore, the apparent leader of the group, not counting the mystery hobgoblin.

Hammerfist and Elfgina ignored Tim, their attention focused completely on Julian as he started jogging backwards. They didn't even seem to notice or care that a hulked-out Cooper was rapidly, if not directly, approaching.

"H-h-horse!" Julian cried out, just as the two hobgoblins were about to reach him. A shabby brown horse popped into existence about four nanoseconds before it got tackled by two angry, axe-wielding hobgoblins.

Unlike most of the magical horses that Julian habitually murdered, this one had some fight in it. It was the first one back up on its feet, and looked to be pretty pissed off by the events occurring during its first six seconds of life. Just as Elfgina was getting to his feet, presumably wondering where the fuck a horse had suddenly come from, the horse kicked him in the breastplate, sending him flying into Cooper, who would have otherwise missed the fight entirely, running past it in a close tangent.

While Hammerfist was distracted by the horse, Tim fired a bolt into his back.

"Ow!" Hammerfist yelled. "That hurt, you little shit!" He grabbed Tim and cocked his arm back to throw. No Magic Missiles would save him this time.

"Here I am!" said Dave, finally waddling onto the scene. "Is everyone—"

Tim sailed right into him. Plate mail armor is hard. A lot harder than Tim's face.

When he was able to stand up and orientate himself again, Tim surveyed the battle scene, or at least the forty foot diameter dome of it that was visible to him. Cooper was on top of Elfgina, beating the shit out of him with his bare fists. Julian and his horse were missing. Hopefully they were together and both alive. Hammerfist grinned as he followed a target steadily with his bow. Just as he loosed the arrow, Ravenus swooped out of the darkness and rammed his beak into the hobgoblin's ear.

Hammerfist's agonized roar was echoed by the shriek of a horse. The horse shriek cut off suddenly and was followed by a splash.

Hammerfist swatted at Ravenus, but the bird was too fast. He gazed out into the darkness in the direction he had fired the arrow.

"God dammit!" Hammerfist and Julian shouted at the same time. Hammerfist picked up his battleaxe and started running in the direction Julian's voice had come from. Tim grabbed his crossbow, plucked the glowing arrow out of Snarlgore's neck, and gave chase. There was another splash just ahead of him. He loaded a bolt as he ran, and his lack of attention to where he was running nearly put him in one of the wide pools of the meandering stream. He stopped himself just in time and planted the Light arrow into the bank.

"Where are you, you long-eared freak?" Hammerfist shouted as he brought his axe down on what Tim guessed was a random bit of water. He got nothing for his effort but a splash. He sliced into a different spot of water. "You can't hide under there forever, coward!"

Tim fired a bolt into Hammerfist's back.

"Yeeeaaaoooorrrrrrgggghhh!" Hammerfist roared. This bolt had obviously relieved him of significantly more Hit Points than the last one had. "What? You again!" He turned around to face Tim. His height, along with the length of the shaft on the axe he wielded, gave him more reach than Tim had accounted for. He was in striking range.

"Ray of Frost!" Julian shouted poking his head and finger up out of the water. A film of ice crystallized around the hobgoblin's head. Julian stood up, grabbed his quarterstaff with both hands, and smashed the brittle ice to a billion shining fragments. Hammerfist collapsed into the water.

Tim and Julian each grabbed a foot and hauled the unconscious hobgoblin body out of the water. Tim wedged the Light arrow between two plates of his armor so that he could see where they were going. Halfway back to the original fight scene, Hammerfist started to cough and spit up mud. Tim dropped the leg he was dragging and shot the hobgoblin in the chin, up into his oral cavity. He stopped choking.

When they reached the others, Cooper was still pounding the shit out of Elfgina, and Dave was just standing there watching him. Amazingly, the poor hobgoblin bastard's face was still intact.

"Cooper!" said Tim. "It's over. You can stop now."

"Huh?" said Cooper. He stopped beating Elfgina and stood up. "Everybody okay?" The Barbarian Rage left his body, and he shrank from massive to merely huge.

"Yeah," said Tim. "How about you?"

"My knuckles are a little tender," said Cooper. "But I'll live."

Cooper dragged the three bodies back to the cave entrance.

"Well," said Julian. "Just one more to go. Who wants to go in first?"

All eyes, as they did in situations like this, gravitated toward Cooper. Cooper, however, sat on the ground, blissfully picking his nose, unaware that everyone was staring at him.

"No," said Tim. "It can't be Cooper this time. He's blind."

"Oh yeah," said Dave.

"Why don't you go, Dave?" said Tim. "You've got more Hit Points than either of us, and you really didn't do shit during that last battle."

"I'm sorry," Dave snapped. "I can't help it if I'm slow."

"It makes sense," said Julian. "You're a dwarf. You've got Darkvision, and you've got knowledge of caves and shit, right?"

"Fine," said Dave. "I'll go." He cautiously stepped into the cave. Tim was about to step in behind him, when Dave said, "What the hell?"

Tim froze. "What is it? What's in there?"

"Nothing," said Dave. He walked out of the cave. It goes back another twenty feet or so, and opens up into a little room. There's a couple of mats and a few shovels, but that's it."

"What do you mean, that's it?" asked Tim. "Where's the seventh hobgoblin?"

"Dunno," said Dave. "Maybe he just went home or something."

"Shit!" said Tim. "We can't go back with six heads. That nymph bitch will turn us all blind." He started pacing back and forth. "What are we going to do? We should have left one of these guys alive to interrogate."

"Elfgina should still be alive," said Cooper.

Tim stopped pacing. "You punched him repeatedly in the face for like ten minutes straight. How could he possibly be alive?"

"I was punching him with Subdual Damage," said Cooper. "You know, just in case it was Dave again."

Dave's face went pale. His eyes grew big and round, like he'd just walked in on his grandparents fucking. "Um... thanks?"

Tim put his ear to Elfgina's chest. "He still has a heartbeat! Cooper, sit on him. Dave give him a zero-level Heal spell, just to wake him up. Julian, back off a bit, would you?"

Cooper sat on Elfgina's chest and Julian stepped back.

"I heal thee," said Dave, touching the creature's head.

Elfgina groaned as he slowly came into consciousness. His eyes opened just a sliver, and then suddenly as wide as golf balls. "What do you want? Let me go! I'll give you anything!"

"Tell us where the seventh hobgoblin is!" Tim demanded.

"What?" said Elfgina. "There's only the six of us!"

Tim pulled the dagger out of his boot. "I'm not fucking around, dude. You better talk."

"He's telling the truth," said Julian, stepping into the hobgoblin's view. "He's a coward. If the seventh hobgoblin was his own mother, he'd sell her out in a heartbeat."

Elfgina's body writhed under Cooper's weight. "Who are you calling a coward? You filthy elf! You disgusting abomination!"

"Fuck this," said Tim. "Just kill him."

"But he's an unarmed prisoner," said Dave.

"But we need his fucking head," said Tim. "We've got one too few as it is."

"Give him a weapon," said Julian. "Let him go."

"Here," said Tim, placing his dagger in the hobgoblin's hand. "Stand up, Cooper."

Elfgina sprang to his feet and ran at Julian like a rabid dog.

"Ray of Frost," said Julian, pointing at the hobgoblin. The thin blue ray hit the creature in the nose, freezing its eyeballs solid. It dropped to the ground.

Ravenus quickly flew in to take advantage of a new spin on an old delicacy. "This is fantastic," he said. "Nice and crunchy, and the nerve just snaps right off."

"I'm starting to think zero-level spells are severely underrated," said Dave.

After chopping off the three heads they had available to them, they followed the stream to where their original fake campsite had been. They removed the head from the one-armed corpse, and then Ravenus guided them to the site of the battle where they'd killed Bonecrusher and Pepper.

After removing Bonecrusher's head, Cooper chucked it unceremoniously into his bag. "Well, that's six heads. Now what?"

They couldn't put the question off any longer. "There's only one thing to do," said Tim. "We take her what we've got and explain to her that she was misinformed."

"Oh that'll go over great," said Dave. "Hi sadistic tree woman. Here's something less than what we promised you. By the way, you're stupid too."

"We're not calling her stupid," said Tim. "We're just saying she's misinformed. Where's she getting her information from? Birds. Birds are stupid as shit."

"Hey!" said Julian.

"I'm not talking about Ravenus. I'm talking about normal birds."

"Maybe she'll understand," said Dave. "But are we willing to gamble all of our eyes on it?"

"I am," said Cooper.

"What other choice have we got?" asked Tim.

Dave looked at the ground. "We could let Cooper stay blind for a while."

"Hey fuck you, Dave!" said Cooper.

"I'm not talking about forever," said Dave. "I mean like maybe we'll go find a cleric in town who can sort him out or something."

"There's another option," said Julian.

Everyone with functional eyes looked at Julian.

"It's not the most pleasant option, but it's something worth considering before we gamble on the nymph's mercy."

"Spit it out," said Tim.

"If we can't find another Hot Pockets head,—"

"Hobgoblin," said Tim.

"If we can't find another head, we'll make one."

"And how do you propose we do that?" asked Dave.

"See, that's the unpleasant part," said Julian. "I was thinking we take the wolf's skull, and shove it into some of their skin. I don't know. Maybe a foot or something."

"How the fuck is that going to pass for a head?" asked Cooper.

"It'll be covered in the right kind of hair. We'll cut open a mouth hole and expose some wolf teeth. Cut out some eye holes and say that Ravenus ate the eyes. I'll use my disguise skill to do as convincing a job as I can."

"And how do you plan to explain the fucking toes growing on the guy's face?" asked Tim.

"Give me some credit, dude," said Julian. "Naturally we'll cut off the toes. We'll make it look like a giant wound. We'll have to cover the whole thing with enough gore to make it look like it was beaten pretty badly. It doesn't have to pass a close inspection. It's psychological, you see. If someone hands you a mangled lump of bone and flesh with eye holes and teeth showing and tells you it's a head, you'll probably take their word at face value."

Cooper snorted. "Ha! Good one."

"Somebody please tell me they have a better idea than this," said Tim. "Dave?"

Dave looked at the ground.

A final plea of desperation. "Cooper?"

"I like Julian's idea."

"Fuck."

When the butchery started, Tim climbed up a nearby tree. He couldn't stomach the sight of it. Eventually, he fell asleep. His sleep was fitful and uneasy. More than once he woke up just barely stopping himself from rolling off of his branch. When the sun began to dissolve the darkness, he finally couldn't force himself to sleep any more, though he desperately wanted to.

"Good morning," said Julian. "What do you think?"

Tim looked down. Staring back at him was the most horrifying thing he had ever seen, real or imagined. It was like the Devil had miscarried Werewolf-Hitler's baby. "Jesus Fucking Christ!" he shouted as he fell out of the tree.

He landed on Cooper, which was tantamount to landing on a giant whoopee cushion, except that this one produced actual fart.

"Dude," said Cooper. "There are people trying to sleep here.

Tim stood up on shaky legs, taking care to keep his eyes away from the monstrosity in Julian's hands.

"So," said Julian. "Do you think it will pass?"

"I'll give credit where credit is due," said Tim. "It looks like a head well enough. And nobody is going to look at that thing long enough to give it a proper inspection. Just put it in the fucking bag already, would you?"

Dave was sprawled out on the ground, still in his armor. Tim kicked him awake.

"Huh? What?" said Dave.

"It's time to go," said Tim.

"Did Julian finish the head?"

"Yeah."

"How did it come out? Can I see it?"

"Better not," said Tim. "You might change your mind about not wanting to be blind."

With Ravenus leading the way, the group eventually made it back to the nymph's oak grove. The life tree was again alive with the twittering of birds, and Ravenus excitedly flew up to join in their frolicking. The nymph herself was nowhere to be seen.

"What do we do?" asked Dave.

"Um, hello?" said Julian. There was no response.

Tim marched up to the tree and knocked on it so hard his knuckles hurt. "Hey! Come on out! We've got what you asked for!"

"Good morning!" The chirpy voice came from behind them. Tim, Dave, and Julian turned to face it. Cooper turned and faced a random direction. "It's so good to see you again!"

"I wish I could say the same," said Tim. He'd brought her a bag full of heads. He figured he'd earned the right to be a little testy with her.

"So do I," said Cooper.

"Well, well now, my big man," said the nymph. "Perhaps you shall. Let's see what you brought me."

Cooper upturned his bag and let the contents spill out on the ground.

"Oh my!" said the nymph. "You boys have been busy indeed!"

As the nymph looked down at the heads, Julian and Tim exchanged a nervous glance.

"Excuse me, ma'am," said Julian. "It has been a very long night, and we could really do with some rest. If it's at all possible, we'd like to get our friend's vision back and be on our way."

The nymph smiled as she walked in a slow circle around the heads, never once looking up from them.

Julian cleared his throat. "We've done as you asked, after all."

"You have indeed," said the nymph. "You've brought me seven hobgoblin heads. A very impressive feat, considering there were only six hobgoblins out there."

"Wait, what?" said Tim. "You knew there were only six hobgoblins? Then why—"

"I wanted to see what you would do. I certainly wasn't expecting a seventh head."

"You sadistic bitch!" said Tim. "You—"

Julian bonked Tim on the head with his quarterstaff. "A thousand apologies, ma'am. We meant no offense. You put us in a difficult situation. The deception was my idea. I used a wolf's skull, and—"

"I know what you did, child," said the nymph. "My birds have been watching you this whole time.

Tim had a whole lot of vitriol to spit out, but Julian stopped him short with a quick glare.

"We are at your mercy, oh mighty tree spirit," said Julian, bowing and taking a knee. "What will you do with us?"

The nymph looked down at Julian with a smug, satisfied grin, as if she were finally getting the sort of respect she thought she deserved. "You have exceeded my expectations in fulfilling the primary task set before you."

"We have?" said Dave. "But—"

"You have amused me to no end."

"Jesus Fucking Christ!" shouted Cooper.

Tim, Dave, and Julian looked up at him. He was staring down at the makeshift hobgoblin head.

"Cooper!" cried Julian. "You can see!"

"That's pretty fucked up, dude," said Cooper.

"Come on, guys," said Tim. "Let's get the hell out of here."

As they left, the nymph called out after them. "Feel free to visit again any time!" They quickened their pace.

"I think I need to wash my eyes out with fire," said Cooper.

"How about a big bottle of stonepiss," suggested Julian.

"I suppose that will do."

The End

Buzzkill

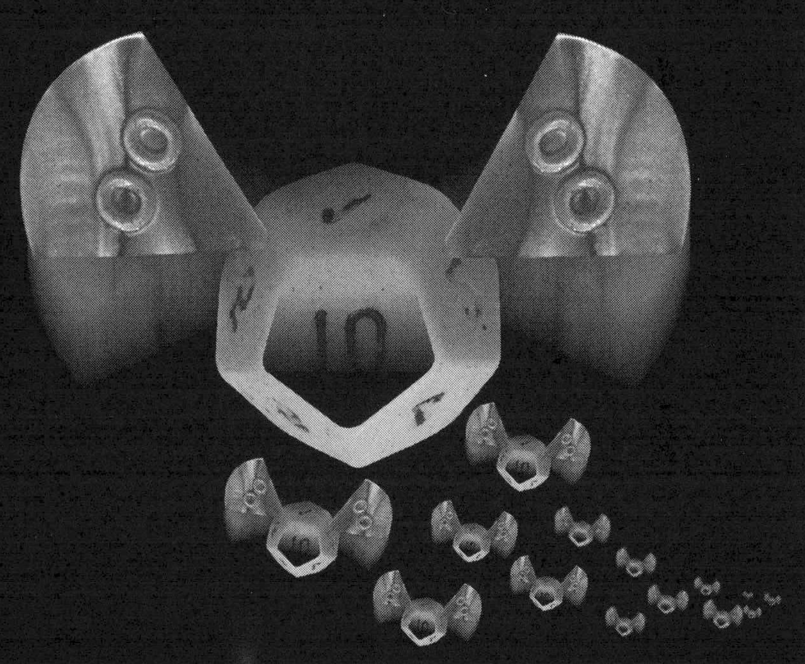

ROBERT BEVAN

BUZZKILL

(Original Publication Date: December 10, 2013)

It's times like these, when your best friend is dangling from the edge of a cliff, and you're hanging onto his leg, and he shits on your head, that you really begin to reflect on the choices you've made in life... particularly those that involved choosing best friends and favorable topography to explore.

"Julian!" cried a voice from above. It was either Tim or a random eight-year-old inexplicably lost in the desert

Julian wiped the shit out of his eyes on Cooper's calf and looked up. Tim's little halfling head peeked out over the ledge. With one arm, he hugged the trunk of the same withered tree whose newly exposed roots Cooper was holding on to. In Tim's other hand was a coil of rope.

The rope fell and the bulk of the coil hit Julian in the face.

"Ow!"

"Grab the rope!" said Tim.

Julian looked down just in time to see the broken pieces of rock, which he and Cooper had been standing on only seconds ago, explode into tiny clouds of dust at the bottom of the canyon below them. He had no intention of letting go of Cooper's leg.

"No!" said Julian. "Pull Cooper up."

"We can't," said Tim. "Dave and I are too short to reach him."

"Well dammit!" said Julian. "Cooper, don't you have a bunch of ranks in the Climb skill?"

"I think I'm taking a penalty on account of there being an elf on my leg," said Cooper. "I can't find any footholds."

"Grab the rope!" Tim repeated. "It's the only way."

"Fine!" said Julian. He closed his eyes and willed himself to be able to let go with one arm. Finding the rope, he wrapped it around his wrist four times and gave it a tug. "I'm letting go of Cooper! Don't you guys drop me!"

"We've got you!" said Dave. "The other end is tied around me. You're not going anywhere but up."

Julian let go of Cooper's leg with his other hand and found himself swinging freely in the wide open air. "Pull!"

Every part of Julian's body except for his stomach immediately started to rise. When he scrambled onto solid ground, he discovered that his stomach had made the trip with him after all. He threw up.

"You okay?" said Tim.

"I'll live," said Julian, standing up on shaky legs, using the tree to support himself. The tree tilted about five degrees toward the cliff's edge. Rocks and dirt spilled down.

"Fuck!" said Cooper, below them.

"Throw him the rope!" said Dave.

Julian began to unwind the rope from around his wrist. The tree gave a little more, the roots on his side breaking up through the earth.

"Hurry up!" said Tim.

Just as Julian freed himself from the rope and tossed the end over the side, the ground beneath the tree disintegrated and the tree disappeared over the edge.

"Cooper!" shouted Julian.

"What?" shouted Cooper.

Julian turned around. Dave and Tim were losing a battle of strength and mass, slipping inch by inch toward the edge of the cliff.

"Grab the goddamn rope!" said Tim.

"Oh right," said Julian. He grabbed the rope and planted his feet firmly into the ground. It slowed the rate at which they were all dragged toward certain death, but did not stop or reverse it. Cooper was just too heavy.

Dave's face was beet-red as he huffed and puffed through his bushy dwarf beard. "Dammit, Cooper! You've put on weight, you fat bastard!"

"We can exchange beauty critiques when I'm up there!" Cooper shouted back. "By the way, you assholes are moving the wrong direction."

Julian let go of the rope. "I've got an idea!"

"For fuck's sake!" said Tim, his hairy feet scrambling for purchase on the ground. "Could you think of an idea that doesn't involve letting go of the rope?"

Julian ran back to Dave and placed a hand on his shoulder. "Bull's Strength."

Dave stopped slipping. His leopard-furred forearm expanded like Popeye. His body grew inside his armor, challenging the integrity of his buckles.

"Gaaarrrr!" Dave shouted as he started stepping backward. The rope went taut, lifting Tim's tiny body off the ground. Dave moved like a steam locomotive in reverse. Five steps later, Cooper came climbing over the edge.

"Whew," said Cooper, wiping the sweat off of his giant sloped forehead. "That was a close one."

"No thanks to you, fucktard!" said Tim.

"How was I supposed to know how weak the ground was?"

Julian pulled at his long elf-ears. "Well you didn't have to go jumping on it like Wile E. Coyote!"

"Ah ha," said Cooper. He crossed his massive arms over his chest and looked smugly down at Julian. "You didn't let me finish. How was I supposed to know how weak the ground was until I tested it? Safety first."

"That's it," said Julian. "I'm going to kill you." He threw the right side of his serape over his shoulder, made a fist, and stepped toward Cooper.

Tim stepped in his way. "Cool it, man. Remember, it's not him. It's his Intelligence score."

"I almost died!"

"We've all almost died," said Tim. "Just take it easy and—"

"Is everyone okay?" said Ravenus, flapping in from above. His head moved left and right as he settled on the ground. "I seem to recall there being a tree here earlier."

"Where the hell have you been?" asked Julian.

"I was hunting," said Ravenus. "Killed me a squirrel, I did. Not much of a meal, I'm afraid. They have tiny eyes, and the rest of him won't be good to eat for a couple of days yet. When I felt you panicking, I came right away."

"If you're still hungry, Cooper said you could have his eyes."

Ravenus stared open-beaked at Cooper. "I say, that's very generous of him, but—"

"Just try it, Fucko," said Cooper. "And I'll be having roasted raven for dinner tonight."

"Just everybody calm down," said Dave. "We've just been through a traumatic experience, and we're all a little testy."

"Speak for your own little testes," said Cooper.

"Shut up, Cooper," said Tim. "Julian, have you chilled the fuck out yet?"

"Yeah, I'm okay," said Julian. "Sorry, Ravenus. You can't eat Cooper's eyes."

"Thank the gods," said Ravenus. "I didn't want to be rude, but he's revolting."

Tim and Dave giggled. Julian was impressed. He'd seen Ravenus tear into a week-old dead dog before, but even he was not immune to Cooper's low Charisma score.

Cooper frowned at Tim and Dave. "What did he say?"

"He said 'Aw, shucks'," said Julian.

Cooper gave Ravenus a satisfied grin. "Tough luck, bird."

"I'm sorry for losing my temper," Julian said to Cooper. "I'm still hungover from last night."

"Don't sweat it, dude. I know what you mean. I think I'm still a little drunk."

"I just can't drink like I could when I was human."

"That makes sense," said Dave. "Elves take a penalty to their

Constitution scores. It's the same reason I can drink like ten times the amount any of you guys can. I feel fantastic."

"That's great," said Tim. "Maybe you can find us a better way off of this mountain than the one Cooper found."

"There was a stream not too far back," said Dave. "If we follow that, it should eventually lead to the Bluerun river, which will take us back to Cardinia."

Cooper frowned. "If we go back to the Whore's Head empty-handed again, Frank will put me back on werewolf duty. Where the hell are all the monsters at anyway? We've been wandering around all day."

"Don't worry," said Julian. "With any luck, we'll get attacked by evil leprechauns on the way home." He didn't know what worried him more. That his statement was only mildly laced with sarcasm, or that he was really starting to consider the Whore's Head Inn home.

The land here sloped so gently that they hadn't even realized they were at a dangerous elevation until he and Cooper nearly fell off a cliff. Dave had a knack for noticing slight variances in topography... something to do with him being a dwarf. He led the group to the stream he'd spoken of earlier. It wasn't much more than a trickle of water, but it flowed in a discernible direction, and that was the direction they followed.

About thirty minutes downstream, through the leafy curtain of some massive willow trees, the stream opened up into a lovely pool. About as wide around as Papa Joe's Pizza, including the parking lot, the surface was covered in a green, slimy film, and dotted with enormous white flowers. It was the sort of place you'd take a hippie chick if you A.) wanted to make sure you got laid, and B.) wanted to see that she had some kind of a wash first. It was so perfectly hidden by the willows that, had they not been following the stream, they would have missed it entirely.

"Oh my God," said Dave, his mouth an open cavern in his otherwise hairy face. The Bull Strength spell had worn off, and he was back to his normal size.

"I never would have thought something so beautiful could exist," said Tim.

Cooper blew a double-barrel yellowish-gray snot bubble from his upturned nostrils. "They should have sent a poet."

A film of green algae covered the surface of the water, punctuated here and there by some rather large flowers. Tim stepped toward the water, but Julian put a hand on his shoulder.

"What?" said Tim.

"You don't know how deep that water is."

"I can swim," said Tim. "You only need to make a skill check if you're fighting a current or being chased by monsters or something."

"But there could be anything in there," Julian insisted. "Sharks, krakens, dire trout."

"Where the fuck are sharks going to come from?" asked Cooper. "The pool is fed from a mountain stream."

Julian put his hands on his hips. "As if that would be the most nonsensical thing we've encountered in this stupid game."

"I don't know," said Dave. "Dire trout might actually take the cake."

Cooper picked Julian up and lifted him over his head.

"What the hell are you doing?" Julian cried.

"Fishing for dire trout," said Cooper as he threw Julian into the pool.

Julian only barely managed to throw his bag away before smacking into the water. It was only about knee-high. He sat up, exposing crystal clear water beneath the algae. He supposed that maybe his concern about sharks was a little silly after all. And he had to admit that it felt good to wash the shit off of his head. But that didn't make what Cooper did any less stupid or irresponsible.

"I have scrolls in my bag, you big idiot! What if they'd gotten wet?"

Cooper frowned. "Sorry."

"How's the water?" asked Dave, already beginning to unbuckle his armor.

"It's not bad," said Julian. "A little slimy on the surface, but clear and refreshing underneath."

"Awesome," said Tim, stripping off his vest, shirt, and pants. Julian averted his eyes and made a mental note to buy Tim some underwear. He'd seen all the tiny halfling dick he wanted to see.

Cooper waded in, tentatively at first, and then dove in with a huge belly flop. When he resurfaced, Julian threw a big glob of algae at his face.

Cooper wiped it off. "Oh you asked for it, elf!" Julian's heart quickened as Cooper rushed at him. Ravenus flew down and started pecking on Cooper's head.

"Ow!" Cooper shouted, trying to swat Ravenus away. "Call off your goddamn bird!"

"Ravenus, stop!" cried Julian. "We're only playing."

Ravenus disengaged from Cooper and perched on a willow branch. "Apologies, master. I felt genuine terror in your heart.

"That's just my survival instinct kicking in," said Julian. "I know in my heart that Cooper is my friend and would never hurt me, but when my brain sees a giant half-orc rushing toward me... um... it's sort of like riding a roller coaster."

"I'm afraid I'm not familiar with that term, sir."

"Of course not," said Julian. "Hmm... let's see. Back where we come from, we sometimes—"

"You guys!" said Tim. "Look at the size of this flower!" He was standing waist deep next to the biggest lily Julian had ever seen. It was a blend of pink and lavender, about the size of a Volkswagen Beetle. The pad it rested on would probably support the four of them.

"Is it a dire lily?" asked Julian.

"Don't be stupid," said Tim. "It's just a big flower."

"Not every oversized thing in this world is dire," said Dave, having finally shed all of his armor and wading into the pool. "Some things are just big. Oxygen levels or evolution or some shit like that."

"Thanks, professor," said Julian.

"Everyone shut up for a second," said Tim, pressing his ear against the giant flower. "It's humming."

With his long elf ears, Julian didn't need to be that close to hear the noise Tim was referring to. It sounded like a refrigerator. "Tim. Maybe you should step back."

"Why would a flower be humming?" Tim mused distractedly.

Julian, though already a probably-safe distance from the flower, took a step back. "I don't know, Tim. That's why I think you ought to—"

His words were lost in an explosion of pollen. The hum-level grew from refrigerator to Vespa-with-a-faulty-muffler as a five-foot long bee flew out of the flower.

"Jesus!" cried Tim, falling back on his bare ass. His head barely poked out of the water.

"Dire bee!" shouted Julian.

"Giant bee," said Dave.

"Oh shit!" said Julian as the bee lifted Tim out of the water. "Magic Missile!"

A golden bolt of energy blasted from his outstretched palm and hit the bee in its striped abdomen, spraying a cloud of pollen dust. The insect's buzz grew sharper as it darted straight up in the air.

"Dammit!" said Julian. He raised his arm toward the bee again. "Magic Miss—"

Next thing he knew, he was underwater with Cooper on top of him. He struggled briefly, but ineffectively, until Cooper finally got off him.

"Sorry, dude," said Cooper.

"What the fuck?" said Julian.

"They were too high," said Cooper. "If you killed the bee, Tim would have fallen to his—"

"Wait," said Julian.

Dave looked skyward. "Shouldn't we be going after—"

"Shut up for a second!" Julian snapped at him. He hoped that he'd imagined the sound, but it was still there, and growing louder. "Guys. Get your weapons."

"Huh?" said Cooper.

Julian sloshed through the water until he was on dry land. He picked up his quarterstaff. "Ravenus! Go after Tim. Do not attack the bee. Just follow it and report."

"Right away, sir!" said Ravenus. He spread his big black wings and took to the air.

"You two idiots get out of the water!" Julian shouted at Dave and Cooper.

Cooper scratched his armpit. "Why do you—"

"BEES!"

Five giant bees rose out of the surrounding lilies.

"Oh fuck!" said Cooper, stomping and splashing through the water.

Dave, even unencumbered by his armor, was a good deal slower than Cooper. Two of the bees caught up to him and planted their pointy asses into his wet and hairy one.

"Yaaaaaaaooooo!" Dave howled. The bees' wings stopped buzzing, and they fell dead in the water, leaving their stingers behind like daggers in Dave's ass.

"Nice going, Dave!" said Cooper. "You took down two all by yourself!"

"Oh, my ass." Dave whimpered. He closed his eyes and plucked the two stingers from his cheeks simultaneously.

Julian readied his quarterstaff home-run-derby-style for the bee which had homed in on him. His timing was perfect, and he smacked that bee right in its big stupid bee face.

The bee spun out of control through the air, disappearing through the willow branches. It was only out of sight for a second before it burst through the branches again, minus an eye and headed straight for Julian.

Julian threw his hand out toward it. "Buzz off!" he shouted as a Magic Missile flew from his open palm. The bee's head exploded and its body crashed to the ground at Julian's feet.

"Lame," said Cooper, swatting his axe at the two bees which had chosen him as their target.

"Let's see you do better," said Julian.

"Hmm..." said Cooper, ducking under a bee attack. "Okay, I've got one." He gripped his axe with both hands by the very bottom of the handle. "Two bees?" As the bees closed in, Cooper swung his axe sideways in a large arc, slicing straight through the face of the first bee and into the thorax of the other, killing them both instantly. "Or not two bees?" He looked at Julian and cocked an eyebrow. "That is the question."

Julian considered it. "Okay, that was good, but only applicable in a very specific—"

"Holy shit!" said Cooper. "Check out the ghetto booty on Dave."

Julian turned around. "Wha!" Dave's ass was purple and swollen, like he'd just come out of the OR after having two watermelons implanted in it. "Jesus, Dave. Are you okay?"

"I don't feel so hot."

"You look like shit," said Cooper. "Maybe you should sit down."

Dave glared at him.

"On second thought, that's probably not such a good idea."

"Cooper, you help Dave get his armor back on," said Julian. "I'm going after Tim." He waved his arm in a circle. "Horse!"

A black mare popped into existence before him, saddled and ready to ride. Julian secured his right foot in the right stirrup and hefted himself onto the horse. "Go, horse!"

The horse bolted forward, coming to a full gallop in a matter of seconds. As experienced a rider as Julian's elf character may have been, the real person inside was still unaccustomed to riding so fast on the back of such a large animal. He held the saddle horn with two white-knuckled hands while he tried to focus his mind on Ravenus. Fortunately, his empathic link with his familiar functioned like a GPS, and he was able to intuit the direction the bird was flying in. A few minutes later, he had visual contact.

Ravenus flew in wide circles around the struggling giant bee.

The bee was flying slowly and erratically, but still very high. Julian guessed that while Tim was small enough for the bee to pick him up, he was still too heavy for it to make good time. The Magic Missile Julian had fired into its ass probably wasn't doing it any favors either.

As Julian followed, the bee began to descend. The little bastard must have been all tuckered out. When it got low enough, Julian would finish it off with one more Magic Missile, grab Tim, and get back to the others. Hopefully that would all occur before it reached its hive.

He followed the bee over one more hill and stopped his horse at the top. The bee was descending toward a deliberate destination, but it wasn't a hive. It was a cottage. Two things immediately stood out as being peculiar about this cottage. The first was that it appeared to be made entirely of stone, and the second was that it was huge. It was at least twice the size of what a normal cottage should be, complete with proportionally large windows and doors.

The bee's descent was toward the side of the house, where a series of large stone boxes, about the size of shipping containers, lay in a row. The stone boxes were surrounded by dozens of giant bees, some coming, some going, most just hovering around. Julian was about to just roll the dice with another Magic Missile when something— or someone – stepped out from the side of the house.

Whoever— or whatever— it was, it was easily twice as tall as Cooper, and maybe three times as tall as Julian. And it appeared to be wearing some kind of Hazmat suit.

Julian snapped his fingers, and the horse disappeared beneath him. He landed on his feet, but let himself fall the rest of the way down. This was not a time to go rushing in with naught but a quarterstaff and a few Magic Missiles. He stayed close to the ground and observed.

The huge man had a tiny metal bottle in his left hand. As he approached the stone boxes, he pulled the stopper out of the bot-

tle, releasing a cloud of thick, white smoke. The bees coming in contact with the smoke stopped flying and settled down to sleep on the ground.

Having calmed the bees in the immediate vicinity, the man slid the lid off of one of the boxes and pulled back his meshed visor. His skin was as grey and rough as the stone his house was made from. He was completely bald. His eyes and cheeks were sunken, giving him a most severe face, like a statue of a king who had not enjoyed his reign. He dipped a gloved finger into the box. When he pulled it out again, it was coated in a thick golden—

"No fucking way," Julian whispered to himself, not believing what he was seeing. "A dire fucking beekeeper."

"Mmmm," said the beekeeper, licking his finger. "That's the stuff. Good work, little bees. You've outdone your—what's this?" His attention was on the bee carrying Tim. He held out one hand under the bee, and with the other hand he waved the smoking bottle around. The bee dropped Tim into the big man's palm and flew sluggishly into the open box. Tim started choking violently in the smoke until the beekeeper stoppered the bottle and blew the lingering smoke away.

"Great Ragnor!" said the beekeeper. Julian was too far away to be sure, but he thought the dude might be crying. "Greta! Come quickly!"

"I'm not going anywhere with all of those blasted bees buzzing around!" shouted a female voice from inside the cottage.

"Love of my life!" said the beekeeper. "The gods have heard our prayers, and they have answered!"

"Speak not idly of the gods, Thorak!" the voice inside the house snapped back at him. "I'll not have it in my house."

"My words are not idle, love," said Thorak, Holding Tim in his cupped hands and patting him gently on the head with his massive thumb. "Our dreams have come true! They have delivered us a child!"

The front door swung open and an equally huge grey-skinned person shook the ground as she stomped out. She was as bald as her husband, but her breasts were like boulders under her apron. This must be Greta.

"What blasphemy do you profane this house with? I tell you, I'll not tolerate—" She clapped her own hands over her mouth as she looked into her husband's. "Blessed be the gods! A little boy!"

"Oh ho ho!" cried the beekeeper. He really was crying now. Tears streaked down either side of his stony grey face. "He's made a little pee-pee right here in my hands!"

"So he has," said Greta. "Well bring him inside. We'll get him cleaned up and I'll wrap him in a fresh nappy. Then we'll see about feeding him."

Thorak's smile faltered briefly as he looked at Tim in his hands, but he beamed down at his wife with a broad smile which Julian thought might not be one hundred percent sincere.

When they brought Tim inside the massive cottage, Julian stood up and looked for Ravenus. He spotted the bird flying high in a tight circular holding pattern directly above the bee-boxes. Julian waved his arms and willed Ravenus to look his way. Shortly after, Ravenus flew down to him.

"Tim's in trouble," said Julian. "Those dire beekeepers think he's a child delivered by the gods."

"Those what, sir?" asked Ravenus.

"Dire beekeepers?"

"The stone giants, you mean?"

Julian's face flushed. "Yes, of course. Do you have any ideas?"

"As a matter of fact, I do," said Ravenus. "As I was flying around up there, I got to thinking. Fish tend to decompose much more rapidly than mammals. If you were to combine the two somehow— say, mash them up together into a paste— you might only have to wait a few hours before it's ready to eat. Maybe spread it on a crust of bread. Or just lap it up straight out of the—"

"I was talking about ideas on how to rescue Tim."

Ravenus lowered his head. "Oh, of course sir. A thousand pardons. No, I'm afraid I don't."

"Dammit," said Julian, tugging on his long ears. "Even with

Cooper and Dave here, I don't think we could take those stone giants in a fight. They're way too big. And if they really believe that Tim is their child, Diplomacy isn't going to be much help either."

"If you don't mind me saying so sir," said Ravenus. "You're a very talented sorcerer. I don't think you always use your magic to its full potential. If you use your imagination, I bet you could—"

"Magic!" said Julian.

"Yes, sir," said Ravenus. "The point I was making is that sometimes we—"

"Shut up for a second. I want to check something out." He closed his eyes and muttered to himself. "Detect Magic." When he opened his eyes again, his vision was in black-and-white. He immediately turned toward the bee-boxes and found what he was looking for. The bottle which the stone giant had subdued the bees with glowed bright pink. He'd left it on top of the bee box.

Julian closed his eyes and shook the spell free from his head. "Ravenus, do you think you'd be able to pick up that bottle over there?"

"I wouldn't think so, sir. "There's not really a spot for me to wrap my talons around."

"It's too high for me to reach," said Julian. "We'll have to do this as a team."

"Have you thought of a plan then, sir?"

"Yes."

"Brilliant!"

Julian smiled. He really liked having Ravenus around. "Thank you. Now here's what we're going to do. I'm going to walk over there, slowly and quietly. The idea is to not let the stone giants hear me and not provoke the bees. When I'm in position, next to the big stone bee-box, you fly over and tip the bottle off the edge. I'll catch it, and we'll both meet back here. Got it?"

"No problem, sir!"

As Julian inched his way toward the massive stone bee box, the air smelled more and more strongly of hickory, which he assumed was from the lingering traces of bottled smoke. He paused whenever a bee flew too close. Proximity was a problem he was going to have to face anyway, though, as he was the one approaching their home.

The bees ignored him for the most part until he stepped within about twenty feet of the box. Then a trio of bees started buzzing past him more aggressively. He stood as still as the stone the boxes were made of as the bees sated their curiosity. They passed so close that he could feel the air move from their wings.

One of the three hovered directly in front of Julian. Its buzz seemed as loud as a riding lawn mower, and it made clicking, chittering sounds with its mouth. Julian didn't need to understand bee-speak to make a guess as to what this bee was trying to tell him. Back your elf-ass up. We would prefer not to leave vital parts of our anatomy inside you, but we will do just that if you step any closer to this box.

Julian conceded defeat. He had been outsmarted by three insects. His plan had failed. He was about to take a step back when Ravenus flew in and tipped the bottle off the top of the box. It landed on the grass below, and the stopper fell out. Smoke poured out and a thick cloud began to form. Ravenus started rolling the bottle toward him.

Julian held his breath and his eyes began to water as the cloud moved his way, but Ravenus's quick thinking had worked. The bee which had been interrogating Julian settled down on the grass for a nice little nap, and his two wingmen had flown away from the smoke. When it was within reach, Julian grabbed the bottle and sprinted back to his rendezvous spot on the hill. It wasn't as tiny up close as the giant had made it seem. It was a little bigger than a 3-Liter Coke bottle. Smoke continued to billow out of the top of the bottle, so Julian held it over his head as he ran so that he could breathe. He felt like a steam locomotive.

When he stopped at the rendezvous spot, holding the bottle over his head no longer had any effect. The smoke continued to pour out, surrounding him. He held his breath again, trying to cover the top of the bottle with his hand. The smoke ran right through his fingers. He turned the bottle upside-down and pushed the open end into the grassy earth. Still no good. Smoke was all around him, and his eyes were burning like sons of bitches. They would need to go back for the stopper. Ravenus could get it.

Julian called out, "Ra—haugh haugh blaugh haugh!" He choked, his oxygen-starved lungs sucking in enormous quantities of smoky air.

As an alternative to passing out and suffocating to death, Julian forced his legs into motion. He ran in a wide circle until his choking calmed down. Then he continued running as he scanned the skies for Ravenus. Where the hell was that bird? He stopped running when a small metal sphere fell out of the sky, thudding into the ground next to him.

"The hell?" Julian muttered before the ever-growing cloud of smoke forced him to hold his breath again. Picking it up, he discovered that the sphere was only the top of the object. It was connected to a cone, sort of like a child's drawing of an ice-cream cone. It took a few more seconds before his smoke-filled brain made the connection. He placed the stopper into the top of the bottle. It was a perfect fit. The air cleared and Julian let out a long sigh of relief.

"Thought you might need that," said Ravenus, flapping to the ground next to Julian.

"Well done, Ravenus."

"Now what's this plan of yours?"

Julian looked curiously at his familiar. "What are you talking about?"

"Your plan to rescue Tim," said Ravenus. "You said you had a plan."

"Oh no," said Julian. "I meant I had a plan to get this bottle. We just carried it out."

"Um..." Ravenus scratched at the ground with a talon. "And a finely executed plan it was, sir," he lied. "But what do we need the bottle for?"

"It's magical!" said Julian enthusiastically. "There must be a thousand and one uses for a continuously smoking bottle." His enthusiasm waned with each word of that sentence.

"Outside of bee subdual," said Ravenus, "I'm hard-pressed to think of one."

Julian frowned, looking at his newly acquired treasure. He'd find a use for it. They wouldn't bother including a magic item in the game if its only practical use was for beekeepers, would they?

"I with Cooper and Dave would hurry up. We need to work out a strategy."

"The stupid one will be along shortly," said Ravenus. "I saw him running this way while I was flying."

"Alone?" Julian stood up and looked eastward just in time to see Cooper's head rise above the crest of the next hill over. "Where's Dave?"

Ravenus shrugged his wings.

"Oh no!" cried Tim from inside the cottage. "Please, anything but that! I'm telling you, you've got the wrong—" The rest was muffled grunts.

Julian desperately wanted to run to Tim, but heading Cooper off was the safer option. If Cooper opened his big mouth and alerted the stone giants to their presence, it could mean death for all of them, Tim included. Also, Julian would need Cooper's help to be able to look in the window.

Holding a finger over his lips, he ran as fast as he could toward Cooper. They met in the shallow valley between the two hills.

"Where's Dave?" Julian asked.

"He's coming," said Cooper. "He's slow. What the fuck is that?"

"Huh?" Julian followed Cooper's gaze to the bottle in his hand. "Oh, it's a magic bottle. It makes smoke. I swiped it from a stone giant's house. I thought it might come in handy for rescuing Tim."

"Shit," said Cooper. "Tim got captured by stone giants?"

"More like adopted. They think he's their baby, delivered by the gods."

"That's fucked up, dude. Wait, so they're like a married couple?"

Julian shrugged. "I guess."

"And they don't know where babies come from?"

"I guess not."

"That's fucked up, dude."

"We should get to the cottage," said Julian. "I think they're torturing him or something."

Cooper put his hands on his hips. "Now that's just bad parenting."

They approached the side of the cottage as quietly as they could. Cooper wasn't particularly stealthy, but Julian felt confident that Tim's continuing grunts and protests would cover them well enough.

"Oh god stop!" cried Tim as Cooper and Julian stood beneath the window. "It's like Pepto Bismol and sand. I can't—" He was stifled again.

"Lift me up," whispered Julian. Cooper grabbed him by the waist and lifted him over his head. Julian took a tentative peek over the sill. Greta sat topless, facing away from the window, pressing Tim's face against her huge gray breast. Thorak rubbed her naked shoulders.

Tim's eyes met Julian's, and he let out a long, muffled groan. Julian put his finger over his lips and nodded.

"What's going on?" asked Cooper in what passed for a whisper for him.

"Shh!" Julian said, looking down at him. He whispered back, "She's breastfeeding Tim."

"No way!" said Cooper, letting go of Julian.

"Ow!" said Julian, his face hitting the window sill on the way down. He landed on his ass.

Cooper jumped up, grabbed the window sill, and pulled himself up to peek over. "Oh shit."

"Hey!" Thorak shouted from inside.

Cooper let go of the window sill. "Dude, I've got some bad news."

"You think?" Julian whispered harshly at him.

"What is it?" cried Greta. "What's happening?"

"Nothing to worry about, love," said Thorak. "Just a pervert. I'll take care of him." His voice seemed extra loud, as if he was giving them a warning, maybe a chance to run.

"Dude, come on," said Cooper. "We've got to go."

"No," said Julian. The seed of an idea began to take root in his head. "You've got to go. He didn't see me. Throw me up onto the roof and start hauling ass."

"But what about—"

"Dude. Don't think. Throw."

"Okay," said Cooper. He picked up Julian and tossed him underhandedly onto the roof. His ninety-five pound elf-body was nothing for Cooper's massive strength.

He landed surprisingly gently on the roof. Even more surprising was seeing Ravenus there staring back at him.

"Well isn't this nice, sir," said Ravenus. "I certainly wasn't expecting to see you up here."

"Keep it down," said Julian. "I'm hiding." He scooted back away from the edge of the flat stone roof and watched Cooper run away. A few seconds later, Thorak was in view chasing after him and carrying a huge, bulging sack. He would have caught up with any of the rest of them with ease, but Cooper had a Movement Bonus as part of the barbarian package. Julian silently congratulated himself on remembering that. He was getting the hang of this game.

"Sir?" said Ravenus.

"Okay, here's the plan," said Julian. "I'll sneak in through the kitchen window, hide this bottle somewhere, pull the stopper, and sneak back out. When the lady stone giant smells the smoke, she'll leave Tim behind to go investigate. Tim sneaks out of this window, and we all run like hell." He crossed his arms and stuck his chin out, proud of himself for coming up with a plan, and for thinking of a practical use for the smoking bottle. "What do you think?"

"If I may say so, sir," said Ravenus meekly. Mustering up his courage, he continued. "Your plan seems just a bit far-fetched."

"What are you talking about?" said Julian. "It's foolproof!"

"Let's, for the moment, take for granted that every part of your plan happens exactly the way you expect it will," said Ravenus. "Mind you, I'm not entirely convinced of that, but that's neither here nor there. How long do you think you'll have to run before she figures out that her baby is missing? She'll catch up to you in a matter of minutes. And what do you think she'll do to her son's kidnapper?"

"I'll admit you raise some thought-provoking questions," said Julian. A moment later, he added, "Shit."

As it turned out, Julian wouldn't have had the time to carry out his plan anyway. Thorak didn't chase Cooper very far. He reached into his sack and pulled out a boulder roughly the size of a beach ball. He hurled it at Cooper, who only just managed to duck out of the way before the huge, round rock exploded into a nearby outcropping.

"The next one's for your head, you filthy pervert!" the angry giant called out after Cooper. "Dishonor my wife again, and I'll make you into a stew!" He hefted his sack of rocks over his shoulder and trudged back toward his house.

Julian took cover behind the chimney. Just as Thorak was getting close enough to make Julian nervous, another figure crested the hill to the east. It was Dave, out of breath and naked from the waist down. He held his helmet over his junk, but his ass must have still been too swollen to don the lower half of his armor.

Upon seeing one another, Dave and Thorak paused in mutual disbelief.

"Jesus Christ!" said Dave.

"Another one!" Thorak growled. "Perverts everywhere!"

"Huh?" said Dave. He looked down at his helmet. "Oh, no. You don't understand. I was just—"

A boulder smashed into Dave's breastplate, sending him tumbling backwards down the hill and out of sight.

"What's become of this world?" Thorak grumbled to himself as he walked to the front door. The house shook when he slammed it behind him.

"Go see if Dave is okay," Julian said to Ravenus.

"Right-O!" said Ravenus as he flew off.

"Did you get rid of the perverts?" asked Greta.

"They won't be bothering you again anytime soon," said Thorak.

After hearing the ferocity with which the giant had shouted at Cooper and Dave, Julian only now picked up on how very gently he spoke to his wife.

"You didn't..." Greta started.

"No, love," said Thorak. "Of course not. We are not savages. Oh, but I gave them a warning they'll not soon forget."

"I'm worried about little Krum," said Greta. "He's not taking down much milk at all."

"You named him Krum!" said Thorak. His voice was positively jolly. "After my own father. What a lovely gesture!"

"Your father was always kind to me."

"He keeps spitting up on me. Do you think he's sick?"

There followed a sound like a plunger being pulled out of a clogged toilet, then a loud, liquid splat.

"Mayhap the gods sent him to us with a full stomach, so not to overburden us on our first day of parenthood."

"Oh!" said Greta. "They are wise and generous indeed!"

"Now why don't you go in the kitchen and wash up? I'll look after little Krum here." A moment later, he spoke again. His voice was quieter, sterner, and more direct. "Sit down. We haven't much time."

"Are you people crazy?" said Tim. His voice was raw and raspy. "I'm not what you think I am."

"I know what you are, halfling. Do you know that I rescued you from being devoured by the queen of my bees? 'Tis true! You owe me a debt, and I intend to collect." After a short pause, he continued. "You've been through an ordeal. You must be hungry. Here, have some cheese."

"Thank you," said Tim. His next words were a little muffled, which Julian guessed was due to a mouthful of cheese. "Look, I'm sorry for your recent loss, but I can't replace your child."

"You do not understand," said Thorak. "We have suffered no loss. My wife suffers from a condition which makes her unable to bear a child. It has maddened her with grief. She prays to the gods every night. It breaks my heart to watch her suffer so."

"Hold on," said Tim. "If the problem is a physical one, then why the fuck is she lactating?"

"Mind your tongue, halfling," said Thorak. His voice carried a not-so-subtle warning. "It's just one more symptom of the same condition. The gods can be cruelly ironic. True, 'tis a continuously painful reminder of our plight, but it makes for a fine cheese."

The sound that followed was either a paper bag full of marshmallows exploding or Tim spitting out a mouthful of cheese. Julian guessed the latter.

"Fucking hell, man!" said Tim. "You might want to give a guy a heads up before you feed him your wife's tit cheese!"

"Speak not such foul words under my roof! You are unfit to bear my blessed father's name!"

"I didn't ask for your fucking father's name," said Tim. "Just like I didn't ask to be dressed in a diaper or suck spackling paste from your batshit crazy wife's tit."

Tim was starting to lose his shit. Julian had seen this happen before. His little mouth was about to get him killed.

"I'm warning you, halfling!"

"Take your best shot, Kojak."

"Another word and I'll feed you to the queen bee myse—"

"What's all the commotion in here?" Greta had entered the room again.

"Our little Krum is cranky," said Thorak. "Perhaps it's time for a nap."

"Perhaps it's time for you to eat my ass, Daddy Warbucks," said Tim.

"Did he just call you Daddy?" said Greta.

"How is that the only word you heard, you crazy bitch!"

"On second thought," said Thorak. "Perhaps he's finally hungry."

That shut Tim up real quick.

"Would you look at that!" said Greta. "You were right, dear. He's all tuckered out. You've taken to fatherhood quite well."

There was some moving of furniture, and then Thorak spoke softly. Even with his improved hearing, Julian had to crawl closer to the window and strain his ears to hear.

"Now there's a good lad. Get some sleep. Daddy has to go to town on business for a couple of days. When I come back, maybe I'll teach you how to tend the bees."

"Oh, must you really leave today?" said Greta. "Our son has only just arrived."

"All the more reason for me to handle my affairs responsibly," said Thorak. "I'm not the only beekeeper in the realm. If I displease my customers, they'll get their honey from one of my competitors."

"But what if the perverts come back?" She didn't sound frightened exactly. If Julian had to guess, he'd say she almost sounded hopeful.

"I have shown them mercy once. The gods are appeased. Should they choose to ignore my warning, you may chop them up and feed them to the queen with a clear conscience."

The good news was that, if they waited a little while, there should be only one stone giant to deal with.

The bad news was that, even after encountering the group's two strongest fighters, the giants saw absolutely nothing in the way of a threat. The only concern Greta had with being left without her husband was a question of the morality of using them as bee food.

Julian sat back and sorted through his scrolls. He always kept a few extra Magic Missiles handy, but he'd already ruled those out. He had a Mage Armor, which he'd definitely use if it came to a fight, but it wasn't helpful in formulating a plan.

Grease? No.

Ventriloquism? No.

Mount? Always good for the getaway, but not so useful for the rescue.

Feather Fall? He'd be using that one shortly.

Enlarge Person? Hmm.... He might be able to enlarge Cooper, and then he could keep her busy while the rest of them ran off with Tim. No, that plan sucked. Judging by the size of the rocks that dude was throwing, even an enlarged Cooper would be no match for a stone giant. He'd just be swapping out Cooper for Tim, and Cooper was the sort of baby that a mother would just feed to the bees. Now if he had a Reduce Person, they might all be able to grapple with her, tie her up or something, and then make a break for it. But he didn't have one, so there was no point in dwelling on that.

Julian frowned as he rolled up the scrolls except for the Feather Fall and packed them back into his bag. Dave and Cooper were more experienced in this game. Maybe they would be able to come up with something.

He listened carefully for movement within the house. When he judged it safe enough to do so, he whispered the incantation to the Feather Fall spell. As he spoke them, the words disappeared from the parchment. He jumped off the roof, and his stomach lurched as he dropped at a conventional falling speed. He thought he'd screwed up, but five feet into his descent, the spell took effect, and he glided gently to the ground. He ran as fast as he could away from the stone giant house.

Julian scanned the uneven terrain for signs of his friends. As if reading his mind, Ravenus took to the air to serve as a beacon for Julian to locate Dave and Cooper. As Julian got closer to the position beneath Ravenus's holding pattern, he no longer required the bird's service. He could find their position by sound alone, because they were making a hell of a lot of it. Banging and clanging, as if they were trying to tunnel through stone with a frying pan.

He was almost right on top of them when he finally made visual contact. They were crouched down, hiding behind a five-foot outcrop. He winced at the sight of Dave's huge, purple ass. He was completely naked now, banging on something with a rock.

"What the hell are you guys doing?" asked Julian. "I could hear you a mile away."

Dave stopped his task. "I'm pounding out the dent that big bastard put in my breastplate."

"Are you okay?"

"Yeah, but it was close. I think my sternum was touching my spine."

"Ouch."

"I had to use up all of my Heal spells."

"All of them?"

"I've still got a couple of zero-levels left, but yeah. And, wouldn't you know, they didn't do a goddamn thing to bring down the swelling in my ass."

"Well I've got some good news," said Julian. "The husband is leaving tonight to go sell honey in town, so we only have the wife to deal with."

"Great!" said Dave. "Now it'll take a full twelve seconds for us all to die instead of six."

"Maybe try to be a little more constructive?" Julian suggested.

"We can't take on a stone giant," said Dave. "We simply aren't high enough level for that."

Julian opened his bag. "Then we'll have to think of something else."

As the sun descended toward the western horizon, Julian, Dave, Cooper, and Ravenus discussed different options, taking into account Julian's repertoire of spells and the magic smoke bottle. It wasn't exactly a Mensa meeting, though, and they didn't come up with much more than Julian had thought of on his own.

"Dave could stand in the doorway," said Cooper. "You cast Enlarge Person on him so that he gets stuck, blocking her exit. We grab Tim through the window and make a break for it."

"You're such an ass," said Dave.

"You're one to talk, J-Lo."

"Cooper!" said Julian. "That's brilliant!"

"The J-Lo thing? Thanks, but he kinda walked right into it."

"No, the Enlarge Person thing."

"You know what?" said Dave. "Fuck the both of you. Tim's in real trouble, and you guys have got nothing better to do than make fun of me?"

Julian ignored him. "Ravenus, fly back to the house and stake it out. As soon as the big guy leaves, come back and report."

"Roger that, sir!" said Ravenus, and he launched into the darkening sky.

While they waited, Julian shared his new idea with Dave and Cooper and the three of them worked out some of the kinks. It wasn't foolproof by any means, and would actually put them in a much worse situation if Julian's timing was off. But they all agreed it was the best chance they had.

*

Under the cover of darkness, they approached the cottage. Greta was humming softly and Tim was weeping openly.

Wearing nothing but a coil of rope, Cooper took his position below the window of the room Greta and Tim were in.

Dave nakedly walked around to the other side of the house and stood outside the kitchen window.

Julian stood outside the front door, unrolled the scroll in his sweaty hands, licked his dry lips, and nodded to Ravenus, perched up on the roof.

"Caw!" said Ravenus. It was the agreed-upon signal, for Cooper's benefit.

Shortly after, Cooper began shouting the famous Bourbon Street chant.

"Show your tits! Show your tits!"

"What in the name of the gods?" said Greta. "You again!"

"Show your tits! Show your tits!"

"How dare you show your face again! You will rue this day!" Only a little more calmly, she spoke to Tim. Julian could only just make out what she was saying over Cooper's chanting. "You stay here, Krum. Mommy will take care of that filthy pervert."

Julian felt the earth tremble slightly as she stomped through the house, and that's when Dave joined in the chanting.

"Show your tits! Show your tits!"

"The nerve of you!" Greta screamed. "Why can you not leave decent people alone? Oh, the bees shall eat well in the coming weeks. I can promise you that!"

The ground shook more violently with each step she took closer to Julian. His hands were trembling so much that he could barely make out the magical writing on the scroll. He took a deep breath to calm himself, and then heard the latch being undone on the other side of the door.

"Enlarge Person!" Julian shouted as soon as the door swung open.

"Wha!" screamed Greta and slammed the door shut. He must have startled her.

"Did it work?" shouted Dave.

"I don't know," Julian shouted back. "She closed the—"

A foot crashed through the window next to the door. It was almost as long as Julian was tall, but surprisingly feminine for a foot so large.

"Um..." said Julian. "Yeah, it worked." He ran around to Cooper's side of the house in time to see Tim climbing up the rope and out of the window.

"Horse!" said Julian. A sturdy grey horse appeared before him.

"Horse!" he said again, and a brown horse appeared next to the grey one.

"What the hell are those for?" asked Dave, coming around the corner. "Let's just walk. She's not going anywhere."

"There's something I forgot to mention," Julian lied. "That spell is only going to last for a minute." That part wasn't a lie at all.

"What the fuck, man!" cried Dave. "I can't ride a horse. Look at my ass!"

"Hey Dave," said Cooper.

"What?"

Cooper punched Dave in the face.

"What the fu—"

Cooper punched him again, this time knocking him out cold. "Let's go." Cooper mounted the grey horse, leaned over, and picked up Dave by the arm.

Julian and Tim mounted the brown horse, and they galloped back toward the pool by the willow trees.

"Come back here, you filthy perverts!" Greta screamed after them. "Come back with my son!" Gradually her screams faded as the group lengthened their distance from her. She was fast, but she wasn't horse fast.

When they reached the pool, Cooper tossed Dave's unconscious body into the water. A few seconds later, Dave was on his feet, coughing and cursing.

"My fucking face!" he cried, covering his face with his hands.

"Your ass feel better?" said Cooper.

"I really hate you, Cooper," said Dave. "And thanks."

"Don't mention it."

"Are you okay, Tim?" asked Julian.

"Physically, I'm fine," said Tim. "But psychologically, I don't know. That was pretty messed up."

"Oh boo-hoo," said Cooper. "Poor little Tim had to suck on giant titties all day."

"Dude, they dressed me in a diaper!" Tim spread his arms out to show off the thick, white, fluffy fabric wrapped around his waist. "It was humiliating."

Cooper waved his hand dismissively at Tim. "You're describing some men's wildest fantasies."

Everyone stared silently at Cooper.

"What?" he said defensively. "Not necessarily mine. I'm just sayin'."

Julian suddenly remembered the smoking bottle and took it out of his bag.

"Is that the smoking bottle the giant was using?" asked Tim.

"Yeah."

"Nice grab."

"I'm sending it back."

"Like fuck you are!" said Tim.

"I don't feel right keeping it," said Julian. "Thorak needs this for his livelihood.

"For his lively—" Tim stammered. "Thorak? When the hell did you two become such good buddies?"

"I feel sorry for them," said Julian.

"They just tried to murder you and feed you to bees!" cried Tim. "They put me in a diaper and sexually assaulted me! Dave, Cooper, are you listening to this bullshit?"

Dave frowned and averted his eyes from Tim's glare. "I don't know."

"Have a heart, man," said Cooper. "She just lost a son."

Tim shook his head. "Un-fucking-believable. Fine. Do whatever you want. Let's make absolutely sure that this entire expedition was another glorious waste of time."

Julian secured the bottle to the brown horse's saddle and gave instructions to the horse. "Go that way. Stop when you reach the house." The horse ran off into the night. About a minute later, way off in the distance, Julian heard the dreaded equine scream and knew that he had once again sent an innocent magical horse to its death. He was pretty sure it was far enough away such that the others wouldn't have heard it, so he mourned his short-lived companion in silence.

"We should get moving," said Julian.

Dave and Cooper scavenged Tim's clothes, which were barely sufficient to cover their junk. Tim remained in his diaper. Only Julian was fully clothed as they walked back to Cardinia.

Tim reached into the folds of his diaper and pulled out a large hunk of white cheese. "I grabbed this before I left, if anyone's hungry."

"Nice!" said Dave, smiling through his blood-crusted beard.

"Oh hell yes!" said Cooper. "I'm hungry as fuck."

Julian smiled at Tim and politely declined.

The End

Cooper's
Christmas Carol

ROBERT BEVAN

COOPER'S CHRISTMAS CAROL

(Original Publication Date: December 22, 2013)

Cooper grimaced down at the dead boar he carried under his right arm. Ravenus had eaten its eyes, but Cooper still felt like the boar was looking back at him, mocking him, with the inside of his testicle even now drying on its tusk. Dave's Heal spell had repaired Cooper's nuts well enough, but it hadn't done anything for the lumpy rash spreading out from his left armpit. That much, at least, he couldn't blame on the boar. Still, fuck boars.

Nobody else was in any better a mood as they trudged back to the Whore's Head Inn. A boar was good for a bit of food. And to be fair, this was a decent-sized boar. But it wasn't treasure. It wasn't a prize the four of them could hold their heads up high while offering. It was a notch above a completely wasted day. Cooper knew this. But just in case he didn't, Tim had mentioned it about forty thousand times since they started back home.

"Frank is going to be pissed," said Tim. "Four guys. Twelve hours. That's forty-eight man-hours, and what have we got to show for it? A pig."

"It's not all that bad," said Julian. "Look at the size of it. That's enough meat to feed the whole pub for a couple of days."

"Look at that thing," Tim snapped. "Half of its hair is missing. It was coughing up blood before we even attacked it. It's obviously riddled with disease and parasites. And that's not even taking into account that it's been marinating in Cooper's pit-juice for the past hour and a half."

"Still," said Dave. "It's not like we're coming back completely empty-handed."

Hopefully, Tony the Elf would be on door duty when they arrived. They didn't exactly like one another, but at least he didn't fuck around with secret passwords and all that kind of bullshit like Gorgonzola. He'd just slide the window open, roll his eyes like he was hoping you had died out there, and then open the door. Cooper didn't need a warm welcome. What he needed was a cold beer... maybe a shot of stonepiss.

When they arrived ten minutes later, the question of who was on door duty turned out to be moot. The door was wide open, with four dumbasses trying to shove a pine tree through it.

"What the hell are you guys doing?" said Cooper.

"Oh, good!" said a dwarf whose name Cooper had forgotten. "Could you give us a hand?"

"I can give you a foot in the ass if you don't get that fucking tree out of my way." Cooper didn't like many of the dwarves at the Whore's Head Inn, but he couldn't quite put his finger on why. Dave was easy enough to figure out. He didn't like Dave because Dave sucked. But he didn't have that specific a reason not to like the guy asking him to help move the tree. The best he could come up with was that the game dictated that half-orcs and dwarves just didn't get along. He didn't like that explanation because it made him feel like a racist.

"You don't have to be a dick about it," said the elf who called himself Scorn. "Come on. We don't need his help."

"I'm sorry," said Cooper. He dropped the boar and palmed the chopped up base of the trunk. He shoved as hard as he could, but the tree wouldn't budge. It was jammed in there real good.

"Okay guys," said the dwarf. "On three!"

"Fuck that," said Cooper. "I've got this." He cracked his knuckles and his neck on both sides. "I'm really angry!"

His heart-rate picked up the pace as hot blood surged through his body. His man-tits ballooned out into mighty pectoral muscles. The growth spread out to his arms and legs, all the way out to his fingers and toes. His vision turned pink.

"FUCK YOU, TREE!" he shouted, shoving the tree effortless-

ly through the doorway. Most of the branches on the bottom half broke, but there was no avoiding that. His task successful, he ceased his Barbarian Rage. He inhaled deeply, inviting in the soothing scent of pine.

As his muscles relaxed and his vision lost its blood-tint, Cooper found that he had knocked over a number of tables and chairs, and caught several patrons in the branches of the great tree. He stood vulnerably amongst the silent crowd staring at him.

"Merry Christmas!" said Frank, clearly plastered. Gnomes got a bonus to their Constitution score. He had obviously skipped the beer and gone straight for the stonepiss. For some reason, he was wearing a Santa Claus hat, but not a shirt. If his skin, for whatever reason, were to turn blue, he'd be the spitting image of Papa Smurf. Cooper tucked this observation into an easily accessible pocket in the back of his mind for further consideration at a later time.

"What the hell?" said Tim. He and Julian had followed in the path of furniture carnage Cooper had left in the tree's wake. "It's barely autumn."

People were laughing. Booze was flowing. The man they most feared was shitfaced and shirtless. It was just like Tim to start asking questions at a time like this.

"We do this every couple of months," explained the booze-sodden gnome-shell of Frank. "It helps keep morale up." He hiccoughed and raised his mug. "Merry Christmas!"

"Good enough for me," said Cooper. He picked his kill up off the floor, took it behind the bar to the kitchen, and set it on Barney's preparation table.

"What the hell am I supposed to do with that?" asked Barney.

"Cook it."

"That's the most sickly-looking boar I've ever seen. Did you kill it, or just find it dead in the woods?"

"Dude," said Cooper. "This is fresh meat."

Barney picked up a meat cleaver and chopped into the hindquarter of the dead animal. The muscle beneath the patchy-haired skin was tinted green and crawling with little worms.

Cooper frowned. "Those will die in the oven, right?"

Barney crossed his arms. "I'm not cooking this thing."

"Fuck you, dude," said Cooper. "I'll cook it myself."

"Do you have any ranks in the Cooking skill?"

"I didn't even spend a skill point to get Literacy," said Cooper. "You think I'm going to blow one on Cooking? Seriously, how hard can it be?"

"Suit yourself," said Barney. "I'm done for the night. The kitchen's all yours."

Cooper opened the oven door and looked inside. There was still a pretty strong wood fire burning beneath the rack. Nothing to it. He shoved the boar carcass onto the rack. A few of the worms fell out of the post-mortem wound and into the fire, making a satisfying popping sound.

"Merry Christmas, you squirmy fuckers," said Cooper. He closed the oven door and went back out to the bar to get a drink.

The few resident druids at the Whore's Head Inn had healed the broken lower branches of the tree. It stood upright in a corner, its trunk planted in a barrel. Cooper had to admit, it didn't look half bad.

"All right!" said Frank, waving a stonepiss bottle in the general direction of the tree. "Now the magic users. Work your magic!"

All of the wizards and sorcerers, who far outnumbered the druids, crowded around the tree and began to cast their spells. The dull corner suddenly exploded with light. Glowing, illusory ornaments hung from every branch. Multi-colored lights twinkled and orbited the tree in haphazard directions. Someone even cast a Light spell on an armored glove to place on top of the tree. It was a sight to behold.

Cooper wiped away a tear and sniffed back some snot, but then decided it wasn't worth the effort. People were used to seeing fluids seep out of his face. He let it flow.

"Now that's a fucking Christmas tree!" said Frank.

Cooper necked one mug of beer and poured himself another

to take back to the kitchen. He opened the oven door to check on his boar. It didn't look any different than it had when he put it in there.

"It's not going to cook if you keep opening the door," said Julian, his slender elf body silhouetted against the twinkling Christmas lights beyond the doorway.

"Thanks," said Cooper. "But I got this. Does your bird ever lay eggs? We could make some nog."

"Ravenus is male," said Julian. "And even if he did lay eggs, I don't think he'd appreciate you drinking his potential offspring."

"Just a thought." Cooper opened the oven door again. No perceptible change. "I think I need to turn it over." He reached into the oven and grabbed the dead boar. It was hot to the touch, but not painfully so. His half-orc hands were leathery and rough, and were usually coated in a protective layer of filth. Having a Charisma score of 3 had its perks. No need for oven mitts.

The hair on the bottom half of the boar was singed. Cooper gave it a satisfied nod, flipped it over, and shoved it back into the oven.

"You don't have to eat that, you know," said Julian. "There's plenty of food out there that isn't crawling with disease."

"That fucker gored me in the nuts," said Cooper. "I'm going to eat him."

Julian shook his head. "Just make sure you let it cook a while longer. Come on. Let's go top off your beer."

The communal area of the Whore's Head Inn was bustling with Christmas spirit. Bards played Christmas carols, and everyone drunkenly sang along. Cooper had drunk half a dozen more mugs of beer before he remembered his boar in the oven.

"Fuck!" he said.

"What's wrong?" said Julian.

Cooper scrunched up his face at Julian. "You sneaky bastard. You used Diplomacy on me to make me forget about my boar, didn't you?"

"I just didn't want you to get sick."

Cooper stomped back into the kitchen, bumping against the door frame on his way in.

"Come on, man!" Julian called after him. "Let it go! You killed the thing. How much more revenge do you need?"

"I will have my revenge when I turn that tusky bastard into poo!"

Cooper pulled the oven door open, expecting a cloud of black smoke to billow out. There was no smoke. The fire had died down to barely glowing embers, and the meat only looked to be charred on the bottom. Perfect. He took the boar out of the oven, held it before him, and prepared to bite into it.

"Cooper!" said Julian, standing in the doorway again. "I'm begging you, man. Don't do it."

Cooper flashed his own tusks at Julian before ripping into the boar's belly. It was juicy and tasted of salt... and something that he couldn't quite put his finger on.

"That's so fucking gross," said Julian.

"Tastes like vengeance!" said Cooper, boar juice flowing down both sides of his mouth onto his chest. Once his tongue had had enough time to explore the subtle complexities of flavor, he had to admit, if only to himself, that Julian was right. It actually tasted pretty shitty.

"Oh my god!" said Julian, looking at the boar when Cooper lowered it. "That's not even meat you're eating. You bit into its intestines."

That explained the shit taste. Cooper swallowed. "I could use another beer."

He left the boar on the preparation table, halfheartedly intending to come back and finish it. He and Julian rejoined the party. It took three more mugs of beer before Cooper was able to taste anything but pig shit.

Cooper scanned the crowd. He was happy to see that even Tim looked to be having a good time. Dave, for all his dwarven bonus to Saving Throws vs. Poison, looked well on his way to being hammered, fucking up the lyrics to Holly Jolly Christmas. Some-

one had even magically changed the leopard fur on his forearm to green with red spots.

Looking back at the table where Dave and Tim had been sitting, Cooper saw it was littered with empty beer mugs, shot glasses, stonepiss bottles, and Dave's gloved gauntlets. A foul idea began to brew in Cooper's head even as something even fouler brewed in his bowels.

Sneaking over to the unattended table, Cooper tripped over four chairs and knocked over two other tables. Fortunately, the only people who seemed to notice were the ones sitting at them. Having reached his target, he swiped Dave's gauntlets and made for the front entrance. He had a bomb ticking in his gut, and it was going to be a photo-finish race.

He slammed the door shut behind him, only just managing to get Dave's gauntlets under his loincloth before his ass exploded like an angry volcano, spraying the inside of the gauntlets as well as the outside of his own forearms with worm-riddled liquid shit. He wiped his arms and the outside of the gauntlets on his loincloth until they were passably clean.

He was just about to knock on the door when he spotted Julian's familiar, Ravenus, staring down at him from his perch atop the sign for the Whore's Head Inn. That fucker had seen everything.

"Not a word from you, understand?" Cooper knew Ravenus couldn't understand his words, as the bird was only able to communicate in the Elven tongue, but he hoped his threatening grimace communicated his warning well enough.

Ravenus squawked back at him and flew away. Cooper pounded the door with his fist. He was sweating, and he wasn't quite sure that he had done all the shitting he needed to do. His stomach was turning like a contortionist trying to escape a straightjacket.

The window of the door slid open. Julian was on the other side. His eyes widened.

"Cooper! What's wrong with you? You look like shit. I mean,

even for you."

"Just open the door, would you, I've got to—" He doubled over and puked on the wall of the neighboring building.

The door opened behind him, and Julian was soon at his side. "Are you okay?"

"Better now," said Cooper. "Thanks."

"I told you not to eat that boar, you ass!" Julian scolded him. "Look at you! You're sweating and shitting and puking and— Hey, are those Dave's gauntlets? Why do you have those?"

Cooper's heart was racing and his vision was beginning to blur as the world spun around his head, but he still managed a weak laugh. "I took a shit in them."

"Why the fuck would you do that?"

Cooper steadied himself against a post. "Don't get your pussy in a knot."

"My what in a what?"

"It's just a prank. Trust me. He'll think it's—" Cooper dropped to his knees and splattered Julian's shoes in vomit. "—hilarious."

"No he won't, you stupid asshole," said Julian.

"Come on, man," said Cooper, climbing up the wooden post to get on his feet again. "Where's your sense of Christmas spirit?"

"That's what you call Christmas spirit?" said one of the four Julians swirling around each other. They all looked pissed. The tips of their big elf ears were almost glowing red. "I've never felt more proud to be Jewish. Now come on inside. You need to get cleaned up and rested. Leave those out here."

Cooper looked down at his hand to see what Julian was pointing to. He had a pair of gauntlets in his hand. "Where the fuck did these come from?"

"Jesus Christ," said Julian. "You're delirious. Just drop them."

Cooper dropped the gauntlets and took a step toward the swirling images of his friend. He slipped in his own vomit puddle and slammed the ground hard with the back of his head. The world slowly faded to black.

*

When Cooper woke, his mind was clear and his vision focused. He looked down at his hands. They weren't covered in shit. He was in a bed much too large for him. The polished wooden bedposts were as thick around as he was. Each had a sconce attached about five feet above the comforter, holding a torch. The dim, flickering light from the torches was not enough for Cooper to see the top of the bedposts. They might have continued up forever for all he knew. He felt like a kitten. But as huge as it was, the bed felt warm and safe, which was more than he could say for the dark void beyond it.

The silent illusion of security inside his torchlit sphere was shattered by a sound from the outside. It was faint and distant, but it was definitely a sound, and it was getting closer. It didn't take Cooper long to identify the sound as chains, rattling in a rhythmic pattern, which Cooper soon judged to be that of approaching footsteps.

"Who's out there?" cried Cooper, pulling the comforter up over the lower half of his face. He was all but paralyzed with fear.

"Coooooooper," a not entirely unfamiliar voice called back to him.

Chink, clink. The chains rattled.

"What do you want?"

"Coooooooper," the voice called again, this time a little louder.

Chink, clink.

"I'll kick your ass!" said Cooper. "Fuck off!"

"COOOOOOOOOOOOOOOOOOOPER!" the voice bellowed. It obviously didn't appreciate being threatened. It sounded like it was nearly right on top of him.

The rattle of the chains was now deafening. Chink clink, chink clink. A black man covered in chains stepped into the torchlight. His hands were manacled together, as were his feet. Seemingly purposeless chains were wrapped arbitrarily around his body, the ends of them dragging behind him.

Cooper swallowed hard and mustered his courage to speak. "Django?"

"No, mon," said the figure. He grinned at Cooper, and his white teeth shone like high-beams. Suddenly, his voice, his face, his dreadlocked hair all clicked together in Cooper's mind.

"Bob Marley?"

"Ya, mon."

Cooper lowered the comforter. "It's an honor. I'm a big fan. That song... um... I..."

"I Shot the Sherriff?"

"Dude, it's cool," said Cooper. "I chopped a guard's head off."

"What?"

"I'm sorry. I'm confused."

"You don't know any of my music, do you, mon?"

Cooper hung his head. "I'm sorry. I swear it's not because you're black."

"I beg your pardon?"

"I just never got into reggae. Jesus, this is so embarrassing."

Bob Marley lifted his chained hands in a peaceful gesture. "Don't sweat it, mon! I'm not here to talk about music."

"Why are you here?" asked Cooper. "And why are you all chained up? I've got to say, I'm not entirely comfortable with this imagery. I mean, between the whole black-dude-in-chains, and your shitty Jamaican accent, I just feel like there's some racial insensitivity going on."

"It's your dream, mon," said Bob Marley. "If there's sometin' here you uncomfortable with, maybe you need to look inside yourself."

"Thank you for your insight, Bob Marley. Can you please go away now?"

"I cannot!" said Bob Marley. He seemed to resent the question. "I am doomed to walk in these chains for all eternity. And you will be too, unless you change."

"My loincloth?" He lifted the comforter to look down at it, and his eyes started to water at the smell of escaping fart. He had a mean dutch oven going on down there.

"Your heart, mon!" said Bob Marley. "You be a miserable excuse for a human being."

"I'm a half-orc."

Bob Marley shook his head. "I got no more patience for you, mon. I'll say what I came to say, and then I'll be on my way."

"Is that from one of your songs? It's beautiful."

"You will be visited by tree spirits. They—"

"What, like nymphs?"

Bob Marley rattled his chains. He was getting flustered. "Tree spirits! One, two, tree!"

"Oh, three spirits. I'm sorry. Does that include you?"

"No, mon. Three more. I should have made that clear." Bob Marley was pretty chill if you didn't provoke him.

"Should I prepare somehow? Are they going to ask me questions?"

"It's time I must be goin', mon." Bob Marley stepped backwards, out of the torchlight.

"No, Bob Marley!" cried Cooper. "Don't leave me alone in the dark!"

"Change your heart, mon." The voice was no longer coming from a focused point of origin. It echoed in from every direction.

"Bob Marley! Please, wait!"

"Change your heart!" It was fainter, but more commanding.

"Don't go!"

"Chaaaaange your heeeeeaaaaaaart..." This time it was barely a whisper.

"Fuck you, Bob Marley!"

Once again, Cooper was alone in complete silence, with only the quickened beat of his pulse to keep him company.

*

Cooper lay on the bed for what might have been minutes or

months. Time was murky in this place. Panic eventually gave way to boredom, and he thought about having a wank, but he didn't know whose bed he was in.

He was just drifting off to sleep again when he heard a sound which did not come from his own body. It was a mixture of grunts, snorts, and pants, like a fat guy running to catch a bus. Cooper sat upright, determined to face this demon without fear.

The grunts and snorts grew louder until Cooper was able to pinpoint a direction. He stood up on the bed and waited, fists balled at his side. Finally, the creature emerged from the shadows. It was the sickly boar that Cooper had killed. It was burned black on one side and slightly singed on the other, just as it had been when he'd taken it out of the oven. It even had a large chunk missing from its underside.

The boar looked up at him. "Donald McKinley Cooper?" It's voice was husky and dry.

"Who wants to know?"

"I'm the ghost of Christmas past."

"Shit," said Cooper. "I wish I'd known that back when you gored me in the nuts. We could've worked something out."

"You seem out of sorts. Do not be afraid. I mean you no harm."

"I'm just a little concerned about my heart. Bob Marley said I needed a transplant. But then, I don't expect he's a licensed cardiologist."

"Because he's black?"

"Fuck you, pig!"

The boar's empty eye sockets squinted as it snorted and wheezed at him. Cooper assumed that's just the way cooked boars laugh.

"Come, Cooper!" said the boar after it had finished laughing at him. "Take my hoof. I have something to show you." It stood on its hind legs and reached out a charred, blackened foreleg to Cooper.

The torches on the bedposts flared bright for an instant and then went out completely. Cooper was in total darkness holding hands with a dead pig. They were floating in the void, for the bed beneath him was gone.

"Open your eyes, Cooper," said the boar.

Cooper hadn't even realized his eyes were closed. When he opened them, he was sitting on the curb in the parking lot outside a Waffle House. The boar was next to him. The torches had been replaced with electric lamps. It was still dark, but the night was filled with stars.

"What the fuck are we doing at Waffle House?" asked Cooper. "You want to fuel up before a long trip?"

"The long trip is at its conclusion," said the boar. "This is our destination."

"You wanted to show me a Waffle House?"

"Not just any Waffle House, Cooper. Come, follow me." The boar waddled across the parking lot toward the entrance of the restaurant, right into the path of a Ford Taurus with some drunk asshole at the wheel.

Cooper jumped to his feet. "Pig, watch out!" He flinched as the car met the boar, but his fears were unwarranted. The car passed through the animal like it wasn't even there.

The boar turned around to face him. "You needn't fear the physical objects of this world. We currently exist on the Ethereal Plane. We can do nothing here but observe."

"Sweet!" said Cooper. He ran out onto the I-10 just in time to catch a tractor-trailer moving at least ninety miles per hour. It rushed through him fast and noisily, like a hurricane wind. It was exhilarating.

"Cooper!" the boar shouted at him. "Get back over here right now!"

Cooper did as he was told. The boar walked through the front window of the Waffle House, and Cooper followed. Walking through a pane of glass wasn't as much fun as being hit by a truck, but it was still pretty cool.

The restaurant was empty, except for the beast of a woman behind the counter. She looked like the Hutt that Jabba had rejected for the prom. She was an easy deuce and a half, with a dark, hairy birthmark on the left side of her face. Nice big titties though, and probably an easy lay. A chill ran down Cooper's ethereal spine at such a thought.

"Does she look familiar, Cooper?"

"She looks like she fell out of the ugly tree and... I don't know, fucking ate it or something. What does the Waffle House or that fucking yeti have to do with Christmas past?"

"These are your memories, Cooper," said the boar. "I am but a guide. This is a Christmas seven years ago. You spent it at the casinos on the coast."

Cooper grinned. "I remember that Christmas. I nailed this chick in the bathroom of a Waff—" Clearer memories began rushing into his head. The Waffle House. The fat chick. The Ford Taurus. The drunk asshole. "NO!"

The bell on the door rang behind him, and Cooper quickly turned around. A younger, human version of himself stumbled through the entrance.

"Ho ho ho, baby!" said the bumbling idiot through a cloud of his own cigarette smoke.

"What can I get for you?" said the thing behind the counter.

"Maybe it's me who's got something for you," said human Cooper, staggering toward the counter like he was being controlled by an unskilled puppeteer.

The big girl raised a bushy eyebrow and laughed. "You couldn't handle this, sugar. Not in your condition. Seriously, what do you want?"

"Beer's fine," said Cooper, finally slumping down on a bar stool.

"We don't have beer."

"Jack and Coke?"

"Do you know where you are?"

He looked up into her eyes. "I know where I want to be."

"Jesus fuck!" said ethereal Cooper, trying to slap his human self. His huge half-orc hands just breezed through his human head, not even stirring a hair. "Knock that shit off!"

He sat through two cups of coffee and some of the most painful and desperate flirting he'd ever heard. Eventually, she started to succumb to his drunken charm.

During his third cup of coffee, the she-beast came out from behind the counter.

"Where is she going?" Cooper asked the boar.

"I think you know."

She locked the front door and hung up the "Closed" sign.

"No!" cried Cooper. "You can't close the Waffle House! The Waffle House is never closed!"

She turned around and gave human Cooper a come-hither look. Spirit Cooper wanted to puke his ethereal guts out, but human Cooper had a conspicuous bulge in the crotch of his jeans. She took his hand and led him to the women's restroom.

"Let's go, man," Cooper pleaded with the boar. "I really don't want to hear what goes on in there."

"You shall hear!" the boar shouted at him. "And furthermore, you shall see!"

"No, ghost pig!" cried Cooper. "You can't make me!" But even as he said it, his ethereal body drifted involuntarily toward the bathroom door.

As he got nearer, the sounds coming from within the bathroom grew louder and more disturbing, like a mop wringer.

Cooper's head was level with the boar's, facing the women's restroom door and almost touching it.

The boar turned to Cooper. "It is time. Behold!"

Their heads went through the door simultaneously. On the other side was a ghastly sight. The first thing Cooper homed in on was his own bare ass. He was standing upright, pounding away into her from behind. She was bent over the sink, just a stack of moaning fat rolls. It looked like he was raping the Michelin Man.

"Make it stop, spirit!" cried Cooper. "Please make it stop!"

"Okay," said the boar. "I can't take much more of this either."

Sight and sound began to fade until Cooper was once again in silent oblivion.

*

Cooper's sensory deprivation was so complete that he even started to doubt his own existence until he felt cold stone beneath his feet. He dropped to his knees and pawed at the ground, looking for a clue as to which way he should proceed.

The dilemma was solved when two torches burst into life on a wall directly in front of him. Between them, they illuminated an ornate golden door. A pair of cherubs, one high and one low, held either end of a staff, which served as the door's handle.

Cooper stepped forward and gripped the handle. Testing it, he found the door moved freely in either direction. He pulled it open just enough to take a peek at whatever might be on the other side.

"Cooper!" a voice boomed from within the next room.

There was no point in trying to hide. He'd been made. He opened the door wider. Mordred sat on a gilded throne at the far side of the room. His stupid purple cloak had transformed into a plus-sized Hugh Hefner smoking jacket, exposing more of his pasty man-cleavage than Cooper could stand to look at. He looked like the king of the Bacchus parade.

"Come in and know me better, man," said Mordred. His voice echoed in the chamber like a god's.

"This is well more than I ever wanted to know you," said Cooper.

"I'm sorry," said Mordred, cupping a hand around his ear and leaning forward. "Could you speak up?"

Cooper's eyes readjusted. The room was far larger than he had first assumed, which made Mordred proportionately larger as well. He must have been about forty feet tall. It might have been his giant bed Cooper had woken up in. He was glad he'd reconsidered masturbating in it. That would have been weird.

Cooper raised his voice. "What do you want?"

The giant Mordred smiled and shrugged. "Peace on Earth. Good will toward men."

"So you're the ghost of Christmas present."

"What do you think?"

"It makes sense," said Cooper. "You've got more than eighteen hundred fathers."

Mordred frowned. "It's brothers."

"I know," said Cooper. "That was just a cheap shot at your mom. The implication was that she's a big whore."

"Yeah," said Mordred. "I got it."

"You mind if we get this show on the road?" asked Cooper. "I'd kind of like to hurry through this part. I'm still pretty pissed at you for sending us here and giving me perpetual diarrhea."

Mordred stomped his great booted feet on the ground and rose from his throne. The room shook. "Is that any worse than what you did to me?" he bellowed. "Blame me not for the consequences you bring upon yourself! Your heart is dark and your deeds are wicked!"

"What the fuck are you talking about?"

Giant Mordred grabbed a torch from a sconce on the wall and walked toward Cooper. He must have been shrinking as he walked, as Cooper's perception of his size never changed. By the time he reached Cooper, they were approximately the same size. "Take my sleeve."

Cooper did as he was told, and the chamber began to crumble around them. Giant chunks of the stone ceiling smashed into the floor, obliterating both on impact. The walls crumbled away to nothing. The great throne melted away. When it was all done, he and Mordred were standing on a quiet, snow-covered street. It took Cooper a moment to realize they were standing outside the Whore's Head Inn.

"Hold on a sec," said Cooper. "Why's it snowing? It's not even cold out."

"Your mind is confusing your current reality with more conventional images of Christmas," Mordred explained. "Pay no mind to the snow."

In front of the door, Cooper saw his own body lying unconscious on the ground. "Am I dead?"

"Ho ho ho!" Mordred chuckled a hearty Santa Clause laugh. "Not yet, friend."

"Is this what you wanted to show me?"

"This much even you could have figured out on your own," said Mordred. "Be patient, man. Watch."

He didn't have to wait long. The door opened, spilling out multi-colored flashing lights and the sounds of merrymaking. Julian led Dave and Tim to Cooper's unconscious body.

"Can you help me drag him inside?" said Julian, the only one who looked even remotely sober.

"Is it snowing?" asked Tim.

"Of course not," said Dave. "You're just trashed. Hey, what are my gauntlets doing out here?"

"Wait, Dave!" cried Julian. "Don't—" but it was too late.

"What the fuck?" said Dave, pulling his arm back out of the glove. It was slimy and brown. The leopard fur band on his forearm was slathered in half-orc shit.

Spirit Cooper nudged Mordred with his elbow. "What did I say, huh? Fucking hilarious."

"Do you see anyone laughing?" asked Mordred.

"Julian's too uptight, Tim's so trashed he barely knows where he is, and Dave's the butt of the joke," said Cooper. "Of course no one's laughing now. But they'll come around tomorrow."

"Will they?" asked Mordred. "Will they laugh when Dave dies of dysentery? Will they laugh when Tim shrivels up to a mere husk of a halfling and loses the use of his legs?"

"No!" said Cooper. "Not Tiny Tim! Hold on... I didn't shit in Tim's gloves. How's he going to get dysentery?"

"Let's go back to Dave for a moment," said Mordred. "He's the real Bob Cratchit of this story."

"Wait a second. How many Bobs are in this story?"

"Just the one."

"But what about—"

"Your mind jumbled the memories of Bob Cratchit and Jacob Marley, creating Bob Marley. It's because you're stupid."

"Ah, I see."

"Why do you treat Dave so badly?" asked Mordred. "What have you got against the guy?"

"Dave sucks."

"Can you be anymore specific?"

"No," said Cooper. "It's a general suck."

Dave threw the gauntlet down at Physical Cooper. It bounced off his face. Cooper grunted. His eyelids twitched, and he put his finger in his nose.

Spirit Cooper turned to Mordred. "See?"

"You felt that was undeserved?"

"He attacked me while I was sleeping."

"Come on, guys," said Tim. "Let's get back to the party. Leave this dickhead in the snow."

"What snow are you talking about?" said Dave.

"You two can stand out here and freeze your asses off if you want," said Tim. "I'm going back inside."

"What are you talking about?" said Dave. "It's not even cold."

"Screw this," said Tim. "I need a—" His little halfling arms flailed out as he slipped in Cooper's vomit puddle. Dave caught one of them to keep him from falling down, thus answering the question of how Tim contracts dysentery.

Dave led Tim back inside the Whore's Head. Julian hesitated, looking down at Cooper, but eventually abandoned him as well.

Spirit Cooper frowned. "I didn't want to hurt anyone. It's my Intelligence. You said so yourself. I'm stupid."

"Let's take a walk," said Mordred. "I have one more thing I want to show you."

Cooper gloomily followed Mordred to the apothecary across the street.

Mordred pointed his torch into the alley between this building and the one next to it. "After you."

Cooper walked into the alley. It was dark, in spite of Mordred's torch behind him, so he proceeded cautiously, keeping one hand on the brick wall to maintain direction. The alley went on far longer than it should have. He seemed to be walking for miles, and maybe even descending.

After an indeterminate length of time, Mordred spoke. "Stop. We have arrived."

"How can you tell?" asked Cooper.

Mordred walked past Cooper and thrust his torch forward. The flame flared bright, illuminating the end of the alley.

They were at a dead end. Ahead of them, two emaciated children— a boy and a girl— were shackled to the wall. Their eyes were milky white, and they snapped their teeth at Cooper, as if trying to eat him, but their chains held true.

"Jesus Christ!" shouted Cooper. "Who the fuck are they?"

"His name is Intelligence and hers is Charisma," said Mordred.

"What the fuck are they doing chained in the alley?"

"I should probably remind you that you're dreaming right now," said Mordred. "Weird shit happens in dreams."

Cooper nodded. "Fair enough."

"Beware them both," warned Mordred, "for they are not your friends. But blame them not for your actions. The choices you make are yours alone."

The light from Mordred's torch began to fade swiftly. By the time Cooper turned around, he was in complete darkness. It wasn't the void, like the previous times, as he could still hear the snarling and snapping of the kids chained to the wall.

"Mordred?" Cooper called out. There was no answer. "Mordred!" The word simply echoed down the long, dark alley. "You fat fuck! Don't leave me alone with these freakshow kids!"

He reached out, and was relieved to find the brick wall where it was supposed to be. He walked briskly away from the two rabid children, and was surprised to find the journey back to the street only took a few seconds.

Cooper ran out into the middle of the street and waited. He

was still shaken up by the two kids shackled in the alley, but he was more excited by anticipating who might represent the ghost of Christmas yet to come.

He stood in the middle of the street, closed his eyes, placed the clawed tips of his index fingers on his temples, and tried to will Doc Brown to blast onto the scene in his DeLorean. It was his dream, after all. Surely he could choose the last ghost.

Several minutes passed without any lightning-engulfed cars or wild-eyed mad scientists. Now that he thought about it, nothing at all was going on. The street was eerily quiet, even for as late at night as it must have been. He gave up on meeting Christopher Lloyd and walked back to the Whore's Head Inn.

The first thing he noticed was that the front windows were broken. He must have missed a hell of a party. He peeked into one window to find that the place was empty. A layer of dust covered the floor and furniture, suggesting that it had been empty for quite some time.

"Hello?" he called inside. There was no answer.

He walked over to the entrance, surprised to find it wide open. Also surprising was the fact that his own body was missing. Had he woken up? Had the guys had a change of heart and dragged him inside?

A loud caw startled Cooper out of his speculations. Ravenus looked down at him from his perch on top of the tavern sign.

"Goddammit!" said Cooper. "Not you! Anyone but you!"

"There is no one else but me!" said Ravenus.

"Whoa," said Cooper. "How come I can understand you?"

"Because you're dreaming, fucktard."

"Oh, right."

"Follow me," said the bird. He flew in short bursts, perching on tree branches or lamp posts as he waited for Cooper to catch up.

Cooper followed Ravenus out of the Collapsed Sewer District, to the outer-regions of the city where there were more open spaces than buildings. In the middle of one such open space stood a single tombstone.

Ravenus flapped down to land atop the stone. "Behold!"

Memories of Scrooge McDuck started to manifest in Cooper's head, and his heartbeat quickened. "Whose grave is this, spirit?"

"What kind of question is that?" asked Ravenus. "Read it."

Cooper hung his head in shame. "I'm illiterate. It's part of being a barbarian."

Ravenus shook his bird head. "Unbelievable. It's Dave's, you moron."

"Oh, thank fuck." Cooper breathed a sigh of relief.

Ravenus stared at him with his beady little judgmental bird eyes.

"What?" said Cooper. "It's a bummer about Dave. I'm sorry about that. I just thought... wait a minute. What did you mean before when you said there's no one else but you?"

"How many ways can you interpret that?" asked Ravenus. "An epidemic of dysentery swept through the city. Dave here was lucky to be one of the early ones. He got a proper burial at least. Most residents wound up being dumped into mass graves and burned."

Cooper's lower lip quivered as he asked the first question that came to mind. "Tim?"

"Dead!" cried Ravenus. "All of them are dead. You killed Dave. You killed Tim. You killed Julian, damn you!"

"And me?"

"Don't worry, Cooper," said Ravenus. "You're alive and well. You survived because your body was accustomed to constantly shitting itself. I survived because I'm a carrion eater. I eat nastier shit than you can poop out on a daily basis."

"Say it isn't so!" cried Cooper. "I'm stuck here forever, alone with you?"

"Oh, I wouldn't say alone," said Ravenus, spreading his black wings wide. "This is a city of death now. My kind has taken over." He let out a loud caw.

The caw was answered by at least a dozen more in the near

vicinity, and then a hundred from the darkness beyond, and a thousand more beyond that.

Cooper looked up at a nearby tree. Every branch was covered in ravens, standing shoulder to shoulder, eyeing him hungrily.

Cooper backed away, but there was nowhere to go. The night was alive with the flapping of black wings.

"You can't eat me!" he cried. "I'm not dead, and I'm disgusting!"

"We're willing to overlook all that," said Ravenus. "Just this once." He bolted from his perch toward Cooper. Ravens swarmed in from everywhere, scratching and pecking at his skin.

"Nooooo!" Cooper cried, but his plea was drowned out by a cacophony of cawing and screeching. He could neither see nor breathe. He was literally drowning in black feathers. Consciousness faded, and he was once again in the void.

*

Cooper awoke to the warmth of the sun on his face. No, that wasn't quite right. It was still dark, and this warmth was liquidy. He opened his eyes to discover a stray dog pissing on him. He sat up and spit out the dog piss that had run into his mouth.

"What day is it?"

The dog didn't answer. Instead it sniffed at one of Dave's gauntlets, still lying undisturbed on the ground, presumably still full of Cooper's shit.

"Merciful spirits!" cried Cooper. "There's still time! Make haste, dog! Run and fetch the prize turkey!"

The dog stared blankly at him.

"Go on. Get the fuck out of here." He took a threatening step toward the dog, and it ran off.

The door to the Whore's Head Inn opened, and Julian, Dave, and Tim stepped out.

"He looks okay to me," said Tim.

"Hey," said Dave. "What are my gauntlets doing out here?" He took a step toward them.

"No!" Cooper shouted. He jumped repeatedly on the gauntlets until they were mangled beyond repair. The pain in his feet was eclipsed by the joy in his heart.

"What the fuck, man!" cried Dave.

"You're welcome," said Cooper.

"How hard did he hit his head?" asked Tim.

"Pretty hard," said Julian.

Cooper picked up Tim and squeezed him against his chest. "Oh, Tiny Tim! I'm so happy you're alive!"

"Please don't call me that," said Tim. "And put me down. You smell like shit."

Inside the inn, the party was still going strong. Cooper switched from beer to stonepiss to drown out the pain in his head and feet. His "Tiny Tim" moniker spread quickly, made even more hilarious by how pissed off Tim got every time someone said it. No matter what universe you happen to be stuck in, there are few things in life funnier than an angry midget.

Frank's face was beet red from laughing so hard. "Please, sir. May I have another?"

"That's not even the right fucking story!" screamed Tim. He climbed up on a table to address the drunken crowd. The bards stopped playing their instruments and the crowd quieted down and looked at him.

He raised his little arms and extended both middle fingers. "God damn you, every one!"

The End

Sticky White Mess
A Love Story
ROBERT BEVAN

STICKY WHITE MESS

(Original Publication Date: February 3, 2014)

Julian stared at the yellowed, musty pages of a random spellbook he had picked up from a nearby shelf. The magical runes were easy enough to decipher into pronounceable syllables, but they made no sense to him. It was like trying to understand a foreign language after only having cracked its alphabet.

He honestly didn't give a damn what was in the book. The only reason he'd picked it up was to give him an excuse to sit at one of the tables, across from a stunningly beautiful female elf. She had curly golden hair that a goddess would envy, and ears that could sail ships. He and Ravenus shot each other a mutually curious glance. It was only since arriving in this world that Julian had come to include 'enormous ears' as something he looked for in a woman.

A Norwegian forest cat, white around the muzzle but otherwise covered in splotches of brown and black, lay curled up next to the elven girl's book. It looked like his aunt's cat, only fatter and presumably with even more tenuous ties to Norway. It kept a lazy watch on Ravenus, each of them likely fantasizing about making a meal of the other.

Ravenus was growing impatient. Julian could sense it, just as he knew the bird could sense his own feelings of jittery inadequacy in the presence of such beauty. He scratched a talon on the rough wood of the table. The sound was amplified by the otherwise silent library.

The elven maiden blew a golden curl out of her eye. "Do you two mind?" she said. "I'm trying to study."

"Gryffindor?" asked Julian.

"What in the Abyss are you talking about?" she said.

Julian looked at Ravenus. "Slytherin."

The elf girl likewise turned her attention to Ravenus. "What is he talking about?"

Ravenus shrugged his wings. "I'm sorry ma'am. I honestly don't know."

The tips of Julian's own giant ears were burning. He was making a fool of himself. What good was a Charisma score of 17 if he couldn't even competently talk to a girl?

"Begging your pardon, miss," said Ravenus. "I believe my master fancies you."

"Ravenus!" said Julian. "Get out of here!"

"I was only trying to—"

"Right now! Wait outside."

"Yes, sir," said Ravenus. "Right away, sir." He flew out of the library through one of many small openings high in the wall which seemed to have been placed there specifically for flying familiars to enter and exit through.

"I'm really sorry," said Julian. "I don't know what's gotten into him. I'm just here to study as well." He closed his book and held up the cover for her to see.

"Illusory Spells, Volume VI," said the elf girl. "That's some pretty heavy reading. What spell are you working on?"

Julian flipped open to the first random page he could find with emboldened title runes. "This one." He sounded out the syllables. "Mis...lead." He slapped his palm against his forehead. "Shit."

The elf girl smiled. "You're doing a fine job of it."

"Look, I'm sorry," said Julian. "Ravenus was right. I only grabbed this book off the shelf so I'd have an excuse to sit next to you. You're... I'm... You've got really pretty ears."

She rolled her eyes, but her cat purred. Julian grinned.

"Lucifer!" she said. "Stop it!" She picked the cat up off the table and tossed him onto the floor. "Go find some rats." The cat gave her a small whine of disapproval before scampering off.

The pudgy critter was quicker than Julian would have guessed it could.

"You named your cat Lucifer?" asked Julian.

"It's Draconic for 'Light Bringer'".

"Yeah, I know that," Julian lied. "It's just that..."

"What?"

"I don't know, it's just..."

"Listen, I'm flattered that you like my ears or whatever. You have lovely ears yourself. But I've only got a week to learn this Invisibility spell, or else I'm not going to graduate this year."

"Invisibility?" said Julian. "I've looked into that spell. It's only level 2."

"Well excuse me," she said. "I'm sorry if I came off as some great wizardess. I didn't mean to Mislead you."

"I said I was sorry about that," said Julian. "If you'd ease off a bit, I might be able to help you."

"Do you even know the Invisibility spell?"

"Not yet," said Julian. "But it's high on my list of spells to learn."

"So you're saying what?" she said. "You want to be study partners or something?"

"Not exactly," said Julian. "In fact, I think you're wasting your time here."

She raised a perfect golden eyebrow. "Is that right? And how powerful a wizard are you to advise me such?"

Julian lowered his eyes. "I've only dabbled in wizardry," he admitted. "I wasn't very good at it. But I'm a practicing sorcerer now."

"Ha!" she said. "Sorcery. Lazy man's magic. There's no discipline in sorcery. You fling spells around without understanding the magic behind them, and to what end? When I'm enchanting swords for the king's personal guard, you'll still be performing at children's birthday parties."

"I don't think that's—"

"Listen, pretty boy! I didn't work my ears off for two years at

Mystical Melinda's Preparatory Academy for Girls just so some mage-clown could come sweep me off my feet in a public library. Now if you don't mind, I've—"

"You spent two years trying to master a second level spell?"

"I wish you'd stop talking like that. What are these levels you keep talking about?"

"Never mind that," said Julian. "It doesn't matter how you approach your magic, or whatever path you choose to follow in life. In this world, there's one surefire way to advance."

"And what's that?"

"Kill monsters."

The female elf pursed her lips and furrowed her brow at Julian. It was adorable. "You're saying that if I practice the spells I've already mastered, I'll be better equipped to understand new magic?"

"No," said Julian. "I'm saying that if you go kill some monsters, you'll gain experience."

"Kill them with magic?"

"If you like. Stab them, hit them with sticks, throw them off cliffs. Whatever you like. My friend Cooper uses an axe. Tim's more partial to a crossbow. Dave usually just stands around and gets the crap beaten out of—"

"Stop talking," said the female elf. "How is any of that supposed to help me master this invisibility spell by next week?"

Julian stood up. "Depending on how far along you are already, you might have that spell mastered by this evening." He flashed a smile, making a conscious Diplomacy check. "Come on, what do you say? I'll buy you dinner."

She stood up and bit her lower lip. "I suppose I should eat at some point." She slammed her massive, leather-bound book closed and shoved it into a rough suede backpack. Her cloak was made out of the same material. It looked just loose enough to allow her the range of movement she'd need to cast spells while still being thick and rugged enough to deflect a casual attempt at a stabbing. "Okay, sorcerer. I'm willing to waste a few hours while I let my brain recharge. What did you have in mind?"

"First I'll introduce you to my friends," said Julian. "What's your name?"

She broke eye contact for a split-second before answering. "Um... You can call me Diamond."

Julian smiled. "That's a pretty name. I'm Julian."

Diamond stood up and strapped on her backpack. "Let's go then, Julian the Sorcerer."

"What about Lucifer?"

"He'll catch up."

Julian led the way out of the arched front entrance of the Great Library of Cardinia. A grassy quad, about the size of a football field, served as a communal open area for the library they stood in front of, the university to their left, City Hall directly across from them, and the Cardinian Multi-faith Grand Temple and Medical Center to their right. Along the perimeter of the quad, between each of these four prominent structures, stood an assortment of tents, specialty shops, food vendors, minor potions and scrolls dealers, showmen, and charlatans. If he cared to look hard enough, he could probably spot a few residents of the Whore's Head Inn hawking their meager wares.

Ravenus flew down from the roof of the library and perched atop his quarterstaff. "May I rejoin you, sir?"

"Of course," said Julian. "Did you find anything to eat?"

"No, sir. I merely sat on the roof."

"Oh, that's—"

"Waiting."

"You didn't—"

"Alone."

"I'm sorry, Ravenus," said Julian. "You just... She was... You were speaking too candidly. Human conversations are more complex than that. There are subtleties and—"

"What do human conversations have to do with anything?" asked Diamond.

"Oh, sorry," said Julian. "I meant elven."

"You are a strange one," said Diamond. "Where are these friends of yours?"

They weren't hard to find. While there was no shortage of dwarves, halflings, and half-orcs roaming the quad, it was rare to see any of them interacting with any other than their own kind, and most of them seemed to have something better to do on a weekday morning than sit on the grass and get wasted.

"There they are," said Julian. Cooper was waving a jug at him.

"Those are your friends?" said Diamond.

"Yeah."

"Wow," she said. "I wasn't expecting such a... um... diverse group."

"Try not to take offense at anything Cooper might say," said Julian. "He's a good guy, but he tends to come off a bit abrasive before you really get to know him."

"Which one's Cooper?"

"He's the half-orc waving the jug."

"Thanks for the warning."

"Hey guys," said Julian as soon as they were within reasonable speaking distance. "I'd like to introduce a friend of mine." He ignored the amused glance exchanged by Dave and Tim. "This is Diamond."

"Sweet," said Cooper. "Is she a stripper?"

Tim coughed some beer out of his nose.

"Cooper!" said Julian. "I'm sorry, Diamond."

"It's quite all right," said Diamond. She smiled politely at Cooper. "I'm afraid I'm nothing quite so exciting as that. Just a boring university student."

Cooper nodded. "I like your pussy."

Tim lost it. He fell backwards, barely holding on to his bottle in one hand while he pounded the grass with the other. Even Dave choked on his stonepiss.

"God dammit, Cooper!" shouted Julian.

"I love it when they stretch like that."

Julian pulled his ears down to his cheeks. "What the fuck is wrong with you, man?"

"Why thank you," said Diamond.

"What?" cried Julian.

"His name is Lucifer."

Julian turned around. Diamond's familiar had shown up, its front paws stretched out in front of its yawning face.

"Have you considered shaving it?" asked Dave, only barely managing to keep his laughter under control. Everyone looked at him.

"What a random and oddly inappropriate question," said Cooper.

Diamond picked up her cat. "Yes. I must say that was kind of weird."

"I was just advising Diamond," said Julian, "on the best way to master a new spell."

Cooper pointed past Julian. "I think there's a library over there."

"Thank you, Cooper," said Julian. "That's very helpful. I was hoping someone might have an idea of a more efficient way to accumulate the requisite experience necessary to achieve said mastery." If one of the guys were to bring up monster-killing, it would give him some credibility.

"Practice makes perfect," said Dave. "I've often found that if you want to learn how to do something, the best method is to just dive right in and do it, mistakes be damned. Sooner or later, the perseverance will reward you with—"

"Shut up, Dave," said Julian. "Tim, do you have any ideas?"

Tim narrowed his eyes and nodded slowly, licking his lips as if he had picked up on a bit of innuendo that Julian hadn't intended to transmit. He took a quick swig from his bottle and then smiled up at Diamond.

"Let me assure you," said Tim. "My friend Julian is an accomplished tutor of the arcane arts, and his rates are competitive." He pulled the scroll tube containing his character sheet out of his bag. He unrolled the paper and ran his finger down the center.

"We might be able to work you in for an hour tomorrow afternoon."

Julian hung his head.

"Huh," said Diamond. Her tone was slightly amused, but largely unimpressed. "Are you guys trying to swindle me?"

"No!" said Julian. "Of course not!" He glared at Tim. "Well, I suppose he was, but I'm not."

"Sorry, dude," said Tim. "I thought you were dropping a hint."

"I was," said Julian. "I was talking about killing monsters."

"Oh right," said Tim.

"Of course," agreed Dave. "Much more efficient."

"Beats the shit out of studying," said Cooper.

Julian looked at Diamond. "Convinced?"

"I only agreed to this out of curiosity about you and your strange friends," said Diamond. "This is time I'm allowing myself to waste. I never believed for a second that throwing rocks at the tarrasque was going to advance my academic career."

"Who's the tarrasque?" asked Julian.

Diamond looked at him skeptically. "Is that a serious question?"

"Of course not," Julian lied. "Does that mean you're willing to give it a try?"

"I'm willing to watch whatever crazy show you have in store for me."

"That begs the question," said Tim, swaying on his feet. "What crazy show do you have in store for her?"

"I was thinking about that little cave we ran across yesterday," said Julian.

"The one with the giant spiders crawling around outside of it?" said Dave. "Didn't you use your stupid Diplomacy skill specifically to keep us from going in there?"

"I've had a change of heart."

"It's amazing what hormones can do."

"What did you call me, runt?" said Diamond, dropping Lucifer and drawing a dagger from her left sleeve. The handle was marbled red and black. A pair of entwined serpents was etched along the center of the blade. Lucifer's fur bristled as he hissed at Dave.

"Whoa!" said Julian. "He didn't mean it like that."

"How many ways could he mean it?" Diamond snapped back at him. Then to Dave, "Don't think I won't willingly die defending my honor. And if it comes to that, I promise I'll take you into the Abyss with me, dwarf."

"Seriously, Dave," said Cooper. "That was uncalled for. What's gotten into you?"

Dave stood, mouth agape.

"Hormones!" said Julian, trying to crank up the Diplomacy. "One word. They're chemicals in our bodies that regulate our growth and influence our motivations."

Diamond tucked the dagger back into sleeve. "I'll take you at your word this time, only because I haven't understood a single thing you've been talking about since I met you. Just keep the dwarf away from me. He gives me the creeps."

"I don't know that I'm in any condition to go spider hunting," said Tim. "I'm a little wasted."

"Well who told you to start drinking so early in the day?" said Julian. "Did you even get the trigger mechanism on your crossbow fixed?"

Tim grabbed his crossbow from off his back and frowned at it. "Umm... no. I forgot to do that."

"That's the whole reason we walked all the way to the city center!"

"We got distracted," said Cooper. "We ran into a booze stall while we were looking for a weapon repair shop."

"Here," said Diamond. "Let me see it."

Tim handed over his crossbow. Diamond held it close to her face, and squinted into the trigger area. She pulled out her dagger. After a few pokes, prods, clicks, and twists, she successfully cocked and released the weapon.

"Good as new," she said, handing it back to Tim.

"Impressive," said Julian.

"I'm an only child," said Diamond. "It was important to my father that I know how to handle a variety of weapons." She looked down at Tim. "You really should take better care of that. The time you're most likely to discover it doesn't work is likely the time you most need it."

"Wise words," said Julian.

"My father's," said Diamond. "Now who's up for this great spider hunt? If we don't get started soon, I'm going to go back to studying."

"Okay," said Julian. "Let's go. Time to sober up, Tim."

Tim took a swig from his bottle. "Fuck it. I'll take my chances."

Half an hour later, they were beyond the protection of the city walls, headed northwest, away from the main road, across the grassy expanse between road and woodland.

"Stay low," Julian whispered to Diamond. "There may be owlbears out here."

"I'll fear no owlbear in the company of such brave men."

"I can't tell if you're being sarcastic."

"She is," said Dave.

"Just keep your distance, dwarf," said Diamond, any trace of mirth now gone from her voice. "And if you keep staring at my bottom, you'll find yourself minus an eye."

Dave's face turned red. "It's not my fault," he said. "I'm slower than you are, and I'm short."

The top of Tim's head appeared over the top of the tall grass. He was jumping, but not as high as he wanted to. "Are we almost to the trees?" he said. "I've got to piss."

"Just piss in the grass," said Cooper. "That's what I've been doing."

"I know," said Tim. "I've been stepping in it, asshole."

"Keep it down, guys," said Julian. "We're almost there."

When they finally did arrive at the tree line, Julian was relieved. The grasslands may be generally safer than the forest, and it was certainly easier to spot larger predators from farther away. But there could have been smaller, yet just as deadly, creatures lurking mere feet away crouching in wait, and he'd have been none the wiser until they made their move.

While Tim saturated the stump of a felled oak, Cooper rubbed his ass against the trunk of another, leaving behind a crumbly streak of green and brown. Somewhere, a druid was crying.

"Ravenus?" Julian called out as loudly as he dared.

"Up here, sir," said Ravenus, perched on a branch of the tree Cooper was busy defiling.

"What are you doing?" asked Julian. "You were supposed to be scouting the area."

"There's not much to scout, sir," said Ravenus. "The whole area is quiet. Unnaturally so, if I may offer my opinion."

Julian concentrated. Ravenus was right. Outside of the waning trickle of Tim's urine and the scratching of Cooper's leathery ass against bark, the place was silent. No tittering birds. No chirping crickets. No chattering squirrels. "What do you suppose—"

"There!" said Diamond, reaching into her sleeve.

Julian whirled around just in time to spot a nondescript pile of underbrush before Diamond threw her dagger into it. Much to Julian's surprise, the pile of sticks and leaves shrieked and stood upright. It had a reptilian face and hateful red eyes.

"Kobolds!" said Dave.

An instant later, a dozen or more bowstrings twanged from every direction.

"Ow!" said Cooper. His torso was peppered with arrows. "That hurts, you little shitbags!"

Dave touched Cooper's elbow. "I heal thee."

Cooper let out a long, soft fart that sounded like a weak outboard motor while most of the arrows fell out of his body.

The kobold Diamond had hit with her dagger called out two sharp barks and a yelp. Based on his comrades' reactions, Julian guessed the order was Chihuahuan for 'retreat'. They fanned out in different directions.

Cooper started to run after one kobold while Dave charged after a different one in the opposite direction.

"What's going on?" asked Tim, unstoppering a fresh bottle of booze. "Where the fuck is everybody going?"

"Stop!" shouted Diamond. She spoke with such presence that Cooper and Dave stopped dead in their tracks. Even one of the kobolds paused long enough for Julian to shoot him in the face.

"Have some," said Julian as the confused reptile collapsed to the ground. He looked to see if Diamond had seen the shot. She hadn't. She was busy shouting at Cooper.

"Don't split the party," said Diamond. "They'll only regroup and hunt you individually. Go after the leader!"

"Holy shit!" said Tim. "Kobolds!" He raised his crossbow and pulled the trigger. His bolt lodged into the trunk of a nearby tree about eight feet from the ground and not even close to any kobolds. "Fuck."

Diamond took off after the kobold she had hit with her dagger. Julian and Dave followed, and it wasn't long before Julian heard Cooper stomping through the brush, hot on his heels. He cast a glance behind him and was relieved to see that Cooper had Tim tucked under his arm like a football.

They almost all piled into each other when they caught up with Diamond. She was just standing there, hands on her hips, her head turning right, then left, then right again.

"What happened?" asked Julian. "Where'd he go?"

"He just disappeared," said Diamond.

"Did you see him disappear?" asked Julian. "Could it have been a spell?"

"I don't think so. He was in too much of a hurry to be casting spells. I lost sight of him for a second, and then he was gone. He's around here somewhere."

Julian looked up into the treetops. He supposed a creature that small would be able to hide in the foliage, but it was unlikely it would have been able to climb that high without being seen.

"Maybe we should just let them go," said Dave.

"They tried to kill your friend," said Diamond.

"Don't worry about me," said Cooper. "It's cool." He set Tim down and plucked an arrow out of his chest.

"The leader still has my dagger," said Diamond.

"We can get you another dagger," offered Dave.

"That one was special."

Dave chuckled. "How special could it be? It didn't even kill a kobold."

Diamond glared down at Dave so severely that it might have killed a kobold. "My father gave me that dagger."

Dave lowered his head. "I'm just going to shut up now."

Tim staggered into the tense air between Dave and Diamond. "You guys are going about this all wrong. You've got to look at it logically." He walked aimlessly as he talked, constantly changing directions, as if moving was the only thing keeping him from falling over. He finally steadied himself against a tree with one hand and waved his bottle around with the other as he continued. "This is the time to apply Occam's Razor."

"You have a magical blade?" Diamond sounded skeptical.

"It's not a weapon," said Tim. "It's a principal of logic. When you have... give me a minute, I'm a little wasted." He bit his lower lip. "Okay, I've got it. Let's say you have two entities, and—"

Cooper snorted. Everyone looked at him.

"What?" said Cooper. "He said titties."

"Ha!" said Diamond, her face lighting up. "I suppose he did."

Dave scrunched up his face and punched a tree trunk.

"If you halfwits would shut up for a minute," said Tim, staggering away from his tree, toward a spot of slightly elevated ground to sit down on. "I'll solve your little— FUCK!" A rectangular panel of earth gave way beneath his ass, and he fell into a concealed hole.

The fake ground was mounted on an axle at its center, and the whole thing swung around like a giant garbage can lid to reveal an identical display on the opposite side. Settling into place, it was nearly indistinguishable from the natural forest floor surrounding it.

"Well I'll be damned," said Cooper. "Is that how a rogue's

Trapfinding ability works?"

"Seems counterproductive if you ask me," said Julian.

Dave poked the head of his mace at the trap door, opening it just a crack. It was dark inside. "Tim?" he called.

"Yeah?" Tim called back.

"Are you okay?"

"Yeah, why?"

"'Cause you just fell in a pit."

"Oh, right," said Tim. "It's cool. There's a safety net or something. I can't tell. It's dark down here. I can't find my beer."

"You've probably had enough for now anyway."

"Screw you!"

"Okay," said Dave. "Just hang on a bit. We're going to figure out a way to get you out of there." He removed his mace, and the gap closed. "What do you think?" he said to the rest of the party.

"Throw him a rope?" suggested Julian.

"Tim's got the rope."

"Fuck it," said Cooper. "Let's just jump in after him. What's the worst that could happen?"

"Do I seriously have to answer that question?" said Julian.

"You heard him," said Cooper. "He said there's a safety net."

"That doesn't strike you as odd?" said Dave. "I mean, who puts a safety net at the bottom of a pit trap? Doesn't that entirely defeat the purpose of leaving a trap in the first place?"

"You think too much," said Cooper. "There are times for thinking, and there are times for action."

Dave rubbed the leopard fur on his wrist. "Well I think this certainly qualifies as a time for—"

"Action," said Cooper, shoving Dave into the pit.

"Shiiiiiiit!" said Dave, disappearing into the hole.

"That was a dick move, Cooper," said Julian. "Even for you."

"I was just having some fun with him," said Cooper. "We were all going to jump in sooner or later. It's not like we had a whole lot of choice. We weren't just going to leave Tim down there and go hit the pub, were we?"

"There are always options."

"Like what?"

"We could have sent Ravenus down to bring back one end of Tim's rope."

Cooper stroked his fat, leathery neck. "That's a good idea. You should have brought it up before I—"

A screeching, howling roar reverberated through the forest, like Satan had just stepped on a Lego.

"What was that?" asked Dave.

"Owlbears," said Diamond.

"Dammit," said Julian.

"They've caught our scent," said Diamond. "Whatever options there were are gone now. We have to jump in."

"I told you," said Cooper.

"But there could be anything down there," Julian protested.

Diamond hugged Lucifer close to her chest. "Between anything and owlbears, I'll choose anything." She jumped into the pit.

"That was irresponsible reasoning," said Julian.

Another piercing scream-roar shook the air. This one was closer than before.

"Have fun with the owlbears, fucker," said Cooper, and cannonballed through the revolving trap door.

"Well, shit," Julian said to Ravenus, the only one there left to listen. "You coming?" He held the trap door open with his quarterstaff, just wide enough for Ravenus to get through. The bird dove through the gap and into the darkness.

Julian was nudging the trap door with his foot, trying to muster up the courage to jump into some strange abyss, when an owlbear crashed into view. It might have been the adrenaline talking, but the beast looked to be as big as a house, with a beak like the sharpened hood of a Volkswagen Beetle. When its eyes met his, he suddenly found he had the courage to run away. He jumped into the hole.

The drop was a little longer than Julian had been anticipating.

It was just long enough for him to have time to wonder if he had missed the alleged safety net before he finally connected with it.

His impact made a reverberating ripple in the rest of the net, on which he could get a sense of where everyone else was around him without actually being able to see them. A slow and steady wave met him from beyond his feet. A dull moan came from the same direction. Dave. A lighter, but more rapid, pulse came from his left, accompanied by the sound of vomiting. Tim. A solid presence was somewhere above him, conspicuous due to its relative lack of movement. The dense mass was laughing. Cooper. A final mass, proportional to his own, was see-sawing with him in a steady rhythm. It asked "Are you okay?" Diamond.

"I'm fine," said Julian. "Just getting my bearings is all." Despite the constant waving of the net, Julian managed to sit upright. It was a little more challenging still because his clothes and skin stuck to the fabric. "Ew... why's it sticky?"

"Oh good," said Cooper. "You feel that too? I thought it was just my skin."

"I still can't find my bottle," said Tim. "How about some light, Julian?"

Julian pulled a copper coin out of his belt pouch and cupped it between his hands. "Light." When he uncovered the coin, his immediate surroundings were bathed in soft, golden light. They were in a roughly spherical earthen-walled chamber. The net they were all sitting on bisected the chamber horizontally. While it appeared to have been put there for the unlikely purpose of safety for those who fell victim of the trap above, it did not appear to be man-made. It was a dense and haphazard weave of sticky, silky strands of... something. It was stronger than it looked, too. The whole net was paper thin, but supported all of their weight easily. Fingering a few strands of it, Julian guessed he'd have a hard time ripping through it if he wanted to.

Movement in the shadows just beyond the radius of his Light spell caught his attention.

"What was that?" he whispered.

"Um," said Dave as the shadows moved in closer, taking more definite forms. There were dozens of them. "You know those spiders we were hunting? I think we found them."

The spiders closed in, forming a perimeter around the group. They ranged in size from Dave to Cooper, either venom or saliva dripping from their fangs. Neither boded well for Julian and his friends.

"We are so fucked," said Dave.

Even a straight fight on solid ground would have been nigh-impossible to win. There were just too many of them, and they were so big. And here they were on the spiders' turf, where those eight-legged fuckers could move about like Fred Astaire, but he and his friends would struggle to crawl. Julian hated to admit it, but Dave had made what he felt was an astute observation.

Interestingly enough, the spiders didn't close in and devour them all. Not just then, at least. They kept a safe distance while chattering to each other in their spider language. The biggest one stood tall on its exoskeletal legs and scurried through the crowd into the darkness beyond the Light spell.

"Hello," said Julian to the nearest spider. He spoke slowly and loudly. "We mean you no harm. We are sorry for invading your home. We would just like to leave."

The spider opened its giant mandibles and hissed at him.

"Do you have magic to speak with spiders?" asked Diamond.

"No," said Julian.

"Then what good do you think you're going to accomplish?"

"I don't know. It's better than nothing, right?"

"I'm not so sure that it was."

The spider chatter rose steadily in volume and pitch until it stopped abruptly. The spiders in Cooper's direction parted to form an empty lane on the massive web. The large spider which had scurried away now returned. It was not alone. Behind it were two even larger creatures. They, too, walked on arachnid legs, but their torsos and heads were like those of elves, only black.

The male stood tall and proud, white braids hanging down

from either side of his black, angular face. White ink tattoos of bladed weapons ran the length of each muscular arm and across his broad chest. The female wore her hair in a short flapper bob. The cleavage of her pert black breasts was barely contained by a corset that looked to be woven of spider silk.

"Driders," said Dave. His voice was less than enthusiastic.

"What are driders?" asked Julian.

"Half drow, half spider," said Dave.

"Drow?" said Julian. "Oh wait, I remember. Those were the black people, right?"

"Dark elves."

"Is that like the game equivalent of African American?"

"No, it's—":

"Silence!" said the male drider.

Julian and Dave ceased their discussion at once.

The male drider grinned, showing off a mouthful of shiny white teeth which matched his pupil-less eyes. "You have done well, my pet," he said, patting the giant spider at his side. "You shall be rewarded." He turned to the female drider. "The Dark Goddess smiles upon us this day, my bride. We needn't make do with a single measly Kobold after all."

"That kobold," said Julian. "Was it carrying a dagger? Because—"

"Silence!" the male drider roared. He elevated his body on his great spider legs until he was able to curve his abdomen underneath them. From the rear tip of his abdomen, he squirted a sticky white fluid at Julian, covering him from shoulder to knee.

"Hey!" said Julian, earning him another squirt. He found he was unable to move his arms away from the sides of his body. His legs were likewise stuck together. The substance began to crystallize into strands similar to the ones which made up the web they were all standing on.

"Dude," said Cooper. "Did you just jizz on my friend? That's not cool, man."

"You will mind your tongue, foul creature!" said the female

drider. She sprayed a coating of web at Cooper.

"Fucking hell, man," said Cooper, struggling to tear through the fluid before it crystallized. "Your missus packs quite a load as well. I totally didn't see that coming."

Both driders focused their spray on Cooper, and he was soon overwhelmed in a thick, white cocoon, completely covered except for his head.

"This is so humiliating," Cooper groaned. "I feel like a Japanese secretary." He wriggled around on the web like a giant maggot.

The rest of the group were barely able to stand up on the web, much less defend themselves. One by one, the driders coated them all in individual cocoons.

After they were all helplessly squirming on the web, the giant spiders grouped themselves into teams, squirted a bit more web onto each of their feet, and started dragging them out of the chamber.

"Reginald," said the female drider. "Can't we just eat the little one now? It's been so long since we've had proper mammal. I grow so weary of kobold flesh."

The male drider, Reginald, looked back at his wife sympathetically, but shook his head. "When the Dark Goddess bestows such gifts upon us, it is unwise not to make the most of them. The kobold who preceded this group is not like to survive the night. If we eat the halfling now, the kobold meat runs the risk of spoiling. We shall dine on kobold tonight. We can have the halfing tomorrow, dear Lidia."

Lidia lowered her head, pouting.

Reginald placed his index finger under Lidia's chin and lifted her head until their eyes met. He was smiling. "I know a certain someone who has a birthday next week," he said. "I can't think of a better reason to feast on dwarf."

Lidia's white eyes brightened. "Oh Reginald! You are right of course. I will wait!" Then she frowned and looked down at Cooper. "And what shall we do with the half-orc? I fear his meat has

already begun to spoil."

"Fuck you, lady!" said Cooper. "That's my natural musk."

"My children!" Reginald bellowed, his arms spread out before him. The spiders all stopped simultaneously. "Put this group in the storage chamber. Bring my beautiful bride and I the wounded kobold. Please me and you shall all dine on half-orc tonight!"

The spiders glanced uncomfortably at one another for a moment. A few of the nearest ones gave Cooper a sniff and backed away. One of the spiders chattered.

Reginald lowered his arms. "Well then do it because you've been ordered to, ungrateful vermin! There's nothing stopping us from dining on spider, you know."

With that, the spiders returned to their duties. A few of them scurried ahead. Julian and his friends were dragged through a ten foot wide earthen-walled corridor which led downward at a slight angle out of the pit-trap chamber.

A few minutes passed before Julian heard weak moaning coming from the other direction. "What's that noise?"

"I can't move my head that way," said Dave. He was one of the two of the party who was able to see in the pitch-black darkness they were being dragged through. They were now well beyond the light of Julian's enchanted coin. The spell had probably expired by now anyway.

"I see it," said Cooper. "The spiders that ran ahead are dragging something back this way."

"The wounded kobold," said Julian.

"See if he's got my dagger when he passes," said Diamond.

"Ha!" shrieked the kobold as he was dragged past them. "This is your fault! You deserve this. I'll die with a smile on my face."

"Where's my dagger, you little reptilian bastard?" said Diamond.

"Damn you all to the depths!" shouted the kobold. His voice was fading. The spiders were moving faster.

"I didn't see any daggers on him, but he was covered in spider splooge, so he might have had it under there or something."

Eventually they arrived at some sort of a destination. The way the sound echoed off the walls, Julian guessed they were in another large chamber. The texture of the floor felt like web, though it wasn't suspended in the air like in the other chamber. This was just web on solid ground.

"What's going on?" asked Julian.

"I think we're in the storage chamber," said Dave. "The walls, floor, and ceiling are all covered in white."

Cooper snorted. "It looks like Dave got set loose in an elementary school."

Tim laughed.

"Fuck you, Cooper," said Dave.

"Cease your stupid bickering right now," said Diamond. "What are the spiders doing?"

"About half of them are climbing up the walls," said Dave. "The rest are just hanging around. There's something hanging from the ceiling. Two somethings actually. They might be kobolds."

"Are they alive?" asked Diamond.

"It's hard to tell from here," said Dave. "They aren't really moving or anything. They look— Oh my God, I wish you guys could see this!"

"What's going on?" asked Julian.

"The spiders are descending from the ceiling in groups of three. They're suspended from their own threads, but they're swinging around one another, braiding the threads together. It's remarkable."

"I'm glad you're enjoying this so much, dwarf," said Diamond. "But shouldn't you be focusing more on a way to get us out of here?"

"I'm just reporting what I see," said Dave. "Nobody ever likes my ideas anyway. I'll leave the escape to the brainy one."

"Who's the brainy one?"

"Tim."

"The drunk halfling?"

"I've really got to piss," said Tim.

"Something tells me his mind isn't completely focused on the task at hand," said Diamond.

"Then Julian can think of something," said Dave. "He's got a knack for thinking up crazy stupid ideas that always manage to work."

"Well thank you, Dave," said Julian. "I'll take that as a— Shit, what's going on?" His feet were being pulled again, but not forward. This time they were being pulled up.

"We're being hoisted up to the ceiling," said Dave.

Julian ascended slowly for a couple of minutes. In the darkness, it was impossible to tell just how far up he was. Shortly after he stopped ascending, the spiders scurried away.

"Whassup?" said Cooper. Something growled in response. Presumably, one of the kobolds Dave had mentioned.

"You shouldn't be so hostile," said Julian. "We're all in this together now. The only chance we have of escaping is by working together."

"Ha!" one of the kobolds barked. "You think you're going to escape? There is no escaping here. The only way you're getting out of here is when those driders shit out your remains. There were eight of us hanging up here last week. Jirrick told us about what you did to him. Now he's being devoured as well. You all can rot in the Abyss."

"Jirrick?" said Diamond. "Is that the kobold leader? Did he mention having a dagger on him?"

The kobold merely growled at her.

Julian had no intention of being drider shit. He started swinging his body back and forth. "Dave, how high up would you say we are?"

"I don't know," said Dave. "Pretty high."

"I mean, do you think we'd survive a fall from this height?"

"It would definitely hurt. And you'd probably land on your face."

Julian stopped swinging. He'd go back to that if he didn't think of anything else.

"Cooper," said Julian. "Do you think you're strong enough to bust out of your web?"

"I don't know," said Cooper. "Those fuckers bukakked me pretty good. I'm trying. I feel like I'm close, but not quite strong enough."

"Use your Barbarian Rage," said Julian. "That should bump your Strength up more than enough to break through."

"I already used it today."

"When?"

"This morning, while you were in the library."

"You guys were all getting trashed on the quad," said Julian. "What did you have to get enraged about?"

"The booze guy needed help moving his stall," said Cooper. "He wanted to make room for a Doomsayer. He said people drink more when they think the world is about to end."

"Dammit," said Julian. Then he had an idea. "Ravenus!" He tried to keep his tone the same as if he were just talking to his friends. "Ravenus, if you're out there, don't answer. Just come to me."

A few seconds later, he heard the familiar flapping, and then Ravenus was perched on his shoulder, hanging upside down from the webbing.

"I'm here, sir. Do you want I should cut you down from here?"

"Jesus, no," said Julian. "Don't do that. I'd probably break my neck. But do you think you could claw through to my hand?"

"Not a problem, sir." Ravenus flew up to Julian's hand and began tearing away at web.

"It'll take that bird forever to get you free," said Dave. "And then what?"

"I'm not trying to get myself free," said Julian. "That's it, Ravenus. Almost there. Ow! Okay, that's enough."

Ravenus stopped scratching. "Sorry, sir. I seem to have nicked you a bit."

"It's okay, Ravenus," said Julian, grabbing one of Ravenus's talons. "I want you to deliver this spell to Cooper."

"Of course, sir."

Julian whispered the incantation. "Bull's Strength." He let go of Ravenus. "Now go touch his face."

"Ow!" said Cooper a couple of seconds later. "Fuck off, bird! Get out of my— Oh, what's this? Sweet!" A few grunts, rips, and swears later, "Almost there. I've almost got— Oh fuck!"

"Cooper?" said Julian.

The next sound was a crash, and then Cooper called out from below. "I'm okay!"

"Not for long, you aren't," said Dave.

"Huh?" said Cooper. "Oh shit."

"What's going on?" asked Julian.

"The spiders are back," said Dave. "They must have felt the vibrations from Cooper hitting the floor."

"Cooper can handle a few spiders," said Julian. He knew in his heart that it was only wishful thinking. He'd seen their numbers. Cooper might be able to take them all down, one at a time, but like this they'd overwhelm him in no time.

"Come on, man!" said Dave. "At least give it your best shot. What are you doing? Stand up and ready your axe!"

"Fuck that," said Cooper.

"What's he doing?" asked Diamond.

"He's just kneeling on the ground," said Dave, "The spiders are closing in all around him, and he's just rummaging around in his bag."

"Shit," said Tim.

"What is it?" said Julian.

"I held it as long as I could. I was hoping this web shit would be waterproof. It isn't. I just pissed in my face."

"Your friend is about to die down there," said Diamond. "I would think you'd be a little more concerned."

"Who the fuck are you?" said Tim.

Julian sighed. "That's Diamond."

"Sweet," said Tim. "Is she a stripper?"

The room lit up from below. Julian looked down. Holy shit that's a long drop. Cooper wielded a torch. The spiders, almost on top of him now, stopped dead in their tracks.

"Cooper!" cried Dave. "Stop! You don't know what you're doing!"

"Poor Man's Fireball!" said Cooper.

"What's wrong?" asked Julian.

Dave shook his head. "He knows exactly what he's doing. You might want to brace yourselves."

The spiders must have had a pretty good idea of Cooper's intentions. They started crawling over each other trying to scramble away from him.

"Not so fast, fuckers!" said Cooper. He dropped the torch at his feet.

Cooper went up in flames, standing at the epicenter of a wave of fire that spread along the webby floor well faster than those hairy bastards could ever hope to run. They crackled and popped like Rice Krispies as the flames spread up the walls.

And that's about the time that Julian caught the meaning of Dave's warning. "Oh shit! Ravenus, fly away!"

Ravenus squawked but did as he was bid. Julian watched helplessly as the flames curved up the round walls to where they would meet at the ceiling. This would not end well.

The one good thing Julian could say about being set on fire was that it freed his arms and legs to brace him for what would otherwise have been a deadly fall. Tim was alive, yelping and excitedly patting out the tiny fires on his now exposed chest hair. Dave's armor made him sound like a garbage truck collision when he hit the ground, but it appeared to have protected him from the fire.

Painful as it was, Julian was pleasantly surprised to find that he didn't seem to have broken anything during the fall. The only explanation was that game mechanics didn't account for broken bones. He was certain, however, that between the fire and the fall, he'd lost more than a few hit points. He rolled back and forth on the ground to make sure he wasn't still on fire like Cooper was.

Cooper walked among the dead and dying spiders, smashing his axe into any of the latter he found. His loincloth had almost completely burned away, displaying his leathery ass to an undeserving world. Flames still licked their way up, threatening to set the garment completely free.

"Hey Dave," said Cooper, putting out a hand. "You mind slapping me a Heal spell?"

"Yeah, no problem," said Dave, touching his hand to Cooper's. A spider took advantage of Cooper's distraction and rose to its feet behind him.

"Cooper!" cried Julian. "Behind you!"

"Oh my God that's refreshing," said Cooper. He farted, sending a jet of blue flame into the approaching spider's face. It's eight eyes melted down the sides of its horror-stricken face before the creature collapsed to the ground. Julian frowned. Nothing deserved to die like that.

"Excuse me," said Cooper.

"What the fuck, man!" said Tim. Whoever said there was no quick way to get sober had obviously not tried setting himself on fire.

"You okay, Tim?" asked Dave, offering him a hand to help him up.

Tim slapped his hand away. "I don't need your hand," he said, glaring at Cooper. "I need my fucking epidermis!"

"Don't be such a pussy," said Cooper. "It worked, didn't it? We're free and alive, and the spiders aren't."

"That's more than I can say for the kobolds," said Dave, poking through their charred remains. "Poor little bastards only get like four hit points or something like that. There's barely anything left of them."

"Wait!" said Julian. "Where's Diamond?" He scanned the room frantically for her, but the light from the burning spiders was beginning to fade quickly. "Diamond? Are you there? Are you okay?"

There was no answer.

"Dave, I fell here, and you fell over there. That means Diamond should have fallen somewhere around here," Julian said, pointing to the spot where he guessed Diamond should be. "Come over here and tell me if you see anything."

Dave stomped over. "There's nothing, dude," said Dave. "Sorry. Just dirt and ash."

"Relax, dude," said Cooper. "She's got to be somewhere. Maybe she snuck off for a piss or something."

"You killed her, you stupid bastard!" said Julian.

"Bullshit," said Cooper. "If she was dead, then there would be a body. Your mind's not right, because it's in your dick right now. She'll turn up."

"My mind is fine," said Julian. "Did you see the kobolds? There was barely anything of them left, because they only had four hit points. Diamond was a first level wizard! She might have had less than that."

"Fewer," said Tim.

"What?" said Julian.

"It's not less hit points," said Tim. "It's fewer. Just sayin'."

"Fuck you!" said Julian. "He just fucking disintegrated Diamond!"

"Who's Diamond?" asked Tim. "I'm sorry. I only just sobered up. Where are we?"

"Fuck all of you!" said Julian. "I'm out of here." He stomped off through the nearest exit he could find.

"You're going the wrong way," said Dave.

"How would you know?" said Julian. He neither looked back nor slowed his pace.

"That tunnel goes down," Dave continued. "If we're trying to reach the surface, we'd do better to go up. There's another tunnel that goes up from here."

Dave made a fair point, but Julian gave him the finger as he continued defiantly heading in the wrong direction.

"We need to go after him," said Tim. Julian's elf ears could

hear their conversation from an impressive distance away.

"Cooper just burned his girlfriend alive," said Dave. "He's going to need some time."

"Hey fuck you, Dave," said Cooper. "How was I supposed to know she only had one hit point. She seemed pretty capable to me. I did the only thing I could think of. Considering my low Intelligence score, I'm pretty impressed with myself. I stand by my decision."

"No one's blaming you," said Dave. "But maybe you should apologize to Julian just the same."

"Yeah, okay."

"There's no way you killed all those spiders. Some of them will have escaped to report to the driders. We need to get moving before they come back."

And so of course the three assholes started following Julian down the wrong tunnel.

"If you don't mind me saying so, sir," said Ravenus, perched on Julian's shoulder. "You might be overreacting a bit."

"I mind," said Julian. "Dave's right. I need some time to myself to cool off."

"Yes, sir," said Ravenus. "Of course, sir. But might you address the small matter of us not being able to see?"

Julian huffed out a sigh. "Fine. Light." The end of his quarterstaff filled the small, descending corridor with light. As he expected, there wasn't anything here worth seeing. Just dirt, dirt, and more dirt. He had been content just to stumble along in the dark.

One point of interest was an opening coming up on the right, and a single giant spider crawling out of it. The spider faced Julian, standing high on its legs, filling the cramped corridor.

This was just the sort of thing Julian needed to settle his nerves. Something to beat the shit out of. He charged at the spider. It was obviously expecting a different reaction. It lowered its body a couple of inches and took a single step back.

Julian battle cried his first incantation. "Magic Missile!" He

threw a glowing red ball of hate-magic at the confused arachnid, which exploded in its thorax. The spider shrieked in pain and took a desperate grab for Julian when he got into range. Julian shrugged off the spider leg and got down to engaging the beast the way he really wanted to... clubbing it repeatedly in the face. It fell on the second or third swing, but Julian kept bashing away until his club was flinging slimy spider guts all over the walls and diminishing the light from the spell.

"Feel better?" asked Dave.

"Huh?" Julian stopped beating the dead spider. "Oh, um... yeah, a little."

"I'm sorry I incinerated your girlfriend," said Cooper.

"It's okay," said Julian. "I know you didn't mean to. I don't think she was into me anyway. I wasn't getting that vibe, you know?"

"Hold on," said Tim. "How does that make it okay to incinerate a person?"

"Just let it go, dude," said Cooper. "Hey. What's in here?" He poked his head through the side passage. "Score! We found their treasure room!" Tim and Dave followed him inside.

"Ravenus," said Julian. "Stay here and keep your eyes open for driders."

"But I can't see, sir."

"Then listen. We won't be long."

Julian stepped inside the treasure room. Unlike the other chambers he'd been in down here, this room was cubical. For a treasure room, it wasn't very impressive. There were a few weapons lying around, but most of them were either broken, or rusted, or both. The room was littered with busted wooden crates, some of them covered with canvas sheets, spotted black and smelling of mold. One large and conspicuous chest sat against the back wall. It looked like the quintessential treasure chest from an old pirate movie.

Cooper opened the chest and frowned. "Empty." He reached inside, as if to confirm by touch what his eyes already told him.

"Something's coming," said Ravenus. "Put out your light!"

"Shit," said Dave. "What are we going to do?"

"We'll fight," said Cooper.

"You know we're no match for driders," said Dave. "They'll spray us down with web again before we get an Attack Roll."

"Hide!" said Julian. It wasn't a great plan, but it was as good as any at this point. He ducked behind some crates and pulled a sheet of canvas over his head. His friends did likewise. They waited in perfect silence, broken only once by a squeaky fart. Poor Dave. He was hiding under the same canvas as Cooper.

A minute later, the patter of what Julian guessed was sixteen giant legs sounded just outside the entrance of the room.

A female voice gasped. "My jewels!" Julian knew the voice. It was Lidia, the female drider.

"My weapons!" cried Reginald. The great treasure chest creaked open. "My gold! All of it gone!"

"And what's that smell?"

"Those little savages will pay for their transgressions!"

"It's not enough that they murder our children," said Lidia. Her voice had a slight sniffle to it. "They had to go and rob us as well!"

"Come on guys," said a voice from outside that Julian wasn't expecting to hear. It was his own voice, or at least a very poor imitation of it. "I found some more spiders over here. Maybe we can rape them before we kill them this time!"

"My babies!" cried Lidia.

"Those fiends!" said Reginald. "Come, sweet wife. They aren't far. They won't escape us again!"

Their giant spider feet rushed out of the room. Julian pulled the tarp off of his head. The air in the room was thick with fart.

Dave inhaled deeply.

"Come on!" said Julian. "Ravenus just bought us a little time. We have to get out of here."

Cooper led the way back to the storage chamber. Julian and Tim, who couldn't see in the dark, stumbled along behind him as best they could, while Dave took up the rear.

Julian knew they had arrived when he tripped over the corpse of a dead giant spider. "Dave, didn't you say there was a passage leading up?"

"Yeah," said Dave. "It's right up there. I don't know how we're supposed to get to it though."

"Cooper," said Julian. "Can you take Tim's rope and climb the wall?"

"I don't think so," said Cooper. "The walls are curved. I'd only be able to make it halfway up."

"Damn," said Julian.

"I've got it," said Tim. "We'll pile up spider corpses and climb up those."

"First of all, ew," said Julian. "Secondly, we don't have that kind of time."

"Tim," said Cooper. "Get your rope. I've got an idea."

Tim dug blindly through his bag for a moment. "Here."

"No, that's okay," said Cooper. "Just hold this end."

"What?" said Tim. "Hey, put me down! Aaaaahh! Ow! Fuck!" There was a brief pause, and then a thud on the ground. "Ow."

"Shit," said Cooper. "I missed. Sorry."

"No!" said Tim. "Not again!"

"Second time's the charm," said Cooper.

"Aaaaaaaahhh!" said Tim. There was no thud this time. Tim had apparently arrived at his destination.

"Okay, Julian," said Cooper. "Your turn."

"What?" said Julian, backing away from Cooper's voice. "Why?"

"Tim can't support my weight by himself." Cooper's voice grew closer with every word. It was pointless to resist. "Don't be such a baby."

Two giant half-orc hands grabbed his upper arms and picked him up. Julian's body swung backward, and then swiftly forward... and up. He sailed through the darkness, flailing his arms for purchase. His upper body landed in an upward-sloping passage and

immediately started to slide out of it. Tim caught his arm, and he managed to scramble up to safety.

"Dave's too heavy for me to throw," said Cooper. "I'm coming up the rope. You two hold it. Ready?"

Julian and Tim wrapped the rope around their wrists and dug their heels into the earthen walls of the tunnel.

"Ready," said Tim.

Cooper started up the rope, and Julian felt like his arms were going to be pulled off. He and Tim groaned but held their ground. When Cooper reached the passage, the pressure on Julian's wrist let up. He and Tim exhaled.

"Dave," said Cooper. "Your turn. Tie the rope around your waist.

"A little light please?" said Ravenus, somewhere below them.

"Light!" said Julian. There wasn't much point in hiding now. "Ravenus, we're up here!"

Ravenus flew up into the passage. "I'm sorry, sir. I distracted them as long as I could, but they're coming back."

"You were brilliant, Ravenus," said Julian.

"Dave, you fat fuck!" said Cooper. "Are you ready yet?"

"Ready!" Dave called back. "Pull!"

Tim and Julian hurried up the passage, with Cooper dragging Dave behind them.

"There's a light up ahead!" said Tim.

Julian shielded the light from his staff and looked up the passage. Tim was right. It was tiny and distant, but it was there. The way out. Their salvation.

"There!" shouted Reginald. Julian could imagine the driders' point of view, looking up at Dave's big dwarf ass struggling into the passage.

Damn. They'd put forth a good effort, but it was done. The driders could climb the walls as effortlessly and quickly as if they were walking on the ground. There was no way Julian and his friends would make it out of the drider lair before they were caught.

Cooper rushed past Julian. "Come on, jackass! They're gaining on us!"

"What's the point?" said Julian. "We've lost. We're out of options. I'll just fire a Magic Missile at them as a final fuck you before we die."

Cooper stopped and looked at Julian. "There are always options. You know what you have to do." Then he turned and continued up the passage.

"What kind of cryptic bullshit was that?" Julian called after him.

Dave squeezed his way past Julian. "Whatever you've got planned, better do it quick."

"But I don't have anything planned!" Julian cried. "What do I have to..." Then it hit him. It was obvious. He'd do the same thing he always did. He looked down the passage just as Reginald started to crawl into it.

"You die first, elf!" said Reginald. His white eyes looked pissed off. He only had just enough room to squeeze his abdomen under his legs and point his spidery ass at Julian.

"Horse!" Julian shouted, just in time for a very surprised-looking horse to catch an assful of web. The poor animal didn't even have room to stand up properly.

"What's this?" demanded Reginald.

The terrified horse whinnied.

"Bwaaaaaaaaaagghh!" shouted Reginald. Lidia joined in half a second later. It was an extended shout which ended abruptly. It translated to "I just got kicked by a horse and fell a long distance to the ground."

"Sorry, friend," Julian said to the magical horse. "But well done." He turned around. "Let's go!" But his friends were well ahead of him. They were nearly to the end of the tunnel, where it widened to about ten feet wide, when Julian heard the horse scream, which ended very quickly. "Hurry up, guys!"

"Wait!" said Tim just before they entered the sweet sweet light of the sun.

"Are you crazy?" said Dave. "They're right behind us!"

Tim got down on his knees and ran a finger along an almost invisible thread. "It's a trap."

"Well thanks for that, Admiral Ackbar," said Cooper. "But I'll take my chances."

"No," said Tim. "The driders must have rigged the exit, but I think we can bypass it if we stay close to the left wall."

The four of them inched their way outside, backs against the wall.

"We did it!" said Julian. "We're free!"

"Wait a second," said Dave. "Is there any rule that says driders can't go outside their lair?"

"Shit," said Tim. "Julian, do you have any more Mount spells left?"

"Just one," said Julian.

"Run!" said Dave. He took off as fast as his thick little legs would carry him. Not nearly fast enough.

"They're hurt," said Julian. "We might not stand much of a chance, but let's see if we can't take at least one of those fuckers down."

"I'm with you," said Cooper, holding his axe ready.

Tim loaded his crossbow. "I'm with you, too," he said. "But I'm going to hide behind this tree."

"Okay," said Julian.

"It's for the Sneak Attack Bonus," Tim explained.

"Okay," Julian repeated. "Seriously, it's fine."

A few seconds later, Reginald was visible, approaching the opening of the tunnel. When the tunnel got wide enough, Lidia took her place beside her husband, running on their monstrous arachnid legs toward Julian, Cooper, and Dave, who had apparently had a change of heart.

Julian took a deep breath to steady his resolve. His grip on his quarterstaff was slick with sweat as he pointed it at Reginald. "Magic Missile." A white bolt of energy flew out of the staff, striking the drider in the chest. Whether or not he even noticed it was anybody's guess. It certainly didn't slow him down.

"Well shit," said Cooper. That summed up their situation pretty eloquently. They had used up all their tricks and all their luck. It was time to admit that they were way out of their league, and now they were going to—

Click. Twang. Swoosh. Thwack. A barrage of swords, spears, daggers, and javelins sprang from the ground surrounding the cave entrance. They were rigged on a series of ropes, strings, and bent trees. The driders were skewered from all sides.

"My weapons!" groaned Reginald.

The tip of a bolt sprouted out the front of Lidia's throat. Another from Reginald's left eye. Their bodies went limp and they shat out white blobs of web.

"'The fuck just happened?" asked Cooper. Then he farted. It was even more pungent than usual.

"Jesus, Cooper!" said Dave. He and Julian stepped away from Cooper.

"Sorry guys," said Cooper. "That one may have been more liquid than gas." He reached down the front of what barely qualified as a loincloth anymore, and pulled out a piece of paper.

"What's that?" said Julian. "Where did you get it?"

"I found it in the treasure chest," said Cooper. "I took it to wipe with."

"Why didn't you show that to the rest of us?" demanded Julian.

"I didn't think it was important. There's nothing on it but some meaningless scribble."

"That's because you're illiterate, stupid!" He snatched the paper out of Cooper's hand.

"Words can cut too, you know."

Julian spread the paper against the trunk of a tree, flattening out the wrinkles, and smearing brown streaks that he was pretty sure had been contributed by Cooper. "It's a letter." His heart skipped a beat. "It's a letter to me!"

"What?" said Tim. "What does it say?"

Julian cleared his throat and read the letter aloud.

Dear Julian,

If you're reading this letter, then that means you're alive, and that's a good thing. It also means you're heading in the wrong direction. The surface is up, silly.

I've got to hand it to you, you were right. You'll be happy to know that, somehow or another, I've mastered the Invisibility spell. It came in very handy for stealing the driders' treasure and sneaking past them. So I'd like to thank you for that, and for a wonderful adventure. You really know how to show a girl a good time.

I regret having to tell you that I'm not in the market for a romantic relationship at present. You're a lovely elf with a big heart, and there's a more deserving female elf that I'm sure you'll make very happy one day. Please respect my privacy and do not try to look for me. We wouldn't want things to get awkward, would we?

Know that I'll treasure the memory of today, and I'll never forget you.

Sincerely,
D.
XOXOXO
P.S.

Julian paused to glare up at Cooper.

"What?" said Cooper.

Julian continued reading.

P.S. When I find a way out of here, I'm going to set a trap with some weapons I found. Keep to the left against the wall and you can avoid getting stabbed to death.

"Oh shit," said Cooper. "Sorry."

P.P.S. Apologize to the dwarf for me. He was just too much fun to pick on. He's so cute when he gets flustered.

"Well that's nice," said Dave, his face flushing red.

Julian lowered the letter. "There's a heart and a smiley face."

"Um..." said Cooper. "She's alive at least. That's good news, right? She must be more than just a first level wizardess."

"I couldn't rig a trap like that," said Tim. "She must have a few levels of rogue in her."

Julian crumpled the paper in his fist. "What a fucking bitch! I wish you had incinerated her."

"You don't mean that," said Tim. "That's just your broken heart talking."

"I bet her name's not even really Diamond."

Cooper slapped a hand on Julian's shoulder. "It never is, friend. It never is."

The End

Clerical Error
20
ROBERT BEVAN

CLERICAL ERROR

(Original Publication Date: March 11, 2014)

The goblins attacked suddenly and with the ferocity of religious fanatics, most wielding morningstars, but Dave estimated that about a quarter of them favored short swords. Some of the latter were even armed with a dagger in their off hand. None of them carried shields. Those who only carried one weapon gripped the handles with both hands, adding to the savagery of their attacks.

"Watch out!" Tim had said when they sprung their ambush, but his warning did the rest of the group little good, as all of the goblins seemed hell-bent on Tim. Cooper had sliced one in half through the abdomen as it attempted to rush past him on its way to Tim, but Tim was still surrounded by six other goblins with a few more impatiently waiting to get into the melee.

Tim was fascinating to watch in close combat; he fought like a breakdancing knife-fighter, ducking and dodging blades and spiky maces while swiping and jabbing with his own little dagger. Give Tim a few more levels, and Dave might have been tempted to just sit back and enjoy the show. But as quickly and deftly as Tim moved, some of the goblins' attacks connected, and for every goblin Tim dropped, another was ready to take its place.

Dave brought the heavy, steel ball at the end of his mace down on the head of a goblin, introducing its brain to its heart.

Julian didn't waste any of his magic on goblins. His quarterstaff could drop them as well as a Magic Missile could, and he hadn't yet learned any offensive area-of-effect spells. Ravenus did his part by scratching and pecking the goblins' eyes out. Most of the little bastards had so few Hit Points that the combined efforts of a bird and an elf wielding a stick were enough to bring them down.

Cooper, of course, was the most effective at goblin butchery. His greataxe sliced through goblins at nearly twice the rate anyone else was able to manage. He carved a path of carnage toward Tim.

When Tim finally got an opening, he bolted, diving under Cooper's legs. He had done a miraculous job of avoiding goblin swords and morningstars, but he was still in pretty bad shape. His right eye was swollen shut, his clothes were riddled with shallow puncture wounds, clinging to his body with blood and sweat, and when he stood back up, he strongly favored his left leg.

Their preferred target out of reach, some of the remaining goblins began to hack and club whoever was nearest them. Most, however, tried to work their way around or through the group.

"What the hell have these guys got against Tim?" asked Dave, crushing a goblin's chest against a tree trunk.

"Julian and I will handle the rest of them," said Cooper. He kicked one goblin backwards into the air. Its head connected with a low tree branch, sending it into an impressive forward somersault before it landed face first on the ground. "Just go heal Tim!"

Dave stepped back from the fight. He reached his left arm out to Tim, who grabbed it with both of his little hands like it was a life-saving rope.

"I heal thee," said Dave.

Tim closed his good eye and smiled, waiting for the healing magic to course through his body. Dave watched Tim's face. It was always satisfying to see the wounds close up, the swelling go down, fractured bones realign. The satisfied sigh would be reward enough for the help he could provide his friend.

No sigh came. No wounds closed up. Tim's smile faded to a frown. "Um... Dave?"

"Hmm," said Dave. "That's weird. Let me try again." He placed both hands firmly on either side of Tim's face. "I heal thee!"

Nothing happened.

Dave pressed more firmly on Tim's face, squishing his cheeks and lips. "I HEAL THEE!"

"Dude," said Tim through his squished-up, bleeding mouth. "That fucking hurts."

"What's the hold up?" asked Cooper. The din of combat had subsided. "You think you guys could stop making out for a minute and help us loot these bodies?"

"I don't know what's wrong," said Dave. He released his grip on Tim's face. "This has never happened to me before."

Tim spat some blood on the ground. "It's okay, big guy. It happens to all of us every now and again. I won't judge." He started limping toward Cooper and Julian. "These guys have any cash?"

"Not a single fucking copper piece between them so far," said Cooper. "We might be able to sell some of these weapons though." He shoved three goblin-sized morningstars into his bag. They looked like toys in Cooper's giant hands.

"We should come away with a bunch of Experience Points from that though," said Julian. "Right?"

Cooper shrugged. "They were just goblins."

"But there were like a gazillion of them!"

"Thirty," said Tim, surveying the carnage. "Forty tops. We'll get a little something, but don't expect to level up or anything."

"Why do you think they were so focused on you?"

"Who knows?" said Tim, kicking a goblin corpse with his right foot. He winced in pain. "It's a common enough tactic to gang up on the littlest guy first, and work your way up from there." He put his hand on a tree trunk to keep from falling over.

"What the fuck is wrong with you?" asked Cooper. "Dave was supposed to patch you up."

"Yeah," said Tim. "Only his magic didn't work."

"Holy shit," said Cooper. "I didn't think it was possible."

"What?" said Julian. "What is it?"

"Dave became more useless."

Dave just gave Cooper a stubby middle finger, and then bent

down to pick up a goblin short sword. The stillness of the late afternoon air was pierced by a wolf's howl.

Everyone turned westward at once. Two wolves, about halfway between the size of a regular wolf and that of a horse, stood atop a ledge, silhouetted against the grey sky. Mounted on the back of each wolf was a goblin rider. The one on the left was dressed in a loose-fitting gown of roughspun wool. The rider on the right, wearing black plate armor, bore a standard. Dave immediately recognized the symbol on the wind-torn, black banner. He'd seen it in a book he'd recently borrowed from the Cardinian public library. The red skull of OuiJas, the goddess of Death, the favored deity of necromancers.

"Guys," said Dave. "I'm not so sure this encounter is over."

"Sure it is," said Cooper. "Those two just showed up. Julian, make some horses."

"Bullshit," said Tim, loading a bolt into his crossbow. "You know they've been up there the whole time as well as I do."

"What difference does any of this make?" said Julian.

"If they were involved in the attack," said Dave. "then they count as part of the encounter."

"So what?"

"So if we run away now, we don't get any Experience Points."

"Well shit," said Julian.

"It's just two more goblins and a couple of dogs," said Tim. "We can take them." The words slurred out of his mouth with a helping of bloody drool.

"No way," said Dave. "It's too risky, especially with my healing on the fritz."

"I could Magic Missile them from here," said Julian. "But then I wouldn't have enough Level 1 spells to get us out of here if we did have to run."

"Sorry, Fucko," said Cooper. "I have to agree with Shithead on this one."

"Do you always have to be such an asshole?" said Dave.

"What?" said Cooper. "I said I agreed with you."

The goblin in the roughspun gown raised his arms and began chanting.

"Well you losers can stay here and jerk each other off," said Tim. "That just leaves more Experience Points for— JESUS!" One of the dead goblins had grabbed him by the ankle.

"I don't get it," said Julian. "What does Jesus need with Exper—"

"Julian!" shouted Cooper. "Horses! Now!" He chopped the undead goblin's head in half. It released Tim's leg. But two more goblin zombies attacked Cooper from behind.

"Horse!" said Julian. A sturdy, brown draft horse appeared next to him. One of the goblin zombies shambling toward Julian unwisely passed behind the horse. It received a hoof to the chest and a free ticket to twenty feet away.

Tim fired a bolt point-blank into a zombie's face, dropping it instantly. He scurried up the trunk of a nearby tree like a frightened squirrel.

"Goddamn!" said Cooper. "These little fuckers really pack a punch when they're dead. He had four undead goblins clawing, biting, and punching him.

Dave would have tried to help, but he had three zombies closing in on him to deal with. He remembered the holy symbol he wore on a string around his neck. If he could turn a few of them, he'd be able to help Cooper. He brandished the holy symbol at two of the zombies coming at him. "Go away!"

One zombie grabbed his outstretched arm and bit into his leopard-fur-covered forearm. Yellow, pointed teeth pierced through skin and muscle, all the way to the bone. It seared like a red hot bear trap. He could feel tears welling up in his eyes. The other zombie punched his breastplate, probably doing more damage to its hand than it did to Dave. He backhanded the punching zombie and ripped his arm free from the biting zombie. That was at least as painful as the actual bite had been.

"Horse!" Julian cried a second time, circling around the first horse to avoid the zombie that was chasing him. A white horse appeared, a bit taller and leaner than the first one. It was time to go.

Dave held his mace low and swung it upward, catching the bitey zombie in the chin. The whole lower half of its face was a smashed mess of blood and bone. It wouldn't be biting anyone ever again, but it didn't seem to mind.

"I'm really angry!" Cooper shouted. His Barbarian Rage kicked in, and his fat and flabby skin grew tight, bulging with expanded muscles. He dropped his axe, reached behind his shoulders, and tore two of the clinging zombies off of his back. These he swung around to beat other zombies with.

Fight fire with fire, Dave supposed. But the undead goblins were still getting punches in here and there. Even with his temporary bonus to Strength and Constitution, Cooper wouldn't be able to take them all down. "Come on, Cooper! Let's go!" Dave's concern for Cooper was not entirely unselfish. He needed Cooper's great strength to help him get his squat, heavy dwarf body onto the back of a horse.

Cooper whirled around with a thunderous roar and bloodshot, red eyes. He threw a zombie at Dave. It wasn't exactly in the strike zone, but the target was considerably larger than a baseball and Dave already had his mace ready. He swung it as hard as he could with both hands. The head of his mace struck between the flying zombie's legs. When it hit the ground, it didn't get back up.

"Foul balls," said Dave.

Cooper grunted. It almost sounded like a laugh. He gripped the remaining zombie below the chin and above the chest, and strained briefly until its head was separated from its body, a good six inches of spinal cord dangling from it.

"Come on!" shouted Julian. He and Tim were already mounted on each of the horses and ready to ride.

Cooper kicked one more zombie out of his way and made for the horses. He lifted Dave onto the back of Julian's horse, and hopped onto the back of Tim's horse.

"Yah!" cried Tim. His horse didn't respond.

"Go, horses!" said Julian. The horses bolted forward simultaneously. As they retreated, Cooper shrunk down to his natural, still-impressive girth. His rock-solid abs melted back into a pot belly, and his pectoral muscles sagged back into man-tits.

Dwarves weren't made to ride horses. Their legs were too short to reach down into stirrups, and their thick, dense bodies made the whole galloping unit top-heavy. Maybe they'd do okay in a customized dwarven saddle, but one thing was for sure. Dwarves were certainly never meant to ride bareback on the rear end of a horse while clinging to an elf at top speed through a forest while being chased by goblin zombies. Dave barely lasted a minute.

Julian shouted something that Dave couldn't quite make out over the rush of the wind and the pounding of hooves on earth. It sounded like "Fuck!", but he wasn't sure. It could just as easily have been—

Julian dipped his head down, and Dave caught a low-hanging pine branch right in the face.

*

"Duck," Dave groaned as consciousness flowed back into his mind. His face felt like a gorilla had slammed it into a brick wall, and he was surprised he could speak at all, or even breathe for that matter. When his vision cleared, he saw Julian and Tim standing over him. Tim's face was already a bruised and beaten mess. Judging by the expression on Julian's face, his own face must have looked even worse.

With a bit of effort and a lot of pain, Dave managed to sit up. Cooper was pissing on the tree whose acquaintance Dave had recently made. He recognized it by the low-hanging branch bereft of a section of bark. He could feel bits of the bark swimming around in his bloody mouth. Julian's horses were gone, which either meant that more than two hours had passed or that Julian had managed to find a way to accidentally kill them before the spell duration ran out. Dave gave each option equal odds.

"Zombies?" Dave forced the question out of his overtaxed lungs.

"Gomblies," said Julian, grinning stupidly.

"What?" Each syllable that escaped Dave's lips caused him an excess of pain which he would have preferred not to have had to endure. He would have appreciated more succinct answers to his questions.

"I made that up while you were out," said Julian. He sounded very proud of himself. "It's a cross between zombie and goblin."

"It was either that or zoblin," said Tim.

"You made..." Dave spat out what was either a chunk of bark or a tooth. "...the right call." The words were flowing easier now, but not so much so that he wanted to use more than he had to. He looked up pleadingly at Julian.

Julian shrugged. "They didn't follow us. I've got Ravenus keeping an eye on them in case they change their minds. Sorry about your face."

"It wasn't you," said Dave. "It was the gods. I'm being punished." He held out a hand to Julian.

Julian helped Dave to his feet. "For what?"

"I don't know," said Dave. "Excessive violence? Maybe they thought I should know what it feels like to get hit in the face with a blunt instrument." He gestured up to the tree branch.

"Doubtful," said Cooper, having finished pissing on the gods' instrument of justice. "I'm way more violent than you. And you're really slow. The fight's usually over by the time you show up."

"Thanks, Cooper."

"Don't mention it. Also, you're kind of a pussy."

"Hey Cooper," said Tim. "Lay off, would you? He's having a rough day."

Cooper crossed his arms. "I was only trying to help. You know, figure out why the gods are pissed at Dave. Didn't you say that there aren't any dumb ideas when you're brainstorming?"

"I wasn't talking about yours."

"Hmph," said Cooper. "Well you should have made that clearer."

"There's an easy enough way to test Dave's theory," said Julian. Everyone looked at him. "Heal yourself. If the gods wanted to teach you a lesson by hitting you in the face with a tree, I think they got their message across. If your healing still doesn't work, it must be something else."

"I guess there's some logic to that," said Tim. "Couldn't hurt to try."

Dave touched the tip his finger to the tip of his nose, discovering it was about half a centimeter back from where it was supposed to be. "I heal me." There was no orgasmic rush of healing magic. No cathartic release of pain. His nose hurt from him touching it.

"Again," said Julian. "I'm sorry about your face."

"Let's head back to town," said Tim. "We need to find another cleric who can heal us."

The walk back to Cardinia was long and agonizing. Dave brought up the idea of camping out for the night so that Julian could cast his Mount spells again, but the suggestion was quickly— and Dave admitted, wisely— shot down. Julian, the elven sorcerer, probably had more Hit Points than the rest of the party combined. If they ran into so much as a dire gnat, they were fucked. With Ravenus scouting ahead of them, they eventually made their way to the relative safety of the city walls early the next morning.

Fortunately, the Temple of Halor appeared to be a twenty-four hour establishment. The exterior of the building was simple brick and mortar. It was larger than any other building in the vicinity, and better constructed, with patterns of bricks poking out just a bit further than the otherwise flat surface in the shape of Halor's Star. Dave recognized the symbol from the—

"Oh shit," said Dave, suddenly wide awake. "I know why the gods are pissed at me."

"Why?" asked Julian.

"A few days ago, I checked out a book from the library."

"You see?" said Cooper. "This is why I don't read."

"Shut up, you dumb shit!" said Dave. The others, Cooper included, stared back at him in surprise. "This is all your fault!"

"What the fuck are you talking about?" asked Cooper. "What did I do?"

"Gentlemen!" said a young half-orcish cleric from the now-open front doorway. He was dressed in a gown of golden silk. His head was clean-shaven, adorned only by a thin, gold-threaded headband. His underbite was not so pronounced as Cooper's. He clearly favored his human parent more, and could almost be considered handsome by human standards. Taking into account the -2 penalty half-orcs get, he must have rolled a hell of a Charisma score. "This is a house of worship. Kindly take your bickering down to the— Oh! It appears you have been injured."

"We were attacked by goblins," said Tim.

"Zombies," said Dave.

"Gomblies," said Julian.

"Come inside at once," said the half-orcish cleric, "and bear witness to the healing power of Halor, Father of Gods." Somewhere from within the temple, a gong sounded.

They followed the cleric inside, except for Ravenus, who asked Julian for permission to catch a bit of sleep on the roof. The walls, columns, and ceiling were coated in some kind of gold-flecked paint. Dave guessed there was some Light magic mixed in with the paint as well. The polished, hardwood floor reflected the light from the walls. It was as bright as noon inside the temple, and only about half a dozen candles burning. The reflection of their flames in the gold flecks of the paint wouldn't account for even close to how bright it was inside. In contrast to the humble exterior, the inside of this place was truly befitting of Halor, the God of Light. There was probably a symbolic reason for the contrast, but Dave's face hurt too much to contemplate it.

Dave was overwhelmed with awe and a compulsion to confess his great sin. On the other hand, his face hurt like a son of a bitch,

and he was afraid he might be refused healing if he admitted his offense to the gods. He reasoned that he could do both, so long as he did them in the correct order.Get healed first. Confess second.

"My name is Tamun," said the cleric as he led them straight down the center of the great room, toward an altar on which stood a statue twice as tall as a man. Halor. Both altar and statue were covered in the same Light-infuse paint. "Brother Benedict!" Tamun called out. "Brother Stansibold! Brother Murkwort!" After a moment, three figures came from three different directions, each dressed in identical golden gowns. Two were human, the third was a goblin.

"You're a goblin?" Julian blurted out.

"Do you have a problem with that?" asked Tamun severely. His tone suggested that it wasn't all that uncommon for visitors to have a problem with that. Dave sensed that some of those visitors may have even taken issue with a half-orcish servant of Halor.

"What? No!" said Julian, fishtailing in the other direction. "That's totally cool. Some of my best friends are goblins."

Tim elbowed Julian in the hip.

The clerics formed a line, shoulder to shoulder, in front of the altar.

Tamun raised his great, half-orc arms. "Kneel before Halor, Father of Gods, and know his mercy!" The gong sounded again. It sounded like it was behind them this time, but Dave didn't remember passing any gongs on his way to the altar.

Dave knelt before Tamun. Cooper and Tim knelt before the two human clerics. Tamun shot Julian an ice-cold, tight-lipped, Sam Jackson stare. Dave looked over. Julian was still standing up. The goblin cleric was staring sheepishly at the ground.

"What?" said Julian.

"Perhaps you would be more comfortable," said Tamun, "if Brother Murkwort changed places with Brother Benedict or Brother Stansibold?" His voice could have frozen nitrogen.

"What? No! Come on, man. It's not like that," said Julian. "I

wasn't even injured. I didn't want you to waste a—"

Tim reached up and punched Julian in the back of the knee. Julian dropped to his knees and stayed there.

The sides of Tamun's lips curved upward, ever-so-slightly, in a satisfied grin. He placed his hand on Dave's head and nodded to his fellow clerics. They, likewise, placed their hands atop his friends' heads.

"Halor," said Tamun. "Father of Gods, Giver of Light!" The mysterious gong sounded again. "Shine your light upon the souls of these, your unworthy children. Mend the flesh. Cleanse the spirit. Make them whole, that they may shine your divine Light upon others. By the Light of the Father."

The other clerics repeated, "By the Light of—"

Dave missed the last part of the repeated blessing, as his face cracked. Blood rushed through his head like the dial had been cranked up from 2 to 10. His vision abandoned him. The only sound he could hear was the rush of blood through his ears. The pain in his face was so intense that he thought maybe the gods weren't finished with him.

When the pain subsided, Dave knew his face was whole again. Before his sight returned, he smelled the evidence of Cooper's successful healing as well.

"Don't be such a baby, Brother Stansibold," said Tamun. "People respond to Halor's healing Light in different ways. It will wash out. Go and change your gown. Brother Benedict, Brother Murkwort, please fetch a mop and bucket."

"Right away, Brother Tamun," the two lesser clerics said in unison.

"Rise, dwarf," said Tamun.

Dave got slowly to his feet, his vision returning but still very blurry. "Thank you. Do we... um...?"

"Speak your mind, dwarf."

"This is awkward," said Dave. "What do we owe you?"

"Halor does not prostitute his Light for coin," said Tamun. "However, it is the custom for one to leave a donation to the temple to show one's gratitude."

"We'll give you what we have," said Dave. "It isn't much. Tim?"

Tim tossed a small coin pouch to Tamun. "You can keep the pouch. It's worth a silver piece."

Tamun opened the bag and looked inside. He frowned. "You are indeed fortunate that Halor does not prostitute his Light for coin."

Dave felt the rush of blood again in his face. "I'm sorry," he said. "We can come back with more later."

Tamun placed the coin pouch on the altar. "Unburden your heart, dwarf. Your body is healed, and yet I sense there is still a rent in your spirit."

"I made a mistake," said Dave. "The gods have stripped me of my own powers."

"You must understand, child. You have no powers. You are but a vessel through which the gods do their will."

"Yeah, okay," said Dave as reverently as he could. "You know what I mean though, right?" Dave had never been this nervous talking to a priest back in the real world, likely because he didn't believe in their god.

"I do," said Tamun. "Speak to me of your sin, and we can see what may be done to set you back on the path of Light."

"I borrowed a book from Cardinia's Great Library. Saint Whistlethorn's Encyclopedia of the Gods."

"I am familiar with the text."

"I was just trying to educate myself, you know? What with me being a cleric and all."

Tamun pursed his lips and furrowed his brow, but eventually nodded. "Knowledge is a noble pursuit."

"I was reading in a quiet, solitary corner of the tavern when I needed to go relieve myself," Dave explained. "When I returned, I discovered Cooper in my seat, looking through the book." He hated the idea of throwing Cooper under the bus, but he had to get the truth out.

"That was an encyclopedia of the gods?" asked Cooper. "I

thought it was porn." Everyone looked at him. "What?" he said defensively. "Some of those goddesses are hot, and they were doing some weird shit in some of the pictures."

"Please forgive him," said Dave. "He can't read."

"Continue with your story," said Tamun.

"So when I get back," said Dave, "Cooper gets up and leaves all hurried like. And when I look at the book, I see he'd sneezed all over the pages. It's just covered in yellow and green slime."

Cooper snorted. "I sneezed? You thought that was sn— Ow!" Julian had knocked him on the head with his quarterstaff. "Dude, that fucking hurts." After catching Julian's reprimanding glare, he added. "Oh shit, right. I totally sneezed. I think I'm coming down with a cold." He sniffed, but for the first time in his existence as a half-orc, his sinuses were clear as could be.

Dave no longer felt any qualms about throwing Cooper under the bus. He hoped it was one of those big double-decker buses they have in England.

Tamun stared, frozen and open-mouthed, at Cooper for a moment. He snapped out of it and looked at Dave. "So the pages were covered in mucus." To Cooper he said "Please allow your friend to finish his story uninterrupted."

"I did my best to wipe it clean," said Dave. "But the ink smeared and the pages stuck together."

"The sin was not yours, but your friend's," said Tamun.

"But it was my responsibility," said Dave. "I was the one who checked it out from the library."

Tamun grinned. His teeth were pointed like Cooper's, but much straighter and whiter. "This is an issue between you and the librarian, not you and the gods. Saint Whistlethorn's Encyclopedia of the Gods is a respected historical work, but it is not considered a sacred text. Tell me, what did you do with the book?"

"I returned it."

"In its sullied condition?"

"Yes."

"Did you bring the defacement to the librarian's attention?"

Dave looked at the floor. "No."

"I'm surprised at you, Dave," said Cooper. "You ought to be ashamed of yourself."

Julian conked him on the head again. "Shut up," he whispered.

"Your friend is correct," Tamun said to Dave. "Such behavior is unbecoming of a servant of the Light."

Dave sighed.

"But I do not think," Tamun continued, "that this is why you have been punished. Shameful as it may be, this is still a minor offense. There must be more to this story."

Dave looked up at Tamun. "Nope," he said. "Honestly, that's about it." He felt some sense of relief, but knew that he still had a problem.

"What did you do after you returned the book?" asked Tamun.

Dave laughed nervously. "I high-tailed it to the door, praying that I could make it out onto the quad before the librarian found the sticky pages."

Tamun's eyes widened. "You did what?"

"High-tailed?" said Dave. "It just means that I walked briskly."

"You defaced images of the gods, and then prayed to those same gods to spare you from the wrath of a librarian? Would you kick a tiger cub and seek protection from its mother?"

"It sounds pretty bad when you put it like that."

"You have heaped insult onto offense," said Tamun. "Your punishment is just. Praise be to the Light, the gods are more merciful than I might have been."

"I'm really sorry," said Dave. "How can I make this right?"

"You must atone," said Tamun. He placed his massive palm on Dave's forehead. His claws dug, straddling the line between uncomfortably and painfully, through Dave's thick hair and into his scalp.

Not daring to try to move his head, Dave looked up as far has his eyeballs would allow. It wasn't enough for him to be able to see Tamun's face. "Um... should I say a prayer or write a letter of apology or something?"

"Your careless words cast you into darkness," said Tamun. "It will take action to put you back on the Path of Light."

"I could wash dishes, or—"

"Do not speak, dwarf," said Tamun. "I require concentration."

A few awkward moments passed while Dave silently bore the discomfort of half-orc claws digging into his head. Finally, Tamun spoke.

"I see the goblin necromancer. He rides upon a black worg. Beside him flies the banner of OuiJas. The goblins who attacked you, did they seem organized?"

"Not particularly, I guess," said Dave.

"They didn't fight like goblins are supposed to fight," said Tim. "They should have been hiding up in the trees to ambush us with arrows. And they should have known that, even if they managed to take down one or two of us, they couldn't have hoped to have survived that fight. And they all went for me. It didn't make sense."

"It makes perfect sense," said Tamun. "You are, at least to the lay observer, the smallest and weakest of your group. It's a common battle strategy to concentrate on a single kill rather than merely wound many."

"That still doesn't explain why they just charged into battle kamikaze style."

"Simple," said Tamun. "Their purpose was to die. If they could take one of you with them, all the better."

"I don't understand what purpose that would serve them," said Julian.

"Theirs was not the purpose being served," said Tamun. "They were most likely magically coerced or promised rewards in the afterlife. The leader pulls their strings. He seeks to build an army of the undead."

"What's the point?" said Julian. "He already had an army of fanatically obedient followers."

"That was no army," said Tamun. "Imagine if he had gotten lucky and killed you all. You would now be his undead servants.

Zombies do not require food. They do not tire. They do not complain or disobey. You yourselves can testify they are stronger dead than they were alive."

"My ass can testify," said Cooper.

"We've heard enough of your ass's testimony today, thanks," said Tim.

"This is good news for you," said Tamun.

"What's good about it?" asked Dave.

"The path to your redemption has been made clear." Tamun tightened his hold of Dave's head. The pain from his claws fell to the back of Dave's mind when he felt the sudden and searing heat coming from the half-orc's palm.

"Yah!" cried Dave as his forehead sizzled.

Tamun removed his hand, and the pain was gone. Dave turned around.

"Whoa," said Julian.

"Wicked," said Tim.

"What the fuck is that on your head?" said Cooper.

Dave felt his forehead. It was still a little tender, but otherwise felt normal enough.

Tim spit on the blade of his dagger and polished it with his sleeve. "Try this."

Dave accepted the dagger and held the blade in front of him. When he adjusted it to just the right angle, he could see his forehead reflected in it. There was a tattoo right smack in the center of it. The center of the tattoo, accounting for the majority of the whole, was a solid black circle, a little smaller than a golf ball. The circumference of the circle was lined with the same luminescent golden pigment which coated the interior of the temple. Wavy golden lines, a millimeter thick at the base, and thinning out into points a centimeter away, radiated out from the round center. A solar eclipse.

"You have been marked as one whose spirit is lost in shadow," said Tamun. "Appease the gods, and you may once again walk in the Light."

Dave pointed to his forehead. "Will that get rid of this... I mean it's cool and all. I just would have preferred it on my chest, or back or something."

"When you have fulfilled the task the gods have placed before you, the mark will vanish."

"What task?" asked Dave.

Julian sighed. "We have to go kill all the gomblies, don't we?"

"And the necromancer goblin," added Tim.

"Shit," said Cooper.

"That's impossible!" said Dave. "We already had our asses handed to us by them, and I don't have any magic. How are we even supposed to find them again?"

"You have an unholy mark on your face," said Tamun. "Evil will find you."

"That's reassuring."

Tim yawned like a man three times his size. "Do you guys have a place we could crash? Maybe get a drink first? I'm wrecked."

"I cannot permit you to stay here," said Tamun. "Your friend's face bears an unholy mark."

"Come on, dude," said Tim. "You put that there."

"I am but a vessel."

Cooper laughed through his nose. His sinuses were nice and clogged again.

"What?" said Julian.

"He said 'I am a butt vessel'."

"No he didn't. And what would that even mean anyway?"

"I have no idea," admitted Cooper. "That's part of what makes it so funny. So much is left to the imagination."

"I must ask you to leave this place at once," said Tamun.

"Come on, man," said Tim. "We've had a rough day. We're fucking exhausted. Just let us crash here on the floor for a couple of hours."

"If you will not leave peacefully, I shall have you removed by force. Brother Murkwort?"

The goblin cleric looked up from his task of mopping Cooper's shit off of the polished hardwood floor. His eyes had been heavy with exhaustion before, but there was a certain glint in them now. He pulled the wooden handle off the head of the mop and held it horizontally atop his open palms. As he whispered a small prayer, the mop handle began to glow with a faint green light.

"He's casting Magic Weapon," said Dave. "We should go."

The others stood, dumbfounded, like it was the first time they'd ever seen someone cast a spell before.

Brother Murkwort held his enchanted mop handle by one end and looked at them severely.

"Do you guys see what I see?" asked Tim.

"I see that we're about to get our asses ki—" Dave saw it.

The four of them spoke in one voice. "Yoda."

Brother Murkwort swung the glowing mop handle in wide, complicated arcs behind his back and above his head. He started slowly, and the movements grew faster and faster until he was standing in a glowing, green cocoon. He advanced.

"Take me!" said Cooper, dropping to his knees. "This is how I want to die."

"NOOOOO!" cried Julian, Tim, and Dave as the Jedi knight brought his lightsaber down to split Cooper's face in half.

"Ow," said Cooper as the only slightly magically enhanced mop handle bounced off his head.

"We should go," said Dave.

"All right," said Cooper, rubbing his head.

"Do not return until you have atoned for your sin!" Tamun called out after them as they exited the temple.

Cooper gave him the finger. "Whatever you say, butt vessel."

Julian laughed. "Okay. It's pretty funny."

The temple door just barely missed Dave's ass as it closed behind him.

"So what do we do now?" asked Julian.

"I guess we head back to the Whore's Head," said Dave.

"Sounds good," said Cooper. "I need a drink."

"What you need," said Dave, "is a fucking urologist."

"I don't think I can make it all the way back to the Whore's Head," said Tim. "I'd rather just crash here on the street."

"Not in this neighborhood," said Julian. "The Kingsguard would pick us up in no time for vagrancy."

"That doesn't leave many options," said Dave. "Best we start wa—FUCK!" He swatted away a giant cockroach that had just flown into his face. The stunned insect fell to the ground. It was as big as Dave's finger, and Dave had thick dwarven fingers. As soon as it got its bearings, it scurried back toward him on its creepy-crawly legs. A shiver ran up Dave's spine from the encounter, but he kept control of himself enough to bring his boot down on the bug.

"This just isn't your night," said Julian. He called up to the roof. "Ravenus! It's time to go."

"Five more minutes!" said the bird.

"Now!"

Ravenus peeked over the edge of the roof. "Oh all right. Ooh! What's that?" He flapped down from the roof and greedily gobbled up the squashed cockroach.

Dave was just getting ready to start the long trudge back to the Whore's Head when two more cockroaches flew all up in his face.

"Yahahahoohahoohooha!" cried Dave as he swatted the huge bugs away. "What the fuck is going on!"

Dave didn't have to worry about these two cockroaches getting in his face again, as they were devoured by rats when they hit the ground.

"Yawahawahaaa!" said Dave, jumping into Cooper's arms.

Cooper, of course, dropped him on his ass. "Fuck, you're heavy."

Five rats were nose to nose with Dave, squeaking at him as if trying to communicate.

"I think they like you," said Tim.

Dave bounced up to his feet and kicked a rat, sending it flying to the other side of the street.

Cooper called out after it, "You were too good for him anyway!"

No matter how Dave stepped, danced, or hopped, he couldn't get away from the growing swarm of vermin. He had to sweep his arms continuously all over his armor like a madman to keep it free of cockroaches. "Make it stop! Make it stop!"

"What's all this noise?" demanded a Kingsguard, coming around the corner of Halor's temple.

"Help me!" cried Dave.

The Kingsguard actually started laughing. "Looks like someone displeased the gods."

"What's so fucking funny about that!"

"Calm yourself, dwarf. The vermin won't hurt you."

Dave did not calm himself. He continued dancing and brushing away cockroaches.

"Excuse me, sir," said Julian. "You appear to have more of an idea of what's happening here than we do. Might you shed some light on the situation?"

"Creatures of the night." The Kingsguard nodded toward Dave. "The rats and bugs, they're attracted to the unholy mark on your friend's head. It's been far too long since the last time this happened."

"I can't help but find it odd," said Julian, "that you take such pleasure in watching my friend writhe in a swarm of vermin."

"Oh, I take no pleasure in that," said the Kingsguard. "It's a disgusting sight to behold for sure. But it's great for the city. We need a good rat purge every now and again. It's probably a good time to mention, I'll need to escort your friend out of the city at once."

"But we need to rest," said Dave. "We've been awake for nearly an entire day." He was too exhausted to continue sweeping the bugs away. They crawled all over him, through his hair, under his armor. While he would prefer they not be there, the worst of the terror was behind him.

"Good luck with that," said the Kingsguard. "I don't know if

you've noticed, but you're covered in cockroaches and rats."

Dave sighed, ejecting a cockroach which happened to be crawling across his mouth at the time. It spread its brown, papery wings and flew right back into his face. He started walking.

Tim, Julian, and Cooper walked in a wide arc behind Dave, giving the growing swarm of rats plenty of room, while the Kingsguard strutted ahead of him like they were in some kind of goddamn parade.

Other guards they passed, as well as the few residents of the city who were up and about this early in the morning, actually cheered as the procession passed. At first Dave assumed they were mocking him like a bunch of self-righteous pricks, but through the squeak of rats and the flap of cockroach wings, he actually began to make out words of encouragement.

"Good luck on your quest!"

"May you walk in the Light again!"

"Thanks for clearing out all the rats!"

One pretty young woman stepped out onto the top balcony of a three story building as Dave passed underneath. She smiled down sympathetically at him, plucked a rose from the vine entwined around the railing, and tossed it down to him. It was, of course, immediately devoured by rats, but Dave appreciated the gesture.

"Seek the Light," said the Kingsguard escort, stopping just before the open gate.

"We're going to die out there, you know," said Dave.

"Have faith, son. The gods will provide you with all you need."

Dave had heard similar bullshit back in the real world, usually only involving a singular god. The Kingsguard's words did little to encourage him.

"So," said Julian after the gates closed behind them. "Should we like set up camp or whatever?" He spoke loudly to account for the distance away from each other they all stood and the noise from all the rats now surrounding Dave.

"Do you honestly think any of us could sleep right now?" Dave shouted back.

"So what then?"

"I'm going to go find those gomblies and get rid of this curse."

"But you know we can't take them. They've probably got more gomblies by now."

"Then I'll die!" shouted Dave. "I'm fucking tired, and I'm crawling with fucking bugs and rats. I can't live like this."

Dawn was breaking as Dave trudged through the meadow, headed to where they'd had their previous encounter with the goblin necromancer and his gomblies. The rest of the group followed. The noise wasn't as deafening out here, presumably because the rats were busy consuming whatever food they could hunt or scavenge in the tall grass.

"Cooper," said Julian. "Would you mind carrying me?"

"What are you, six years old? You can walk just like everyone else."

"It's going to be a long walk," said Julian. "If I can get my four hours of meditation in, I can have spells ready when we meet the gomblies... or in case we need to make a speedy retreat again."

Cooper sighed. "Fuck. All right."

"Oh that's adorable," said Tim.

Dave turned around. Julian was sitting snugly in Cooper's arms, elf head nestled peacefully against half-orc man-tit, slender arms wrapped around fat, leathery neck. They looked like they should be crossing a threshold.

"Keep moving, shithead," said Cooper. Dave turned back around and kept moving.

Only when the thick grass of the meadow gave way to the first trees of the forest did it become clear just how many rats had joined Dave's entourage. It must have been in the tens of thousands.

The sun was high in the sky when Ravenus reported the first zombie sighting.

"He's just over that rise," said Ravenus, settling on higher tree branch than he normally would when giving a surveillance report, presumably to keep a healthy distance away from a horde of hungry rats. "Funny thing is, this one's not a goblin. It's a half-elf."

"That can only mean one of two things," said Tim. "Either it's a wandering zombie not associated with the goblin necromancer or, more likely, that fucker has had a busy night, and his undead army is growing."

"That would be bad," said Julian.

"Hey," said Cooper. "How long have you been awake?"

"A few minutes now."

Cooper dropped Julian and stretched out his arms. "Dick."

"Okay," said Tim. "Dave, you stay here and try to keep your little friends as quiet as you can. The more we can pick off one-at-a-time, the fewer we'll have to face when they finally catch on."

It was as good a plan as any. Dave agreed.

"Julian, Cooper," said Tim. "You guys go hide behind those two trees. I'll run ahead, shoot the zombie, and run past you. When he passes between the trees, you two beat the shit out of him. Got it?"

"Got it," said Julian.

"Good plan," said Cooper. He and Julian took their places behind their respective trees.

Tim pranced silently ahead of them on tiptoes until he disappeared over the rise. After a moment, Dave heard the familiar snap of Tim's crossbow being released.

Seconds later, Tim bolted back into view, darted between the trees, and turned around, already loading his next bolt.

After a few more seconds passed, a jarring sound clanged out from right around where Dave guessed the zombie was supposed to have been.

"What the fuck is that?" asked Cooper.

"It sounds like a cowbell," said Julian.

Tim ran back to the top of the rise. "Hey, man! Knock that shit off!" He fired another bolt. The ringing ceased.

Dave ran up to the top of the rise. There was no point in trying to keep quiet now. A dead half-elf lay on the ground, a bolt in its neck, a bolt in its eye, and a fucking cowbell in its hand. "What the hell was that all about?" His entourage of rats descended on the corpse, leaving behind nothing but bone and bell a minute later.

"We're so fucked," said Tim.

"What's with the cowbell?" asked Julian.

"Why didn't it chase you?" asked Cooper.

"Those weren't its orders," said Tim. "Zombies follow their creators' simple commands. Usually the command is 'Kill anything that comes near', but there's no rule that says you can't have them wander about and raise an alarm."

As if on cue, the undead began to shuffle out through the trees on the northern and western perimeter of their visibility. The first wave was at least two dozen strong, mostly gomblies, but sprinkled here and there with other humanoid creatures. Dave knew that there would be far more than that. He looked down at the skeletonized half-orc corpse and smiled.

"The gods will provide," said Dave.

"Like fuck they will," said Tim. "We've got to get out of here. Julian. Do you have your spells back yet? Can you summon up some horses?"

"No," said Dave. "The gods will provide." He picked up the bell and rang it as hard as he could.

"What the fuck does he think he's doing?" Cooper shouted over the clanging of the bell.

"I think a cockroach must have crawled into his brain," said Tim.

Dave paused in his bell-ringing. "You guys may want to climb up some trees or something." He rang the bell some more. "Praise be to Halor, Father of Gods!" He couldn't be sure over the sound of the bell, but he thought he might have heard a gong.

Sure enough, more and more zombies shambled out from the trees. There must have been over a hundred. When they entered the rat zone, the furry little bastards went to town on them, de-

vouring their feet almost instantly. The zombies stumbled and were overwhelmed by a swarms of rats. The rat mounds shrank like deflating balloons until there was nothing left but bone. Not a single zombie came close to within striking distance of Dave.

When the last of the zombies collapsed before him, Dave saw the goblin necromancer and his standard bearer off in the distance, atop their wolf mounts.

"There they are!" cried Dave. "Get them!"

Cooper hopped down out of his tree. "Julian! Horse me!"

"Horse!" said Julian, and a black stallion appeared next to Cooper. Cooper unstrapped his greataxe and charged after the goblins.

The standard bearer dropped his standard. He and the necromancer began to flee.

"Magic Missile!" shouted Julian. A golden bolt of magical energy left behind a trail of sparkly dust as it swerved around trees and eventually zeroed in on the necromancer, knocking him off of his steed.

The sight of a charging half-orc on horseback brandishing a greataxe must have trumped the black wolf's loyalty to its rider. It bolted, as did the still-mounted standard bearer.

"FUCK YOU!!!" Cooper shouted, swinging his axe underhanded into the stunned necromancer. Dave couldn't be sure from this distance, but he doubted the pile of gore Cooper's axe had just created would be sufficiently in-tact for any other necromancers who happened by to be able to animate.

A couple of cockroaches crawled out from Dave's hair and flew away into the forest. He noticed the congregation of rats seemed less dense as well.

"Dave!" said Tim. "Your tattoo is beginning to fade!" He held out his dagger for Dave.

Dave accepted the dagger and held the blade up, adjusting the angle until he found his reflection. Sure enough, the black was fading, and the gold was losing its shimmer. "Oh thank god," he said. "I'm so fucking tired."

"Well you can rest easy," said Julian. "I only used one Magic Missile, so I can summon two more horses. Tim and I are small enough to comfortably share one, so you and Cooper can each have your own. We'll take it slow so you can even nod off in the saddle."

"You know," said Dave. "I think I just might do that." He gave his body a good shake, and a few more cockroaches fell out of his armor.

"Horse!" said Julian. A short and sturdy brown horse appeared next to Dave. It was perfect for him. In fact, he might even be able to climb up on top of this one without Cooper's help.

"Horse!" Julian said again. A sleek, chestnut-colored mare appeared next to him, perfectly suited for himself and Tim.

"You fuckers ready to roll?" asked Cooper, trotting up on his own horse.

"Just a minute," said Dave, staring at the reflection of the fading tattoo on his forehead. "I don't want to take any chances." When the mark had completely vanished, he handed back Tim's dagger. "Okay, guys. Let's— Ow!"

He looked down. A rat had crawled up his boot and bitten him on the knee. He smacked it off. "You ungrateful little shit."

Just then, all three horses began to scream. Rats were climbing up their legs. Cooper's horse threw him off and started bucking wildly. Four more rats tried to climb up Dave's legs. Even more were scurrying toward him.

"Run!" cried Tim. He, Julian, and Dave ran away from the rats, and the rats let them go, favoring the three immobilized horses.

Cooper ran out of the frenzy with about ten rats still clinging to him. "Ow! Ow! Ow! Shit! Ow!" said Cooper, as he rolled around on the ground shaking rats off of himself.

Dave, Julian, and Tim watched helplessly as, one by one, the horse-shaped mounds of frenzied rats suddenly collapsed as the magical horses inside died and vanished.

The walk back to Cardinia, and even still farther to the Whore's Head Inn, was a long, arduous, but fortunately uneventful one.

They finally arrived in the late afternoon, and immediately crashed on the floor and fell asleep. All except for Dave, who was forced to sleep out back in the animal pen until he sorted out his cockroach problem.

The End

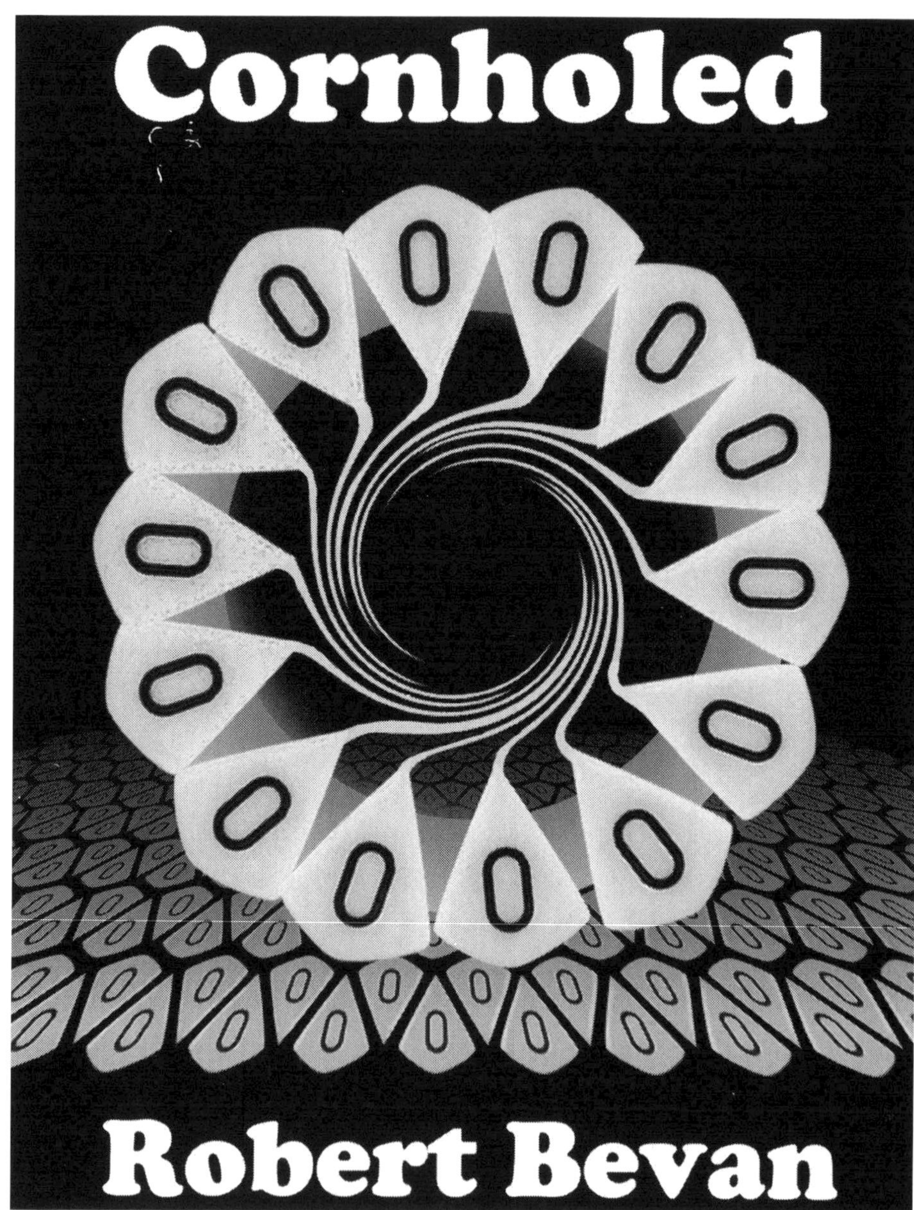
Cornholed
Robert Bevan

CORNHOLED

(Original Publication Date: April 4, 2014)

"This must be the place," said Tim, looking up from the scrap of paper in his little hand.

The house wasn't anything Julian would call fantastic. It was a nice place, large and wooden with a wrap-around porch, but it wouldn't have looked out of place back home. Beyond it was a seemingly endless sea of bright green corn stalks. It reminded Julian of the time he had to drive through Indiana.

Ravenus circled above catching large flying insects, but Julian could feel his familiar's hunger for decaying flesh. His stomach turned with a mixture of desire and revulsion at the thought. It wasn't always pleasant to share an empathic link with a carrion bird.

"You should probably go up and knock," said Tim. Whenever they came across a door, there was an evolving protocol forming for which one of them would approach it. If there was reason to believe the door might be trapped, Tim would check it out first. If they were in a hurry, Cooper would smash it down. If they spent too long talking about it, Dave would get impatient and suffer whatever consequences came from just walking up and opening it. But in a case such as this one, where they were reasonably sure that no one on either side of the door wanted to murder anyone on the other side, the task fell to Julian. He had the highest Charisma score of anyone in the party. He was The Face.

Julian only had time to take a single step off the dirt path when the front door of the house swung open.

"You the boys Skip Wiggins sent?" said the white-haired gentleman at the door.

"Who the fuck is Ski—" Julian, Tim, and Dave all glared at Cooper. He knew better than to talk while Julian was using his Diplomacy. "Sorry."

Julian looked back at the owner of the house and flashed what he hoped was a charming smile. "That's us!" he said, probably a little too enthusiastically.

The man stared back at Julian for a time. His coal-black eyes betrayed no hint of offense or amusement. He was short for a human, but as short as Tim or Dave. He wore a simple white cotton tunic. A beige shawl covered his shoulders, and a matching wide-brimmed hat shielded his sunburnt face from the sun. He had bushy white eyebrows and a handlebar mustache. The most curious feature was the medallion, a red stone a little smaller than a golf ball, the man wore around his neck on a simple silk cord. It wasn't particularly decorative, and didn't really go with the rest of his outfit.

He rubbed the white stubble on his chin as his eyes moved from Julian to Dave, then to Tim, and finally to Cooper. He spat a mouthful of something brown on the sun-baked earth near Cooper's feet.

"Y'all s'posed to be warriors?" he said.

"That's right, sir," said Julian. "We were told that we would be well-suited for—"

"You look like a bunch of cob gobblers to me."

Julian's face remained frozen in a stupid grin. He was unsure of how one was meant to respond to that.

"I guess you get what you pay for," said the man. "The name's Chester. Come on up an' set down a spell. Can I get you boys a drink?"

"That would be lovely," said Julian, leading his friends up the front steps.

"Gertie!" Chester shouted into the house. "Fetch us a pitcher of lemonade."

"Do you have anything stronger?" asked Cooper, ignoring his

friends' glares. "I'm sorry. I'm just fighting a big fucking hangover."

Chester nodded, then shouted back into the house. "Throw a squirt of corn piss in it!"

Julian stopped before reaching the top step. His friends did likewise. Not visible from ground level, the section of porch in front of the door was covered by a great blue rug with a silver floral pattern. It looked very expensive.

Chester sat down on the rug and invited them to do the same. "Don't be shy now. Just take your shoes off first."

Julian and Dave, the only two of them who actually wore shoes, removed them, and they all sat down on the rug.

A moment later, a tall, thin woman emerged from the doorway with a tray. She might have been attractive back in her day, but that day was long past. Likewise, the faded pink dress she wore was likely at one time a tasteful and elegant showcase for the beautiful young woman inside it, conservatively cut below the knee, but revealing well-toned arms in their entirety. Now it was ragged, dirty, and threadbare, and the arms it revealed were flabby, the hands and forearms red and chapped.

"Dammit, Gertie!" said Chester. "This ain't no occasion to be usin' our fine glassware!"

"But your guests."

Chester gestured at Julian and the others. "These are hired mercenaries, not foreign dignitaries. Ain't a one of 'em even human." He turned to Julian. "No offense."

"Um..." said Julian. "None taken?"

"I'll go an' fetch the wooden cups."

"Aw hell," said Chester. "Y'already done wasted enough time. Just set the tray down an' get back inside. Y'oughtta be shamed of yourself lookin' the way you do."

"Yes, Pappa," said Gertie, setting down the tray in the middle of the group.

Chester called out after her as she retreated into the house. "Any these glasses get broken, it's comin' outta your ass, hear?"

No response came from within the house.

Julian, Tim, Dave, and Cooper stared at each other uncomfortably as Chester poured the drinks and passed the glasses around.

"The hell's wrong with your arm, boy?" asked Chester, staring at the leopard fur band around Dave's forearm. "That some kinda gang affiliation?"

"No," said Dave. "It's... I don't like to talk about it."

"Well let's talk business then," said Chester, raising his own glass.

Cooper swallowed his entire glass at once. Dave downed his in a quick series of gulps. Tim only got half as far on his first go. Julian took a careful sip. Gertie had obviously thrown in more than a 'squirt' of cornpiss. The drink tasted like lemon-flavored rubbing alcohol.

"We understand you have some kind of problem in your cornfield?" said Julian.

"Ankhegs," said Chester.

"Gesundheit," said Cooper. Chester narrowed his eyes.

"I'm sorry, Mr. Chester," said Julian. "I'm not familiar with the term."

"Ankhegs?"

"Gesundheit," Cooper said again.

Chester stood up and brandished his crossbow. "You makin' fun of me, boy? I got a mind to put a hole in that big ugly head of yours."

"Please, sir!" said Julian, scrambling for a Diplomacy check. "That won't be necessary." He looked at Cooper. "You say another goddamned word, and I'll shoot you myself."

Cooper pouted.

Chester sat down with a wide grin. "Well there you go, son! That's how you deal with the lower races."

"The lower races?" The question escaped Julian's lips before he had time to think better of asking it.

"Sure," said Chester. "There's a natural order to life. We humans is at the top, with you elves just below us. And then come..."

He looked at Tim, Cooper, and Dave. "... well, the rest of them."

Tim swallowed down the rest of his drink, presumably to give his mouth something to do other than respond to Chester's proposed natural order to life. Dave refilled his own glass, then Cooper's and Tim's.

Diplomacy had taped the wing back onto the burning airplane. Now it was time to hit the eject button. "So, what's an ankheg?"

"Ain't none of you boys been out the city in your whole lives?" said Chester. "I'm gonna have to have a word with Skip."

"Ankhegs are large predatory arthropods," said Tim. He hiccupped. "They burrow under the ground. We've fought them before... back home."

"Well there you go!" said Chester. "At least one of you's got half a brain rattlin' round in his head."

"It was my understanding," Tim continued, "that ankhegs *hiccup* were good for farmland. Don't they aerate the soil or something?"

Julian gave Tim a thankful smile. He knew Tim had a temper, and that rednecks were one of his biggest triggers. He was probably making continuous Concentration checks to avoid punching this asshole in the face.

"So they're like dire worms?" asked Julian.

Chester frowned at him. "What?"

"Arthropods, stupid!" said Tim. "Like lobsters and spiders and shit."

"How the hell am I supposed to know what an arthropod is?"

"You get the Discovery Channel, don't you?"

"All they ever play is fucking Amish Mafia!"

"I may have to rethink the natural order of life," said Chester. "Can one of you tell me what in the Abyss these two are arguin' about?"

Cooper made a show of how tightly his lips were sealed and shrugged.

"We were talking about ankhegs," said Dave. "And how they aerate the soil."

"Now that's right," said Chester. "You have one or two ankhegs in your field, and that's a blessing from the gods. Not only do they aerate the soil, but they keep rodent populations in check. And that's just fine."

Julian listened intently. Even racist assholes were interesting to listen to when they were talking about a subject they genuinely knew something about.

"But sometimes," Chester continued. "Sometimes the balance is tipped. Ankhegs themselves don't have a lot of natural predators, but they's too stupid to watch over their eggs after the mating season. Those eggs is fair game for whatever other critters is crawlin' around underground, and so most of them never even get to hatch. But on occasion, a whole nest will get through the winter unmolested, and then you got problems."

"What sorts of problems?" asked Julian.

"Well it's one thing to aerate the soil," said Chester. "But you get too much aeration, and it undermines the structural integrity of the land. I got sinkholes formin'."

"I guess that's pretty bad," said Julian.

"Oh that ain't the worst of it," Chester went on. "What do you think happens when all the rabbits and rats is gone? All those crawly basterds gotta eat somethin'. They've started attacking my field hands!"

"Do you use zombies?"

Chester glared at Julian. "What kind of sick question is that?"

"I'm sorry," said Julian. "It's just that I know a guy up the road who—"

"Simon Peppercorn."

"Yeah, that's him."

"You boys best steer clear of folks like that," said Chester. "He's a practitioner of the Dark Arts."

"Who the fuck is Simon Pep—"

Julian knocked Cooper on the forehead with his quarterstaff. "I warned you."

"We's a good gods-fearin' family," said Chester, raising his chin and puffing out his chest. "We use slaves."

Dave facepalmed himself. Tim swigged back an entire glass of 'lemonade'. Cooper farted.

"Gods have mercy, boy!" said Chester, waving his hand violently in front of his face. "You practice some Dark Arts yourself, don't you!"

"Excuse me," said Cooper.

"I say it's about time we went and had a look at the cornfield."

"Good idea," said Julian, springing up to his feet.

"Set your skinny ass back down, son," said Chester. "You ain't gonna see nothin' from ground level. Anyways, the ankhegs can sense the slightest tremor in the ground. It's how they hunt."

Julian started to sit back down. "Then how are we going to—"

"Giddap!" said Chester.

Julian's ass met the rug a good half-second before it was supposed to. It took him a moment to make sense of that, but he soon discovered it was because the rug had risen off the porch.

"A flying carpet!" said Tim.

"Awesome!" said Dave.

"Fuck yes!" said Cooper.

Julian just sat where he was, exhilarated and a little terrified, even though they were only about a foot off the ground.

"Heh heh," Chester laughed. "You boys is easily entertained." He brushed his hand along the carpet's surface. The carpet responded by moving in that direction, hovering out past the front steps out over the open ground.

They were now about ten feet off the ground. Falling from that height probably wouldn't even do any damage, but Julian scooted back away from the edge just the same.

"Get this baby moving!" said Tim, hopping up to his feet. "I've got to take a leak!" He stumbled past Dave to the back edge of the carpet, looking as though he was certainly going to fall off. He caught his balance just in time.

"Hold on!" said Chester. The carpet accelerated out of Cooper's fart cloud at a surprisingly smooth rate.

Tim let a stream of urine spray behind them as they circled around the big house. "Woooooo!"

"Sit down before you kill yourself!" said Julian. He took another small swig of cornpiss lemonade to intoxicate the butterflies in his stomach.

When Tim was finished, he returned to the group, tying the rope that held his pants up. "I've always wanted to do that."

"What?" said Julian. "How would the idea even occur to—"

"It's true," said Dave. "He's mentioned it a few times before."

"Ain't no feelin' in the world quite like that, is there?" said Chester. He steered the flying rug past the house and out over the sea of corn.

Julian's long ears sliced through the air as the carpet picked up speed. The view from above opened his eyes as to just how vast this cornfield was; it stretched for miles in every direction. It also made plain imperfections in the otherwise homogenous pattern of stalks.

Chester slowed the carpet until they were hovering over one of these imperfections, a roughly circular hole in the ground, about five feet in diameter, leading downward at a sharp angle.

"Ankheg burrow," said Chester.

"Cornhole," said Cooper.

Dave and Tim laughed. Pissing off the back of a magic carpet must have done wonders for Tim. The rare sight of him laughing all but forced Julian to chuckle along.

"This ain't no pleasure cruise," said Chester, who had obviously not found Cooper's comment quite so funny as the rest of them had. "The observations you make out here might very well save your worthless lives. So you might want to—"

"Bwwaaarrrrrgggghh!" roared something from about fifty feet away. It was a terrible sound, like a bobcat choking on a squirrel which hadn't yet given up the fight. Julian looked toward the noise. Sure enough, a section of cornstalks was shaking violently, some of them tipping over, others sinking straight down.

"Well here you go," said Chester. "The perfect opportunity for you boys to educate yourselves on what you're up against."

The carpet meandered above the stalks until it reached the fight-in-progress. Julian recognized the goblin immediately for what it was. The creature it was desperately hacking at with a sharpened piece of wood, he could only assume was an ankheg. It was only partially exposed. It's head looked like that of a brown grasshopper, but with enormous mandibles. The two exposed legs reminded Julian of steel fence posts, but with hooked claws at the end. The back end of a crossbow bolt appeared in its thorax, right below its leg. Julian looked to his right. Tim had fired the shot.

The creature hissed as it released its hold on the goblin's leg and turned its attention toward them.

Chester, strangely enough, had not yet even raised his own crossbow. He must be wanting to assess their ability. Still, that was some pretty cold shit when one of his own workers' life was on the line.

"Magic Missile!" said Julian. He was too spooked by the ankheg's appearance to focus on a form for the spell, so it just came out as a white glowing blob of magic. It did its job though, exploding into the side of the thing's face, shattering the exoskeletal cheek and part of its right eye. Unfortunately, the parts that did the biting seemed to still be fully functional.

Dave stood at the edge of the carpet, mace ready, waiting for the ankheg to come within striking range.

"Don't be a pussy," said Cooper, kicking Dave in the back.

"Shiiiii-" said Dave on the way down. The end of his scream was drowned out by the crashing of corn stalks.

When the ankheg bent down to bite Dave, Cooper leapt off the carpet onto its back. "Fuck you, you husky bitch!"

Riding piggyback on an enormous insect proved more challenging than Cooper had apparently accounted for, and he dropped his axe in order to hang on. The ankheg swayed back and forth, trying to shake him off, but Cooper had his left arm firmly locked in a chokehold around the creature's neck. He punched into the cavity Julian's Magic Missile had opened up, and then pulled out a fistful of brown and red goop that must have been the mashed remnants of its brain.

The creature stopped writhing and slumped forward over Dave, taking Cooper with it, head first into the ground.

"Ow," said Cooper.

"Impressive work," said Chester. "If not a tad unconventional."

"It might not have killed you to jump in on the action," said Tim. The kettle was beginning to boil.

Chester shrugged off the comment. "Bolts cost money." He looked down at the goblin. The pitiful thing's left leg was torn up pretty bad, but he remained standing. His white burlap shirt had been ripped wide open, revealing skin underneath that appeared to be worse off than the skin unshielded from the sun. It was pink and blistered, like second degree burns. "What you got in your hand, son?"

The goblin looked up like he'd been caught fucking Gertie. "Oh this? Ain't nothin', sir. Just a little chunk of wood is all."

"You know goblin's ain't s'posed to carry no weapons out here," said Chester, fingering the stone that hung from his neck. "Leave it to these here professionals to take care of the ankhegs. You just mind the corn."

"If y'all ain't happened by just when you done, these professionals wouldn't have done me a whole lot of good."

Chester scowled at the goblin with fiery hate in his eyes. For a second, Julian thought he might have to intervene. But the moment passed. Chester's face relaxed, and so did Julian.

"How's that leg of yours?"

"Oh, it ain't too bad," said the goblin. "I might need one or two days to recuperate, but I should be back to work in no time."

"One or two days, huh?" Chester flashed a broad smile. "Why not make it a week?"

"That's mighty generous of you, sir, but I reckon I'll only be—" THWACK A bolt in the forehead dropped the goblin to the

dirt.

"What the fuck!" Tim cried, jumping off of the carpet.

"Give a gobber an inch, and he'll take a mile."

It took Julian a second to realize Chester was talking to him, being the only one left up there on the carpet. His mind reeling, he had no idea how to respond. Was he still even trying to be diplomatic at this point? "Excuse me," he said. He hopped backwards off the carpet, catching the edge briefly with his fingers, hanging on just long enough to halt the momentum of his fall.

"Y'all ain't had to worry 'bout that ankheg," said Chester. "Gobber woulda finished him off."

"He didn't stand a fucking chance, and you know it!" said Tim, plucking the bolt out of the goblin's forehead. Bright red blood poured out of the wound and ran down the creature's dusty face. Tim dragged the body behind the ankheg corpse, which Dave was still struggling to get out from under.

"Ha!" said Chester. "He didn't need to." He raised his eyebrows and tapped his temple. "It's brainpower what makes us the higher race. I have Gertie soak all the gobbers' laundry in a special batch of poison 'fore she hang it out to dry, just for this sort of eventuality."

That explained the chemical burns.

"You sadistic son of a whore!" said Cooper.

Julian whacked him on the head with his quarterstaff. "My apologies," he said to Chester. "My acquaintance has more heart than brain."

"Hey fuck you, dude," said Cooper. "Did you see what—" Julian gave him a look like he was going to hit him again.

"Well that's real sweet," said Chester. "You know I once saw a sick dog suck milk from a sow titty."

"Is that right?" said Julian.

"I shit you not!" said Chester. "Funniest thing in the world, I tell you..."

Julian's eyes remained focused on Chester, to give the appearance that he was still paying attention. But the bulk of his concentration was on Dave and Tim.

"I heal thee," whispered Dave. It was barely loud enough for Julian's hyper-sensitive elf ears to pick up. There's no way Chester's Master Race human ears would have heard, particularly not over the sound of his own blathering. When he heard the sound of muffled groaning, he sighed and turned his attention back to Chester.

"... but that don't matter none on account of we don't have room in the house for another nephew anyway."

"But what about Bosley?" asked Cooper, who had obviously been fully engrossed in whatever Chester was talking about. "How did he react to Eli running off with Leopold's eldest daughter?"

"Bosley?"Chester hunkered down to a squat and cupped a hand around the side of his mouth. "He's the one paid for the gods-damned taxidermist!"

Cooper's eyes widened as he placed his fingertips over his mouth. "Fuck me!"

Chester raised his eyebrows and nodded slowly. "I know, right?"

"Excuse me," said Julian. "I hate to interrupt, but I'd like to know more about the job." Hoping that a little farm lingo might ease the transition, he added, "Daylight's a-waistin'."

Chester stood up and frowned. "So it is. Well, ain't much 'splainin' needs done. You fellers take all the time you need and kill as many ankhegs as you can. When you're done, come on back to the farmhouse, and I'll give you one gold piece for every head you bring back."

"Yes, sir," said Julian.

Chester sat down, and the carpet began to pivot in the air toward the farmhouse. "Good luck!"

Julian waited until he lost sight of the back of the carpet through the corn stalks. "He's gone."

Tim and Dave stood up and stepped out from behind the dead ankheg. Between them stood the shirtless, shaken, but very much alive goblin. His leg was nicely healed up, the hole in his forehead had disappeared, and even the burns on his torso had disappeared.

"Hello," said Julian, attempting a comforting smile.

The goblin responded with a timid nod of his head.

"My name is Julian. It's nice to meet you, Gobber."

"Julian!" cried Dave. "No!"

The goblin's timidity evaporated in an instant. Its red eyes grew wide. "Who you callin' a gobber, you big-eared bitch?" He pushed Dave out of his way and started marching toward Julian.

"Huh?" said Julian, taking a step back.

"I'm pretty sure that's like the goblin N-word," said Dave.

"What?" cried Julian, crashing backward through stalks of corn. "I'm sorry! I thought that was your name!"

"Oh, you a funny man," said the goblin. "We gonna see how funny you is with no teeth." He was somehow incredibly menacing for a three-foot-tall creature.

"Come on, man! We just saved your life!"

"You 'bout to wish you hadn't."

Cooper stepped in front of the goblin. "Just calm the fuck down. Julian didn't mean anything."

"This don't involve you. Best you just step out the way."

"That's my friend," said Cooper. "So yes, it does involve me. If you'd just take a second and chill— The fuck?" Ravenus swooped in and pecked furiously on Cooper's head. "Ow! Fuck! Knock it off!"

"Ravenus!" said Julian. "What are you doing?"

Ravenus narrowly avoided Cooper's fist and settled on top of Juliian's quarterstaff. "I'm sorry, sir. I sensed you were being threatened."

"Not by Cooper."

"Dave?"

"No."

"Surely not Tim."

"No."

"But that only leaves..." Ravenus cocked his head to the side. "You felt threatened by a goblin?"

"I inadvertently made an offensive remark... for which I'm very sorry."

"But he's just a goblin," said Ravenus, just before getting knocked off of his perch by a flying ear of corn.

"Nice shot," said Cooper. The goblin grinned.

"I deserved that!" Ravenus said from behind several rows of corn stalks.

"You speak elven?" asked Julian. It was the only explanation for him being able to understand what Ravenus had said. Well, either that or he was just a major dick.

"That's right," said the goblin in a British accent. "I speak a couple other languages too."

"Hey hey, none of that shit," said Cooper. "You guys speak English."

"What's English?" asked the goblin.

"Or common," said Cooper. "Whatever the fuck it's called. Just knock off that crazy bird language bullshit."

The goblin looked confused, but Julian didn't feel like explaining how game languages worked.

"What's your name?" asked Julian.

"They call me Nutcracker."

"Do I want to know why?"

Nutcracker grinned. "Not firsthand."

"Have you guys sorted all of your shit out?" asked Tim. "We should try to kill an ankheg or two before night falls. You're welcome to join us, Nutcracker."

"And why would I want to do that?"

"We'll cut you in on the coin," said Tim. "Besides, have you given any thought as to what you're next step is? I mean, your master thinks you're dead."

Nutcracker laughed. "I don't reckon he can tell one of us from another."

"Why don't you just leave?" asked Julian. "I don't see any

walls or guards or anything. What's to stop any of you from leaving anytime you want?"

"You seen that big stone Mister Chester wear 'round his neck?"

"Yeah?"

"That's what's called a property stone," said Nutcracker. "Now I don't know the magic behind it, but they got a wizard at every slave auction. They take blood from a newly purchased slave and do what they do. Whatever it is binds us to that stone."

"So what happens if you try to leave?" asked Julian.

"I tried a few times," said Nutcracker. "You reach a certain point and you just want to come back."

"Interesting."

"Same thing happens if you get a mind to do harm to Mister Chester. Like right now, for instance. He done murdered me today, but if he was here right now, I couldn't bring myself to lay a hand on him."

"Because of the stone?"

Nutcracker nodded. "Mmm hmm."

"What if you destroyed the stone?"

"I seen a couple fools try it once," said Nutcracker. "They snuck into the house and grabbed it. This was before Mister Chester took to wearin' it 'round his neck all the time. They banged on that thing with hammers and rocks for a good twenty minutes before Mister Chester come 'round on that flying carpet of his. He shot them both dead, and they ain't put so much as a gods damned scratch on the stone. Damn thing's nigh-indestructible."

"Have you thought about—" The ground rumbled beneath Julian's feet. "What was that?" he asked, having a pretty good idea of what the answer was.

"Take this!" said Tim, tossing his short sword to Nutcracker. He loaded his crossbow.

Nutcracker snatched the sword out of the air by the hilt and made a few practice swipes against some corn stalks. The stalks weren't exactly worthy adversaries, but Julian could tell that this little goblin knew his way around a sword.

"What's going on?" asked Ravenus, poking his head out of the fallen ankheg's giant eye.

"Ravenus," said Julian. "Fly!"

Ravenus flapped his wings, spraying Julian with a bit eyeball goo, and took to the air.

Julian, Dave, Tim, and Cooper stepped this way and that, like they were in a drunken square dance, trying to figure out exactly where the approaching ankheg was most likely to emerge.

Nutcracker stared straight at a certain spot on the ground, sword held high with both hands and pointing down.

The ground disintegrated exactly at the point where Nutcracker had predicted. The massive bug emerged. Brown exoskeleton with a red underbelly, it was easily fifty percent bigger than the previous one.

Nutcracker dug into its underbelly with his sword as it burst out of the hole, putting a nice big gash in its side.

The ankheg swiped at Nutcracker with one of its massive legs, sending the goblin flying into the maize. The little guy had some fight in him, sure. But he still only weighed about forty-five pounds.

When the ankheg had fully emerged from its hole, it was as big as a city bus.

"Yah!" said Dave, swinging his mace at the creature's head. The ankheg dodged Dave's clumsy swing, knocking the weapon out of his hands with a swipe of its mandibles.

"Shit," said Dave as his mace disappeared down the ankheg's hole.

The ankheg made a sound like an old person snoring, only much much louder, and opened its mandibles wide, spraying a jet of dull green liquid into Dave's face. It sizzled on contact.

"Yah!" cried Dave. It was decidedly different in tone and pitch than his previous 'yah'. He covered his face with his hands and ran around like a headless chicken. "My eyes! I can't— Wha? FUUUUUUCK!" He accidentally followed his mace.

"Ha!" said Cooper. "Dave just got cornholed!" He swung his

axe with both hands. The ankheg raised its center leg to deflect the blow, but wound up minus a leg for the effort.

Tim fired a bolt into the creature's back for whatever good that did. It seemed more distracted by its missing leg.

Julian didn't know what else the day had in store for them, and thought it best to conserve his magic for now. He brought his quarterstaff down hard on the ankheg's rear end, but failed to smash through its hard shell.

Understandably pissed off about its severed leg, the ankheg grabbed Cooper with its two front legs and brought its mouth down on Cooper's head. It immediately released him, hissing and standing upright on its hind legs, leaving itself wide open for Nutcracker to charge out from the corn stalks and plunge Tim's short sword deep into its soft underbelly.

There followed a moment of hesitation, as if the ankheg couldn't decide if it was dead yet or not. Tim made the decision for it, firing a bolt right into its face.

Nutcracker rolled out of the way as the giant beast's body smashed a previously unmolested section of cornfield.

"Nice work," Julian said to Nutcracker.

"Yeah," said Nutcracker. "Um... you too." Julian didn't think he meant it to be as condescending as it sounded.

"Hey Dave!" Tim called down the hole. "You okay down there?"

"Yeah," Dave shouted. "Never been better." His tone suggested otherwise.

"Do you need some help getting out?"

"No," said Dave. "You guys should come down here. I think I found something."

"What is it?"

"Some kind of stone surface."

"Probably just bedrock."

"Dude," said Dave. "I'm a dwarf. I know stone. This is man-made."

Tim looked at Julian. Julian shrugged.

"Okay, fine," said Tim. "We're coming down."

The incline of the tunnel was steep enough to slide down, but Julian made his way down carefully, afraid that the whole tunnel could collapse at any minute. Corn roots held the soil together most of the way down, so at least there was a bit of comfort in that, but not quite enough to offset the anxiety he felt at the slightest possibility of being buried alive.

"Hey Dave," said Cooper. "Do you think you could heal me? I got scratched by that ankheg."

"Sorry," said Dave. "My face melted off. I just used up my last Heal spell for the day for that."

"Damn," said Tim. "I didn't realize it was that bad."

"It wasn't. I only used two spells for myself. The rest I used on Nutcracker."

"How many spells did he need?" said Cooper. "He's a goblin. They only have what, like four Hit Points?"

"He must have Fighter levels," said Tim. "He handled my sword pretty well."

Cooper snorted.

"That came out wrong."

"What the hell are you guys talking about?" asked Nutcracker.

"Give me your dagger," Dave said to Tim. Tim held the weapon out in Dave's general direction, but it was obvious that he couldn't see. Even Julian's Low Light Vision was barely functional this far down. Dave, Cooper, and probably even Nutcracker had Darkvision, and could see perfectly fine with no light at all.

"With the proper leverage," Dave grunted as he worked the dagger between two stone tiles. "I should be... able... to..." He sighed as he hefted the three-foot-square, two-inch-thick slab of stone from the place it had been resting, undisturbed, for who knew how many hundreds of years. He slid it onto identical slabs further down the ankheg tunnel.

"I don't know about this," said Julian. "Something feels wrong."

Dave peeked inside. "You guys!" He sounded more excited than Julian had ever heard him sound before. "We've hit the

fucking jackpot!"

"What is it?" asked Tim.

"Gold!" said Dave.

"Gold?" said Nutcracker.

"Sacks of it!"

"Let me see!" said Cooper, crawling past Julian.

"Hey," said Tim. "Stop pushing."

"You guys keep your voices down," said Julian. He had a strong feeling in his gut that something bad was going to happen.

"Damn it, Cooper," said Dave. "Wait a second. There isn't enough room for— Waaaah!"

Dave crashed into the floor below them. The sound of his armor slamming into the stone floor made it pointless to continue reminding anyone to keep their voices down.

"Oops," said Cooper. "Um... are you okay?"

"Fuck you!"

"Don't worry, guys," said Cooper. "He's okay."

"What's down there?" asked Tim.

"It must be some kind of treasure vault," said Dave. "There's gold, but there's also a bunch of these tiny stone statues everywhere. Whoever this belongs to must have a thing for rats. The detail on these is exquisite. I can't even find any chisel marks or anything. And there's hundreds of them. Take a look."

"Not bad," said Cooper, holding a little rat statue in his hand.

"Not bad?" said Dave. "That's a magnificent work of art. I'd love to meet the guy who makes these. It's too bad he wastes all of his talent on rats though."

"Artists are weird," said Cooper. He passed the stone rat to Julian.

Dave was right. It was an impressively detailed piece of stone work.

"We can admire the art later," said Tim. "Tie one of those gold sacks to the end of this rope. Cooper, you go back up the tunnel and pull when I tell you to."

The first sack of gold came up with no problem. It was almost as big as Tim. The comparison was easy to make, as Tim gave it a great big hug and crotch thrust when it surfaced.

"We are getting the fuck out of here tonight," said Tim. "Ready for round two?" He hopped down into the cornhole.

"Holy shit!" said Dave.

"What's wrong?" asked Tim.

"Guys!" cried Dave. "I'm not alone down here. Throw me the rope, quick!" A few seconds later, he cried, "Pull!"

"Jesus Christ!" said Cooper as he, Julian, and Nutcracker pulled on the rope. "Dave has put on some serious fucking weight."

"What the hell?" said Julian. They were barely making any progress. "It's like he's made of..." Julian suddenly remembered the rat statue. "Oh shit. Cooper! Rage now!"

"Good idea," said Cooper. "I'm really angry!"

Julian watched as Cooper's elongated shadow on the fallen cornstalks widened. Suddenly they all started moving backwards very quickly. Tim came out of the hole first. What followed was exactly what Julian feared. The other end of the rope was wrapped around the forearms of a terrified-looking stone statue of Dave.

"Fuck!" said Tim. "He's turned to stone."

"What could do that?" asked Julian.

"Could have been a number of things," said Tim. "Medusa, basilisk, cockatrice, I don't know."

"Can we, um... fix him?"

"Not without a high-level wizard," said Tim. "And likely a shit ton of money."

Julian nudged the sack of gold with his foot. "We've got a shit ton of money."

"That still leaves us short a wizard."

"Old Man Belmont lives just up the road," said Nutcracker. "He's a wizard."

"A powerful one?" asked Tim.

"They all powerful 'round here," said Nutcracker. "This is the Garden District. Rich folks retire here. Most of them is powerful wizards and clerics. Mister Chester's the exception, havin' done made all his money on corn. I can take you there if you like."

"I thought you couldn't leave the farm," said Julian.

"Oh I can go that far," said Nutcracker. "No problem."

"How are we going to carry him?" asked Tim. "Cooper's Rage won't last more than another few minutes."

"I can summon a horse," said Julian. "We could just drag him behind. I don't think he'd feel it, would he?"

"I'm not as worried about that as I am about breaking him." Tim picked up the stone rat and handed it to Cooper. "Squeeze."

Cooper wrapped his gigantic sausage fingers around the stone rat and squeezed. The veins in his forearm bulged out like coaxial cables. After a muffled crunch, he opened his hand. The rat was in at least five or six pieces.

"Yeah," said Tim. "I don't think dragging him behind a horse is going to work."

After about thirty minutes of trial and error, they managed to rig up a harness out of Cooper's leather bag and the rope still attached to Dave's arm. They were fairly confident that, if they took their time, they'd be able to carry Dave and the sack of gold between two horses before Julian's Mount spell duration expired.

"Okay," said Tim. "Do your thing."

"Horse," said Julian. A sturdy gray draft horse popped into existence in front of him. "Horse," he repeated, and a brown horse of similar build appeared right beside it. The perfect horses for this particular situation. His magical skills were improving.

They tied Dave facing headfirst between the two saddlehorns just above his center of gravity so that , if left to his own devices, his feet would fall to the ground. Once Cooper and Tim were mounted, Julian tied Dave's feet to Cooper's waist. Julian and Nutcracker mounted the other horse. As long as the horses walked together, they would be fine.

Julian addressed the horses together, hoping that would keep them nicely synched together. "Horses, walk together slowly." The plan worked better than he had hoped. The horses movements were perfectly synchronized. It was like Riverdance.

Nutcracker navigated them through the maize until they were far enough away from the house that they could safely travel on the road without being seen. They passed a couple of goblins here and there along the way. Nutcracker put his finger over his lips, and the other goblins went back to work like they hadn't seen a thing.

"I was wondering," said Julian, once they were on the road. "And I'm sorry if this is a sensitive question."

"Then don't ask it," said Tim.

"I have to know," said Julian. "How is it that you all came to be slaves?"

"Julian!" Tim snapped.

"It's just that I've seen other goblins around Cardinia. They seem to be doing all right for themselves."

"Well good for them," said Nutcracker. "We ain't slaves because we's goblins." He shrugged his shoulders. "We's cheap because we's goblins. We's slaves because we was captured in war."

"So you're saying there can be slaves of other races?"

"What kind of fool question is that?"

"We're not from around here."

"I ain't from 'round here neither," said Nutcracker, "which, sadly, is the reason I came to be on the losin' side of the war."

"Oh." Julian was curious about how things worked, but he didn't want to pry too deep into Nutcracker's personal history.

"To answer your question, anyone can end up a slave. Don't matter what race you are. I had a human on the auction block on my left, and a minotaur on my right. Both fetched a hell of a lot more coin than I did."

"So all captured soldiers become the slaves of their enemy?" asked Tim.

"Not all," said Nutcracker. "Some choose death."

"Huh?"

"Every soldier gets a choice. Some folks feel they let down their king or country or what have you, and deserve death. Some is more scared of getting' a bad slave master than they is of death itself. Some prefer a quick death from a fellow soldier to the indignity of being a slave. Me, I figure death's gonna come sooner or later whether I want it to or not, so I'll just keep on livin' and see what else life has in store for me."

From there, they traveled in silence but for the perfectly timed rhythm of hooves on dirt. It was only about another hour before Nutcracker pointed out Old Man Belmont's tower on the horizon.

From a distance, the tower looked pretty much like what Julian expected a wizard's tower to look like. Tall, thin, impractical. But as they got closer, he saw that the tower was merely the focal point of a series of smaller buildings. What's more, he could hear children playing and laughing.

"Does Old Man Belmont have kids?"

Nutcracker laughed. "No, not for a long time. He got him some pretty little grandkids though. You best let me off here. Won't do none of us no good for you to be seen with me."

Julian stopped the horses, and Nutcracker dismounted, careful not to jostle Dave.

"See you back on the farm?" asked Julian.

Nutcracker nodded. "Good luck."

"Do you think we can trust him?" asked Tim when Julian started the horses moving again.

"With what?"

"The money."

"I don't see how he has much use for it," said Julian.

"What if he tries to make a deal with Chester?" asked Tim. "Secure his freedom for some information on some hidden treasure?"

"I don't think he'd have time for all that," said Julian. "Chester would most likely just shoot him again anyway."

"I don't like it."

"Ravenus!" Julian called out.

A few seconds later, Ravenus flew into view and settled atop Julian's quarterstaff. "Yes, Master Julian?"

"Would you mind flying back and keeping an eye on the hole

we just pulled Dave out of?"

"Of course, sir!" Ravenus took off into the sky.

"Feel better?" Julian asked Tim.

"A little." It would have to do.

The property was surrounded by a cobblestone, chest-high wall. It must have been meant only for decoration, as it would have kept out only the very laziest of would-be intruders. The wall was interrupted only in one place, by an archway constructed of rough-but-shimmery blue-gray stones. There were no gates, and the arch was just large enough for two riders to enter on horseback abreast of one another. It occurred to Julian as they approached the arch that the sound of children's' laughter was now conspicuously absent.

They stopped just short of passing under the arch.

"Belmont," said Tim, reading a brass plaque mounted on the arch. "I guess we're at the right place."

"Should we just go in?" asked Julian.

"I don't see a bell or anything," said Tim.

"Fuck it," said Cooper. "Let's just go in."

A cool breeze blew through Julian's hair, which was odd, considering he was wearing his sombrero. He looked up and discovered that the giant hat was hovering about a foot above his head. "Well that's interesting."

"OW!" cried Cooper. "What the fuck!"

When Julian turned to look, Cooper was holding a crossbow bolt in his hand. The tip was rounded to a nub, but it still left a nasty welt on his chest.

"That hurt, you little shit!" Cooper said to the little blonde-haired girl who was suddenly standing on the wall, on the left side of the arch. She might have been about nine or ten years old if she was human. Judging by the size of her pointed ears in proportion to the rest of her head, Julian guessed she was half-elven. He wasn't sure how quickly they aged. In her left hand she brandished a wooden sword. In her right, she wielded a miniature, and apparently quite functional, hand-crossbow.

"Who goes there?" said a young male voice. Julian looked at the other side of the arch. A half-elven boy, maybe a year or two younger than the girl, stood atop the wall unarmed, but with his left hand raised confidently in the air. His hair was a thick, wild mess of autumnal colors. His grinning teeth seemed a little too big for his mouth, and his eyes were two different colors. He was going through an awkward phase, but Julian guessed he'd be handsome when he grew out of it.

Julian tried to grab his hovering sombrero, but the little boy jerked his hand higher, causing the hat to ascend just beyond Julian's reach.

"State your business here!" demanded the little girl. "What's that you've got tied up between the horses?"

"None of your business," said Cooper.

"You're ugly," said the girl, matter-of-factly in the cruelly honest way that children are wont to do.

"Your mother's a whore!" shouted Cooper. Julian shot him a severe glare. "...rrible dancer." It was as good a save as Julian could hope to expect.

"No she isn't," said the girl. "My mother is an excellent dancer. She's performed for the Duke and Duchess of Windhollow-Brandyshire." Her tone carried a certain smugness that suggested that she'd just put Cooper in his place.

"Oh," said Cooper. "I guess I was misinformed."

"He's stupid, too," said the little boy, waving his hand in a circular motion, causing Julian's hat to do somersaults in the air above his head. "Let's ask Poppy to turn him into a pig so we can keep him."

Julian had no choice but to move the conversation forward. "Is your Poppy in? We really need to see him."

"He's 'round back by the stable," said the girl, "arguin' with Mamma."

"Come on in!" said the boy. "My name's Stamen. That's my sister, Pistil." He hopped down off the wall, and Julian's hat fell into place on his head.

Julian started the horses through the stone arch. As they passed underneath it, he was blinded by a sudden flash of white light. Before that could even register, he was falling through the air. He almost caught himself with his feet, but fell over backwards, stopping when his back met the unforgiving hard-packed dirt path below him. His vision came back pretty quickly, the light having come and gone like a camera flash.

"Oh, my ass!" said Cooper.

"Oh, your ass!" said Tim, who had landed on his back between Cooper's legs.

The half-elven boy and girl were crippled by fits of laughter. Stamen was rolling around on the grass, while Pistil was hugging the arch to avoid falling off the wall. Both of them were wheezing like hyenas choking on mustard gas. A Tom and Jerry cartoon might well have killed them.

The horses were gone.

Tim rolled away from Cooper's legs and toward the Dave statue. A look of terror swept across his face.

"What's wrong?" asked Julian.

Tim peeked under a piece of Cooper's bag that was wrapped around Dave. "Oh shit."

"What is it?" asked Julian, hoping he was wrong about what he presumed the answer would be. He wasn't.

Tim pulled out a piece of Dave's head. The statue had fractured just above Dave's right ear, diagonally down his face to the mass of beard under his left jaw. "Oh my god, what have we done?"

"Does that mean he's..." Julian couldn't bring himself to say the word.

"Why didn't you keep track of the spell duration for those stupid horses?" Tim snapped at Julian.

"The spell duration had nothing to do with it!" said Julian. "We had a good half-hour, maybe forty-five minutes left before the horses timed out. There's some kind of anti-magic magic in this arch!"

"Dude," said Cooper. "Flip it over and see if you can see his brain."

Julian's first instinct was to club him over the head or at least tell him to shut up, but curiosity got the better of him. He nodded to Tim.

Tim flipped the chunk of Dave's stone head over. Disappointingly, it turned out just to be solid stone on the inside.

"He might not be dead," said Julian.

"His head's fucking cracked in half!" cried Tim.

"We have to try," said Julian. "Hey Stamen. Take me to your Poppy." The boy was still red in the face, tears streaming down from both eyes. "Come on, move your ass. This is an emergency!"

Stamen reined in control of his laughter and stood up. He and his sister led them around back behind the center building. Tim carried the stone head fragment, and Cooper carried the rest of the statue. As they approached, Julian could hear the aforementioned argument in progress.

"You ain't given him a proper chance, Daddy." It was a woman's voice, speaking elven.

"Proper chance!" responded an older man's voice. "Y'all been married ten years already, and I ain't seen a copper piece of rent money."

"He's workin' his tail off," said the woman. "Raisin' two kids is expensive."

"Don't I know it! It's me been payin' for them."

"That ain't fair, Daddy. You know he does the best he can."

"He plays an accordion in a tavern. I reckon I don't have to remind you who bought that."

"Don't even bring that up. You said yourself it was a birthday present." The woman's voice was beginning to crack.

"Aw don't go an' get yourself all worked up again. Everyone makes mistakes, Daffodil. I warned you 'bout gettin' involved with a human. I just hope you won't make the same mistake again once this one finally plays his last note."

"Daddy!"

"I think we can find him from here," said Julian. "I don't know if you kids should be hearing this."

"Ain't nothin' we ain't heard before," said Pistil. "Daddy and Poppy don't get along so well."

They finally rounded the corner to the back of the house, and Julian saw something he never expected to see. A fat elf. The old man had really let himself go by elf standards. Add to that the fact that he was wearing overalls without a shirt, and he wouldn't have looked out of place at Wal-Mart. He also wore a huge burlap satchel, presumably filled with carrots, like the one he was currently feeding to a horse.

"Well what have we here?" he said. He spoke in the Common tongue, the courteous thing to do in mixed company.

"Excuse me, sir," said Julian. "Mr. Belmont, is it?"

"Aye, that's me," said Old Man Belmont. "This is my daughter, Daphne.

"Pleased to meet you," said Daphne, acknowledging only Julian. She curtsied, lifting the sides of a dress made of corn husks and rose petals. The flora of the garment was not at all withered, as if she had tailored it less than twenty minutes ago, or it was being kept alive by some other means. Even the two twigs holding her orange hair up in a bob boasted vibrant green leaves.

And who might you be?" asked Old Man Belmont.

"My name is Julian, and..." He couldn't think of a very good segue. "We were wondering if you could help our friend." He gestured behind him to Tim and Cooper, who held up their pieces of Dave. "His head fell off."

Old Man Belmont frowned. His flaccid jowls sagged like distorted reflections of his pointy ears. "I'm sorry about your friend there, but magic don't come cheap. A spell like that's like to cost more than you fellers can afford. There's costs involved on my end, you see. Spell components, time spent researching, simple supply and demand. This is a business, you see. And I have a reputation to protect. I can't just give away spells to any vagrant who walks in off—""

"We've got money," said Cooper, reaching into his bag.

"Cooper!" cried Tim. "Don't—" But it was too late.

Cooper pulled the sack of gold out of his bag and dropped it on the ground. A few gold coins spilled out of the top. "How much?"

Stamen and Pistil gasped. Their mother's mouth hung open.

Old Man Belmont's fluffy white eyebrows rose as he looked at the sack full of money. "Um... that much."

"Awesome," said Cooper. "What are the odds of that? Talk about a lucky break."

Julian and Tim glared at him.

Cooper frowned. "What?"

"Bullshit!" Tim said to Old Man Belmont. "You give us your honest price, or we'll take our business elsewhere."

"I've told you my price, little feller," said the fat old elf. "Mind you don't jostle those pieces too much on your way out. When those rough edges grind together, tiny little bits crumble away. The more dust you lose, the less of a chance he'll survive the conversion back to flesh."

Tim looked at his hand. His fingertips were already white with dust. He pursed his lips and looked at Julian.

"Cooper," said Julian. "Talk to Mr. Belmont for a minute, would you?"

"Why?"

"Because I need to talk to Tim alone," said Julian. He looked at Old Man Belmont. "And elves have an excellent sense of hearing."

Old Man Belmont shrugged and nodded.

"So," said Cooper. "Magic, huh?"

Julian took Tim by the arm and led him around the side of the house. "We've got to pay him what he wants."

"We could get this done somewhere else at a fraction of the cost!"

"Look at your goddamn fingers!" said Julian. "They're coated in Dave's powdered brain!"

"Ew," said Tim, wiping his hand on his pants.

"Don't get greedy," said Julian. "There's plenty more gold where that came from. The more time we spend squabbling over a few coins here, the bigger the chance Chester takes note of our absence. If he starts asking the right questions to the right goblins, there's a chance he could get to the rest of that gold before we do."

Tim stood quietly for a few seconds, presumably trying to find a hole in Julian's argument. "You're right. Let's go."

Diplomacy. Natural 20.

When they came back around to the back of the house, Cooper, Old Man Belmont, and Daphne were huddled together like they were plotting to kill Caesar.

"Well up to that point," Old Man Belmont was saying to Cooper when Julian and Tim returned, "Rodney hadn't never been with a woman."

Cooper folded his arms and scowled. "And she just left him there on the island?"

"Could you love a man who said the things he did to her uncle?"

Cooper pointed at the ground and raised his voice in anger. "I could love a man who—" He paused thoughtfully. "Wait, where does that leave Bernard's pet pig?"

Daphne put her hands on her hips and leaned in closer to Cooper than most people could stand. "There never was a pig to begin with."

"Of course!" said Cooper, slapping himself on the forehead. "It all makes sense! That heartless bitch!"

"Excuse me," said Julian. "We've come to a decision. We'll pay the money."

"Well all right then," said Old Man Belmont. "Let's get started." He took the carrot satchel off of his shoulder. "Stamen!"

The young half-elf boy stood at attention. "Yessir!"

"Make yourself useful." Old Man Belmont tossed his satchel to the boy, who fell over under the weight of what looked to be a couple hundred carrots. "Follow me, gentlemen. Bring your friend."

The fat old elf led them to the tower.

Aside from its height, the tower was a pretty mundane affair. A simple column of gray stone, punctuated here and there by a seemingly arbitrary pattern of windows. The top of floor was wider around than the rest of the tower, like a tuna can on top of a stack of Coke cans.

Old Man Belmont walked into an unimpressive, doorless entryway, little more than a rectangular hole in the wall.

The inside of the first floor was even more of a letdown. It was magically lit by permanently enchanted stones such as Julian had seen in any number of dungeons, cellars, and even city street lamps at night. But here, why even bother with the light? There wasn't much to see. The inside walls were the same bare, rough stone as the outside. The floor was just plain dirt, bare except for a small circular rug in the center. Most notably absent was any obvious means of getting to the second floor. There were no stairs, no ladders, not even a hole in the ceiling.

Old Man Belmont waddled to the center of the room and sat down on the little rug, almost concealing it entirely with his girth. The rug began to rise vertically into the air.

"My way up is only big enough for one," said Old Man Belmont. His belly shook as he chuckled. "So long as that one is me. You fellers take the stairs. Meet me on the second floor."

"What stairs?" asked Julian, but the old elf disappeared into an illusory plaster ceiling.

"These stairs," said Pistil.

Julian started. He hadn't even realized that she'd followed them. The girl had the makings of a rogue in her.

Pistil grabbed a handful of dirt and threw it at the wall to the left of the entryway. The dirt settled on the first two invisible stairs which presumably wound around the inner wall all the way up to the second floor. The steps were only about six inches tall, and three feet long. The ascent would be a gradual one.

Pistil ran up the first two semi-visible steps and kept on going, running on what looked like nothing but air. When she was about a third of the way around the circumference of the tower, and about six feet up in the air, she jumped over a two-foot expanse of nothing and landed on her feet on some more nothing.

"You have to watch your step!" she called down at them. "There are gaps."

"Gaps?" asked Julian.

"Poppy says it won't do much to stop a determined intruder, but it might piss him off a bit." She continued running up the stairs, jumping over a pattern of gaps that only she knew.

"I'll take the lead on this one," said Tim, handing off Dave's stone head to Julian. He scooped up two fistfuls of dirt and started carefully up the stairs, letting the dirt trickle out of his hands as his feet found each new step.

Julian placed his right foot on the first step. Despite it appearing to be nothing more than a thin layer of floating dust, it felt like solid stone beneath his foot. He brought his left foot onto the step, and there he was, standing with nothing between his feet and the ground but six inches of empty space. He was already dizzy with vertigo.

"Move your ass, dude," said Cooper. "Dave's heavy as fuck."

"Oh right," said Julian. "Sorry." He took another step, and then another, this time finding the second tier of elevation. After climbing a few more stairs, he had the pattern down. Just when he got to the point of confidently placing one foot ahead of the other, he discovered one of the gaps that he'd forgotten having been warned about. His foot plunged down into true nothing, sending his whole body tipping forward.

Must save the head! He was only about six feet in the air, so he resisted his instinct to reach his hands out for something to catch himself. Keeping his arms wrapped tightly around Dave's fragile stone head, he let himself fall. His face met the step beyond the gap pretty hard, invisible stone scraping against his cheek. Painful as it was, it did break his fall, and he might have been able to get back on his feet if he'd had the use of his arms. Unfortunately, the weight of Dave's head just served to drag his face down the side of the invisible stone slab until he found the bottom of it. He free-fell, landing on his head on the dirt floor of the tower. He would surely have broken his neck if the game rules allowed for that.

"Mind the gaps," said Cooper. "The first one's easy enough to spot. It's marked with your face." He stepped over the gap above Julian in one long stride. Julian set aside thoughts of his sore neck, and the dirt that was sticking to his bleeding face and rolled out the way... just in case Cooper shat himself right there and then. It wouldn't have been the first time Cooper had shit on him. His friend had many fine qualities, but continence and timing were not among them.

Further up the wall, on the other side of the tower, Tim was stopped before the third (and hopefully final) gap in the staircase. He tossed what little dirt he had left in his right hand ahead of him. From his position on the floor, and with blood sticking his right eyelids together, Julian couldn't tell if any of the dirt had settled onto a step. It must have, though, as Tim took the leap, landing confidently atop another invisible step. A little further along, and Tim's head was almost touching the ceiling.

"There's no hatch or anything," said Tim, raising his arm. "It's just solid— Oh, there it is." The end of his arm disappeared into the ceiling. "Cool." He kept walking until he completely disappeared into the second floor.

"Sweet!" said Cooper, stepping over the second gap.

Julian groaned as he got back to his feet and limped back toward the first stair.

"Poppy said for me to come and get you." Pistil's voice came from behind and above him.

Julian turned around. The little half-elf girl was descending on her grandfather's miniature carpet. That looked much better than trying to climb those damned stairs again. He hobbled toward the center of the room, arriving there just ahead of her.

"Just will it up, and it will take you," said Pistil, hopping off the carpet.

"You're not coming?" asked Julian, taking a seat. The car-

pet was a little bigger than Old Man Belmont's girth had made it seem. "If this thing can hold your grandfather, I'm sure it can hold both of us."

"Stairs is more fun!" said Pistil. She darted off toward the first step. "Race you to the second floor."

Julian didn't even acknowledge the request enough to refuse it. He concentrated on the carpet. "Up?" he said. The carpet rose slowly, like an elevator.

"Ew!" said Pistil. She had already cleared the first gap, but stopped short before one strangely visible brown stair. "Somebody shit on the stairs!"

She and Julian looked up at Cooper, who had reached the top of the staircase. Evidence of his faux pas was still clinging to his inner thighs. He paused, wide-eyed and tight-lipped. If there's an appropriate thing to say in that set of circumstances, Cooper wouldn't have been the one to know. He turned away and hurriedly disappeared through the ceiling.

Pistil stepped back and got in a few strides before clearing the visible stair.

Julian looked up as the rug brought him closer to the false ceiling. The illusion was remarkable, complete with cobwebs, dust, and knots and imperfections in the wooden beams. It really looked like something he was about to smash his face into. He put his head down, closed his eyes, and hoped for the best.

"Ah, there he is," said Old Man Belmont a few seconds later.

Julian opened his eyes. This was more like what he expected the inside of a wizard's tower to look like. The round walls were lined with shelves full of haphazardly arranged scrolls and leather-bound tomes. On one side stood a wooden desk, atop which sat an assortment of beakers, as well as a long rack of test tubes, filled with liquids of varying textures and colors. Some of them bubbled, some smoked. Julian guessed these were potions in the process of being brewed. Behind the desk stood a cabinet with glass doors, through which he could see what he figured were the finished products, all neatly lined up and labeled in uniform glass jars.

Old Man Belmont stood in front of a smaller table, flattening out a rolled up parchment. "Yes, this should do."

"That's not fair!" wailed Pistil as her head emerged from the illusory floor at the top of the staircase. "I woulda won if this one didn't shit on the floor."

Tim shook his head. Old Man Belmont looked at Cooper.

"I have irritable bowls."

Pistil pointed furiously at Cooper. "You'd better get back down there and clean that shit up, or my Poppy's gonna—" In a sudden puff of smoke, she turned into a black cat.

"What the fuck just happened?" said Cooper.

"She's got a lot of spirit, that one," said Old Man Belmont. He placed the wand he was holding back into the sleeve where it must have come from and bent over to scoop up the cat.

"Is that your granddaughter?" asked Julian.

"Go on now," Old Man Belmont said to the cat. "Play with your brother." He tossed it out of an open window.

"REEEEOOWWWWWW!" Pistil protested on her way down.

"Ow!" screamed Stamen from outside. "She scratched me!"

Tim stood on tiptoes to look out the window. "You have a way with children."

Old Man Belmont looked at Cooper and pointed to a spot on the floor next to his table. "Just put that here, big feller."

"Careful!" said Tim as Cooper set the Dave statue noisily on the floor.

Old Man Belmont ran a finger along the rough surface of the fracture. It came away white. He frowned as he rubbed his fingers together. "Now you bring the rest of him."

Julian touched the floor next to the rug to make sure there was an actual floor there to touch. His hand went right through it. He mumbled a Detect Magic spell to himself, and his eyes were bombarded with color from all sides. He concentrated on the floor. The rug hovered in the center of a ten-foot-diameter circle of illusion, except for a two-foot-wide beam of real floor leading out from the carpet to the main floor of the second level of the tower. Satisfied, he walked across the beam and placed Dave's stone head into place. It didn't feel like it was going to stay put.

"If I let go of this, it's going to slide off."

"Wrap the rope around it," suggested Tim.

Julian did so. "Why didn't the rope turn to stone like his boots and armor and everything did?"

"He wasn't in complete possession of it," said Tim. "We were holding the other end. Cooper, put me up on the table."

Cooper picked up Tim and placed him on top of the table next to the statue.

Holding Cooper's shoulder to steady himself, Tim wrapped the rope around the two pieces of Dave's stone head until they were fastened together as securely as they were going to be. It only amplified the already-present look of terror on Dave's face.

"All right," said Old Man Belmont. "Now you boys take a step back."

Julian, Tim, and Cooper spread out, giving the fat old elf as much room as he could possibly need.

Old Man Belmont cleared his throat and began to read from the scroll. Julian couldn't understand a single syllable of what he said. This was magic well above his pay grade. The incoherent chanting went on for a minute or so, Belmont waved his fat arms about occasionally, but Julian didn't think that was actually a part of the ritual. He was probably just an animated talker, like an excited Italian.

After a loud crescendo of magical gibberish, he removed an expensive-looking dagger from the sleeve that Julian was all but certain he had just put his wand in. He grabbed the blade of the dagger tightly with one hand and winced as he jerked it out quickly with the other. He smeared his own blood over the parts of Dave's head which weren't obscured by rope, being a little more generous with it along the fracture line. Satisfied with the head, he spread his bleeding palm over the rest of Dave's body. He didn't coat it completely; more like a haphazard stroke

of blood here and there, like a preliminary house painter who goes through with a brush and marks the sections of wall that are supposed to be painted. When Dave was smeared up pretty good, Old Man Belmont stepped back to admire his handiwork.

"How do we know if it worked?"

"How in the Abyss do you think you'll know?" said the old elf.

"Oh right," said Tim. "I suppose that was kind of a stupid question."

"You don't have to worry about the spell working," said Belmont. "I'm an experienced wizard."

"That's a relief," said Julian.

"What you've got to worry about is whether or not your friend there will survive the process."

That was less of a relief.

The blood on the statue began to sizzle and smoke. The stone itself took on a decidedly less solid state, the surface writhing and bubbling. Even the parts that weren't meant to be fleshy, such as Dave's armor, expanded and contracted as though life was coursing through it.

From within the writhing stone, Julian could hear the faint beginning of a low moan. The surface of the stone seemed to decide on a shape it liked and hardened. Just when it looked like solid stone again, it began to crack everywhere all at once, like there was a real Dave in there, but coated in a layer of eggshell. His right foot stepped sideways, breaking away massive chunks of the brittle white substance. He lost his balance and fell hard on his face.

"Oh!" cried Dave. "My fucking head!"

"He's alive!" said Julian.

Old Man Belmont nodded. "He has a strong will."

Julian wiped a tear away from his right eye. "He gets a bonus because of his high Wisdom score."

"What? Who? Where am I?" Dave was freaking out. He rolled onto his back, leaving behind flaky white chunks, and pulled frantically on the rope. "Why are my arms tied to my head?"

"Take her easy there, sonny," said Old Man Belmont. "You've just been through an ordeal."

"Who the fuck are you?" cried Dave, pulling even harder on the rope.

"Dude," said Tim. "Chill the fuck out before you strangle yourself."

"What's going on?" Dave was anything but chill.

"Cooper," said Tim. "Sit on Dave while I untie the rope."

"Wait, no!" said Dave. "I'm chill! I'm chill!" He stopped pulling on the rope and sat up.

"Now just sit still," said Tim. He had Dave untied in no time.

"Yaaaaaah!" Dave moaned, cradling his head in his hands. "Why does my head hurt so much?"

"Here you go, son," said Old Man Belmont, thrusting a jar of clear liquid in Dave's face. "Take a swig of this."

"Is that a potion of healing?" asked Julian.

"Naw," said Belmont. "It's just a jar of cornpiss. I buy it off the feller up the road." He grimaced. "Aye, the corn will taste sweeter when it's feeding on his miserable corpse."

Dave was greedily gulping back the cornpiss. Cooper was wrist deep into one nostril. Tim and Julian exchanged a glance.

"Because he's human?" asked Julian.

"Huh?"

"Is that why you don't like your neighbor?" Julian pressed on in spite of Tim's warning look. "I'm sorry, I couldn't help but overhear the conversation you were having with your daughter about her husband. I just got the impression that you don't really care much for humans."

"Aye, that's rich!" said Belmont. "I'm the bigot! I can't even buy a crate of cornpiss without him wantin' to gnaw my ear off all day long 'bout the hierarchy of races, or whatever he calls it. I'll go through two or three jars right then and there just to drown out his yappin', 'fore I can find a polite way to excuse myself."

"I'm sorry," said Julian, "I didn't mean to—"

"And I got nothin' personal against Marlow," Belmont continued. "He's a gentle enough husband and father. He's just not what you'd call a protector or provider."

"Who's Marlow?"

"My son-by-rights," said Belmont. "He's a bard, for crying out loud! Imagine that, my own flesh and blood married to a bard."

"Bards suck," said Cooper.

"You said it, pork pie!" Belmont laughed, slapping his knee. "Course, havin' them all stay here means I get to spend as much time as I like with my mongrel grandkids."

Julian frowned. "Is mongrel really the preferred—"

"Don't matter none anyways. He won't be 'round for long."

"Why?" asked Julian. "Is he sick?"

"He's human!" said Belmont. "God's be damned, boy! Keep up with the conversation."

"I'm sorry," said Tim. "I don't mean to be rude, but I think you've taken enough of our time as well as our money. We really should be heading out."

"Did you really not mean for that to be rude?" asked Julian. "Because it actually sounded pretty—"

Old Man Belmont laughed. "Don't bother me none. Y'all get on your way now. You get into trouble again, just come on back here with another sack of gold."

"Oh my god," said Dave, stumbling toward the center of the room. He held the empty jar in his right hand and rubbed his temple with his left, right where his head had been split in half. "My head feels a lot better, but I think I'm going to throw up."

"Dave!" cried Julian. "Wait!"

"Is there a bathroom in this— WHA!" Dave fell through the fake floor.

Cooper snorted. "Dumbass, you should have taken the stairs." He was descending the staircase, his lower body already obscured by the illusion.

"Fuck that," said Tim. "I'm going out this way." He climbed up onto the window sill, and out the other side, leaving only the tips of his fingers visible. A second later, those disappeared as well.

Julian thought he'd try his luck on the stairs again. Going down turned out to easier than going up. The first third of the way down was tricky. Tim must have run out of dirt by the time he got up that far. After the stair that Cooper had shit on, the rest of the way down was easy, as Cooper was kind enough to leave behind big brown footprints.

"You okay, Dave?" Julian said to the lump of dwarf spread out on the center of the floor.

Dave turned his head toward Julian, gave him a weak 'thumbs up', and puked on the floor. "Better now." He reached out his hand for Cooper to help him up.

"I've carried your fat ass enough today," said Cooper as he walked out the tower's exit.

Julian supported Dave as he hobbled out behind Cooper. They found Tim limping as well.

"That grass wasn't as soft as I thought it would be."

The four of them started back toward the property's front gate.

"Goodbye!" shouted Stamen.

Julian turned around. Stamen and his sister, who had since turned back into a half-elf, were waving frantically at them, bright smiles on their faces. Old Man Belmont and his daughter stood behind their children, also smiling. Julian smiled back and waved. They might have just extorted every last bit of cash he and his friends had out of them, but they were nothing if not friendly people.

"Who the hell were those people?" asked Dave once they were on the road back to Chester's farm.

"Forget about them," said Tim. "What's the last thing you remember before blacking out?"

"Corn," said Dave. "And there was a hole."

Tim's lips quivered. He pressed them together tight.

"Cornhole," said Cooper.

Laughter and snot exploded out of Tim's nose.

"Fuck you guys," said Dave, waddling ahead of the group. "I'm suffering here."

"Dammit, Cooper," said Tim, wiping his sleeve across his face. "There's a lot of money riding on this. We need to know what's down there. Julian, you think you could use some Diplomacy on him?"

"Screw that!" said Dave. "Stay the hell out of my head with your stupid Diplomacy. I'll tell you what I can remember as it comes back to me."

Tim ran to catch up with Dave. "You saw something in the hole. Some kind of creature. You told us you weren't alone down there, and that we needed to pull the rope."

"Yeah, I remember," said Dave. "It looked like a fat Komodo dragon, except that it had eight legs."

"I knew it!" said Tim. "A basilisk. I totally called that."

"There was a door on the other side of the room."

"Of course there was," said Tim. "We accidentally stumbled into the treasure room of someone's secret lair."

"Please don't say you want to go explore the rest of it," said Julian.

"Fuck no!" said Tim. "Anyone with that much gold and a pet basilisk to guard it would kick the shit out of us. We need to go back in the way we came, keep our eyes closed, get the gold, and get the fuck back out of there."

"Dude," said Dave. "That lizard thing was big."

"They aren't very aggressive," said Tim. "And they're lazy. If we don't mess with it, it'll probably leave us alone."

"I'll admit it didn't look terribly ferocious," said Dave. "But I don't know if I'm willing to gamble my life on having to fight it with my eyes closed. I mean, what if there are more of them? What if we get caught by whoever lives in the—"

"Something's wrong!" Julian felt an intense, non-physical tug, like his soul had just been kicked in the nuts. "Ravenus!"

"What's wrong with him?" asked Dave.

"I don't know," said Julian. "Maybe he's hurt. I don't know."

"Maybe he looked at the basilisk."

Cooper laughed. "Stupid bird."

"Goddamnit," said Tim. "If we have to pay to get that fucking bird unfrozen, it's coming out of your cut."

"I have to go," said Julian. He ran ahead of the group as fast as he could.

"Wait!" said Tim. "Shit! Come on, Cooper. Let's go."

"Come on, guys!" said Dave. "Wait for me!"

Julian's heart was pounding by the time he reached the cornfield. He had a compulsion to go to the farmhouse. His gut told him that's where he would find Ravenus.

Figuring he'd get to the house much quicker by going through the field, rather than around it, he turned sharply and barreled through the first stalks of corn. Inertia carried him pretty far, and stubborn determination carried him still farther. By the time he realized that going around the field would have been the quicker option, it was too late. Doubling back and going around would take even more time than just continuing on his way.

"Shit!"

"Get out of the way!" Cooper called from behind him.

Julian stepped aside as Cooper rushed past him, smashing down cornstalks without sacrificing hardly any speed at all.

"Why good evening there, gentlemen!" said Chester once they had made it through the maize. He was sitting on the top step of his back porch. "You know I thought you fellers might turn up. I had Gertie make us up some more lemonade. How goes the hunt?"

"You son of a bitch!" said Julian. "Where's Ravenus?"

"I beg your pardon?"

"My familiar!"

"Oh, you must mean the bird," said Chester. "Don't you worry 'bout him. He's just fine. He's takin' a little nap inside."

Julian stomped toward the porch stairs. "You'd better bring him to me right now, or else I'll—"

"Easy there, son." Chester stood up, not exactly brandishing his crossbow, but making certain it was visible. "Else that little nap might turn into a very long one."

"You think that crossbow scares me?" said Julian. "I've been shot before. How much of a match do you think you are against the three of us? Well... four once Dave shows up."

"It appears you are correct," said Chester, his toothy grin never faltering. "You have me severely outnumbered and outmatched." He scratched at the stubble on his chin. "And yet here I am, not in the least bit afraid. Now why might that be?"

"Fuck this," said Cooper, stepping forward. "Let me just pound some sense into this little bitch."

"Stop!" said Julian. Chester had a point. He was way too confident given his apparent odds should it come to a fight. He was rich, and this was a world full of magic and monsters and shit that Julian didn't know anything about. "What do you want?"

"Come on up and set down a spell, and we'll talk."

"Fine."

Julian, Tim, and Cooper took their places on the carpet behind glasses of lemonade which had already been set out for them. Two more glasses were unaccompanied. One was presumably meant for Dave, and the other for Chester himself.

"Where's the other feller?" asked Chester. "The little fat one?"

"Dave will be along shortly," said Tim.

Cooper snorted. "Good one."

Tim glared at Cooper, and then turned back to Chester. "He's slow."

Chester stood against the railing and peered out into the corn. "That's all right. We got all the time in the world." He held his crossbow conspicuously behind his back. "Hey gobber!" he shouted. "Yeah, that's right, you. Get on over here. I think I dropped somethin'."

Cooper snarled quietly and began to stand up. Julian kept him at bay with a hand on his knee.

"I'm not going to sit here and watch him shoot another goblin in the face," whispered Cooper. "If he pulls that bow, I'm gonna make him eat it."

"Take it easy," said Julian. "We don't know that he's going to— Tim!" he said as quietly as he could while still conveying his alarm and disapproval. "What the hell are you doing?"

Tim was dipping a torn scrap of dirty white fabric into one of the unaccompanied glasses of lemonade. He looked at Julian and placed his finger over his lips.

"That's right!" said Chester. "Right down there." The next thing Julian heard was the unmistakable splatter of urine hitting a surface from a significant height.

"That mother fucker," whispered Julian, pressing down harder on Cooper's even more resisting knee. He looked at Cooper. "Still, it's not worth getting anyone killed over."

"Woo hoo!" cackled Chester. "Gotcha!"

"Yes sir, Mister Chester," said the goblin from below with poorly feigned enthusiasm. "You done got me real good."

"What... the hell... is going on?" said Dave between panting breaths.

"We's just havin' a bit of fun is all," said Chester, giving his dick a vigorous shake. "Get on up here and join your friends."

Julian nudged Tim's arm. Tim nodded, pulled the scrap of fabric out of the lemonade, and shoved it in his pocket just before Chester turned to face them.

Chester took a seat next to Tim, behind the glass of tainted lemonade. Dave took the place between Chester and Cooper.

Chester raised his glass and grinned. "To new business opportunities!"

"I'm not interested in new business opportunities," said Julian. "I just want my bird back."

"Well I am interested," said Chester. "And if you want to see that bird again, you best tell me what you all was haulin' between them two horses earlier today."

Shit. He must have spotted them leaving from his flying carpet. Julian was prepared to give up the gold, and was pretty sure that his relationship with Tim would recover after enough time had passed, but he was only willing to do that as a last resort.

"That wasn't anything," he lied. "We were just... um..."

"It was gold," said Tim.

"Tim!" said Dave and Cooper. Julian, too, was surprised. He wasn't sure what was going on in Tim's head, but he was pretty sure he could rule out concern for Ravenus and respect for other people's property.

"And there's plenty more where it came from."

"Well well now," said Chester. "Seems the little runt knows his place."

"Here's the business opportunity I propose," said Tim. "We take you to the vault hidden under your cornfield, and you give us the bird and let us go on our way. We keep the money we've already stashed away, and we never see each other again."

Tim's lie about them having money stashed away confirmed Julian's suspicion that he was working some kind of angle.

Chester frowned. "I must say I don't much like the idea of a couple of husk suckers like yourselves stealin' money off my property and gettin' away with it, but I'm man enough to admit when I don't have the upper hand. I'll accept your proposal."

Tim smiled and raised his glass. He and Chester clinked their glasses together and drank deeply.

"I want Ravenus first," said Julian. Whatever Tim had in mind, this was a point Julian intended to stay firm on.

"Aye," said Chester. "I'll get your bird. Just remember though. You folks try to double-cross me, and I got o'er a hundred gobbers says you won't make it out of that cornfield alive."

Julian looked at Tim. Tim nodded.

"Deal," said Julian. He clinked his glass against Chester's, and they both drank. It burned going down. The mix had to be at least forty percent cornpiss.

Cooper needed neither an invitation nor a clinked glass to start drinking. His glass was already empty.

Chester stood up and opened the door. "I'll just go and grab us a bit more refreshment." Julian started to speak, but Chester cut him off. "Yes, and your gods damned bird too."

Julian waited until the door closed behind him. "What the hell was that you were dipping in Chester's drink?"

"A scrap of Nutcracker's shirt," said Tim. "He said it was poisoned."

"Are you out of your mind?"

"What? Fuck that guy. He's an asshole."

"That was your big plan?" said Julian. "We poison him and run off with the gold? How can you be so stupid!"

"I've got an Intelligence score of 17!" said Tim.

"Fuck your Intelligence score," Julian snapped back at him. "That guy is an established member of the community. He's rich. If there's an investigation and we get caught, are you going to gamble all our lives on the 'He was an asshole' defense?"

"Relax," said Tim. "That's not enough to kill him. He'll just think he ate some dodgy fish or undercooked meat or something."

"Wait," said Dave. "If you weren't trying to kill him, doesn't the whole plan fall apart?"

"I never said anything about killing him being a part of the plan," said Tim. "I just poisoned his drink for fun."

"That's kinda fucked up," said Cooper.

"So what's the plan then?" asked Dave.

Tim shrugged. "We take Chester to the gold."

Cooper frowned. "This plan sucks."

"I wasn't finished," said Tim. "When—"

The door creaked open as Chester stepped out backwards. In his left hand he held a full pitcher of lemonade. In his right he held a bird cage. He farted.

"Excuse me," he said, uncharacteristically embarrassed. "Dunno what's got into me." He handed Julian the cage. Ravenus lay flat on his side.

"What's wrong with him?" asked Julian.

"He'll be alright," said Chester. "I just gave him a little sleep aid is all."

"You poisoned my bird?" Julian glance quickly at Tim to acknowledge the smug grin he knew was waiting for him.

"I ain't poisoned nothin'," said Chester. "It's just a harmless sleeping potion. He's a noisy critter, he is."

"It's true," agreed Cooper.

"Shut up, Cooper," said Julian.

"Gentlemen," said Chester. "I believe we's gonna have to take this next round to go. Somethin' don't sit quite right in my belly." He sat down and placed his palm flat on the carpet. It rose with a jerk. Cooper rescued the pitcher of lemonade from tipping over and poured himself another glass.

The carpet swerved and dipped as Chester struggled distractedly to follow Tim's directions. The ride this time wasn't smooth like it had been before. It was like a roller coaster, but with neither a track nor the implied guarantee that you weren't going to fall off and die. Julian held onto Ravenus's cage. Dave held onto Julian's leg. Cooper, to his credit, attempted to crane his neck over the front edge of the carpet as he vomited, but everyone wound up getting a little taste of the spray. Tim spilled his corn-piss lemonade onto his crotch, but Julian had a sneaking suspicion that he did it on purpose to conceal a crotchful of actual piss. Chester's face was red and sweaty when the carpet finally touched down near the huge, dead ankheg. Julian was happy to be on solid ground again.

"Go on now," said Chester, stumbling off of the carpet. "Where's this treasure you—" He stopped mid-stride, clutching his gut and shutting his eyes tight. His cheeks ballooned as he puffed out long, controlled breaths. "God's be damned! What did that woman put in the porridge?"

"It's right down in that hole," said Tim. "We'll just be on our way then?"

"Ha!" said Chester. He wiped a hand across his forehead. It came away dripping with sweat. "Nice try, half-stalk. You fellers first." With obvious effort, he waved Tim ahead with his crossbow.

"Okay," said Tim. "Gentlemen?" When he had the rest of the group's attention, but while Chester was still distracted by his own intestinal problems, Tim closed his eyes and held them shut for a few seconds. Julian and Dave nodded their understanding.

"Dude," said Cooper. "Wake the fuck up. This is no time for—ow!" Julian kicked him in the calf. He looked down at Julian.

Julian blinked his eyes hard three times, and left them shut for an entire second on the fourth blink.

"Oh..." said Cooper. Julian could only hope he got the message.

"We can get a move on whenever you two cock munchers are done battin' eyes at one another."

Shit! Julian had been caught. Chester seemed to have regained a bit of his composure. Distraction!

"Um..." said Julian. "Don't your insults usually have a corn theme to them?"

Chester shrugged. "There's only so much you can do with corn."

Cooper sighed. "And I bet you've done it all."

"All right, smart guy," said Chester. "You first!" He pointed his crossbow at Cooper. Get on down that—" He doubled over in pain. "I swear I'm gonna kill that bitch."

"Come on," said Tim. "Let's get this over with." He hopped down into the ankheg tunnel that led down to the underground chamber.

Dave followed after Tim. Julian removed Ravenus from the cage and tucked him into a shirt pocket, snugly under his serape, just in case he should wake up at an inopportune moment and happen to make eye contact with a basilisk. He stepped down into the tunnel. Cooper stepped in behind him, followed by Chester.

"Any you fellers bring a torch?" asked Chester. "I can't see shit down here."

"Why don't you be the light holder?" asked Julian. "It's safer for you that way."

After some labored breathing, Chester said, "Fine. Just hurry it up."

"Light," said Julian as he touched the tip of the bolt loaded into Chester's crossbow. He hoped that Chester might think twice before shooting anyone, lest he lose their only source of light.

"Right down there," said Tim once they had reached the square hole in the chamber ceiling. "Enough gold to double your acreage."

"Why don't you hop down there first so I know it's safe?"

"I'd be happy to," said Tim. He handed Cooper one end of his rope. "Hold this."

Cooper found some decent footholds and planted his feet firmly on the dirt. Tim fed the rope through his hands and gripped it tight before hopping down into the hole.

The rope pulled taut, and only slackened again once Tim had touched the floor below them.

"I can't believe there's all this gold in one place!" said Tim. "I just want to dump it all out and swim in it!"

Chester had heard enough. "Alright, it's my turn." He grabbed the rope and wrapped it around his wrist a few times. "Now you just lower me in. I ain't so spritely as that young feller. I'd most likely break a hip, hoppin' down there the way he done."

Cooper lowered the rope until it started to slacken again.

"This your idea of a joke, son?" asked Chester.

"Huh?" said Tim.

"Where's the gold?"

"What do you mean?" asked Tim. "You can't see it?"

"There ain't nothin' to see," said Chester. "Why are your eyes closed?"

"They're still adjusting to the sudden change of light," said Tim. "What do you mean there's nothing to see?"

"I mean there ain't no gods damned gold!" said Chester. "Only a couple ugly gobber statues.

"Shit!" Tim said what Julian was thinking.

"Boy, I'm warnin' you!" said Chester. "You don't play games with me, or else I'll—" He groaned. "Gods be damned, I can't hold it in anymore. Do me a favor and turn around, would you?"

"Uh... yeah," said Tim.

After a series of precursory farts, Chester groaned like he was having a sword slowly pulled out of his gut.

"You guys okay down there?" asked Cooper.

"I've got a few scraps of fabric if you need them," said Tim.

"Just keep where you are and mind your— Gods be damned! What is tha—"

"Chester?" said Tim. There was no answer.

"Tim!" said Julian. "What's going on?"

"I don't know," said Tim. "My eyes are closed."

"Come back up."

There was a small cracking sound, followed by a crunch. "Shit!" said Tim. "I just ran into Chester. I think I broke part of him off."

"Grab the rope!"

"Okay, I've got it. Pull me up!"

Julian, Dave, and Cooper pulled on the rope. It was heavy lifting, meaning Chester had never let go, but it was still a lot easier than pulling up Dave had been.

Tim emerged first, and helped finesse the squatting statue of Chester through the square hole.

"Check out the size of the deuce he was dropping," said Cooper. It poked out of Chester's backside like a straightened squirrel tail.

"He probably eats a lot of corn," said Julian. "It's weird that his poop also turned to stone."

"It hadn't dropped yet," said Dave. "Technically he was still in possession of it."

"That's all really interesting," said Tim. "But what the fuck happened to all the gold?"

The answer came from the surface, as the cornfield above exploded in goblin laughter and cheer. Either that, or someone had set a badger loose in a cage full of cats.

"What are they so excited about?" asked Dave.

"They've got a bunch of gold?" suggested Julian.

"But what can they hope to do with it?" said Tim. "They're still stuck here on the farm so long as Chester has— Oh shit." He looked at Chester's chest. The medallion was missing. Two fractured ends of petrified string hung down from the statue's neck. "Go! Go! Go!"

Julian scrambled up the ankheg tunnel as fast as his hands and feet would allow. When he surfaced, the cornfield was in chaos. Thin plumes of white smoke billowed out from several random locations. The goblins had made a halfhearted effort of trying to torch the crop, but the stalks were all green, so the fire wasn't spreading.

"Where's the carpet?" cried Tim as he popped up out of the hole.

"Huh?" said Julian. He had forgotten about the carpet. He looked down. Sure enough, it wasn't where they had left it.

Just as Tim looked skyward, a white bundle of fabric hit him in the face.

"Ah! My fucking nose!"

Julian looked up. A black rectangle barely interrupted the already very dark sky. A silhouetted hand waved down to him. "That's for helpin' us out," Nutcracker called down to them. "We's mighty grateful for what you done!"

Julian picked the bundle up off the ground. It was a hastily knotted goblin shirt. He untied it and looked inside. "There's like ten gold coins in here."

"You sons of bitches!" Tim shouted up at Nutcrracker, shaking his tiny halfling fist. "Come back here with the rest of our gold!"

"Sorry folks," said Nutcracker. "We gots to make a new life for ourselves now. That takes coin. Y'all take care!"

"Fuck you!" Tim shouted as the carpet grew smaller against the night sky.

Julian waved goodbye until the carpet finally flew out of view. "Cheer up," he said to Tim. "We did a good thing today, and ten gold pieces isn't such a bad haul."

"Fuck you, too," said Tim. He folded his arms and sat on the ground. It was kind of adorable.

"What's going on?" asked Dave. He and Cooper were hauling

the Chester statue up out of the ankheg hole.

"The goblins made off with all the gold," said Tim. "And the carpet!"

"Ah well," said Cooper. "Good for them. Easy come, easy go."

Tim sulked even harder. "I hate all of you."

"What do we do with him?" asked Dave, his hand on Chester's stone head.

"I guess we'll take it back up to the farmhouse," said Julian. "Let his wife decide what she wants to do with him. She might have to barter off a few acres of the farm to Old Man Belmont. That is, if she even wants him back at— Cooper, what are you doing?"

Cooper was on his knees behind the statue. "Just leaving something for him to remember us by." He broke the end off of Chester's stone turd and shoved it deep into the statue's wide open mouth. "If I had the money, I'd pay to see him get restored myself."

Julian felt movement under his serape. He pulled out Ravenus and set him on the ground. "Hey, buddy! How are you feeling?"

Ravenus shook his head and stretched out his wings. "A bit groggy, to be honest. What happened?"

"We've got a long walk back to the Whore's Head," said Julian. "I'll tell you about it on the way."

The End

ABOUT THE AUTHOR

Robert Bevan took his first steps in comedy with The Hitchhiker's Guide to the Galaxy, and his first steps in fantasy with Dungeons & Dragons. Over the years, these two loves mingled, festered, and congealed into the ever expanding Caverns & Creatures series of comedy/fantasy novels and short stories.

Robert is a writer, blogger, and a player on the Authors & Dragons podcast. He lives in Atlanta, Georgia, with his wife, two kids, and his dog, Speck.

Don't stop now! The adventure continues!

Discover the entire Caverns & Creatures collection at
www.caverns-and-creatures.com/books/

And please visit me on Facebook at
www.facebook.com/robertbevanbooks

Made in the USA
Columbia, SC
15 December 2017